PENGUIN CRIME FICTION

END-GAME

Michael Gilbert was born in 1912 and educated at Blundell's School and London University. He served in North Africa and Italy during World War II, after which he joined a firm of solicitors, where he is now a partner. His first novel, *Close Quarters*, was published in 1947, and since then he has written many novels, short stories, plays, and radio and TV scripts; *End-Game* is his twenty-third book. Michael Gilbert is a founding member of the Crime Writers' Association. Penguin Books also publishes his *The Empty House, The Killing of Katie Steelstock, Mr. Calder and Mr. Behrens,* and *Smallbone Deceased.*

END-GAME

Michael Gilbert

PENGUIN BOOKS

Penguin Books Ltd, Harmondsworth,
Middlesex, England
Penguin Books, 40 West 23rd Street,
New York, New York 10010, U.S.A.
Penguin Books Australia Ltd, Ringwood,
Victoria, Australia
Penguin Books Canada Limited, 2801 John Street,
Markham, Ontario, Canada L3R 1B4
Penguin Books (N.Z.) Ltd, 182–190 Wairau Road,
Auckland 10, New Zealand

First published in the United States of America by
Harper & Row, Publishers, Inc., 1982
Published in Penguin Books by arrangement with
Harper & Row, Publishers, Inc., 1983

LIBRARY OF CONGRESS CATALOGING IN PUBLICATION DATA
Gilbert, Michael Francis, 1912–
End-game.
Reprint. Originally published: New York: Harper & Row, 1982.
I. Title.
[PR6013.I3335E5   1983]   823'.914   83-3976
ISBN 0 14 00.6749 3

Printed in the United States of America by
George Banta Co., Inc., Harrisonburg, Virginia
Set in Caledonia

END-GAME

1

The police car slid quietly down the long, empty street. The widely-spaced lighting left pools of blackness midway between the overhead standards.

"Creepy sort of place," said Detective Sergeant Brannigan.

"More cheerful by daylight," agreed Detective Constable Wrangle. He was driving the car.

"Pull up for a moment. I want to have a look."

The roadway was enclosed on both sides by a wooden wall made of ten-foot planks set vertically in the ground and held together by rows of metal strip. The bottom of the fence was buried in a thick belt of marram grass. Alder and thorn, the trees that grow quickest when men depart, had pushed their shoots through the cracks and were already tall enough to top the wall.

"Been like this long?"

"Long as I can remember," said Wrangle. "Must be more'n six years since they shut the East Docks."

"What used to be there?"

"Offices and sheds. Marine stores, ship repairers, bonded warehouses, places like that. When the ships stopped coming here, they got no customers so they all cleared out."

"I remember it how it used to be in the old days," said Brannigan. "When I was a kid, we lived over on Porthead Road. I remember when the docks was crowded with ships. Albion, Canada, Russia, Quebec, Princess—busy all day long, and most of the night, too, you could see the loading going on. Nothing at all, now."

"Bloody shame," agreed Wrangle. He wondered if this was a moment when he could offer the Sergeant a cigarette. He hadn't known him long enough to be sure. The Sergeant was a recent arrival in the Division and was reputed to be hot on discipline.

"Bloody mismanagement," said Brannigan. "Crowd of bloody old women. Think of nothing but their own pockets." He kicked the planking thoughtfully. "You ever been inside?"

"Once or twice. Few years ago the Friary Lane crowd started using one of the empty sheds as a store for stuff they'd nicked from the goods yard at Malvern Steps. We got a tip-off and raided the place. Caught them with their pants down." He grinned. "Once you're in, there's no way out, see."

"Plenty of ways out on the other side, surely? I remember the kids used to get in and out like rabbits."

"You'd have to be a very small rabbit to do it now," said Wrangle. "They've put up a twelve-foot fence on three sides. Diamond mesh. Not big enough to get your toe in. You'd get over it with a grapnel and a rope easy enough, but not if you was in a hurry."

"So you nicked the lot?"

"That's right. They got a handful each. They'd just about be out by now. Not that they give us a lot of trouble here. There's nothing to attract them."

"Then why do they bother about that?" said Brannigan. He pointed to a notice on the wall which said, "Warning. This place is patroled by Guard Dogs. Keep out."

"That's a load of cock. They did have a dog in there once. Soon after they shut it down, that was. It disappeared."

Brannigan climbed back into the car. He said, "Go on. You tell me. I suppose the rats ate it."

"The rats or the toe-rags. They got some way of getting in and they sleep in the sheds. In the summer, that is."

"Hold it," said Brannigan.

In the shadows ahead something had moved. Wrangle flicked on the spotlight.

"Like I said," said Wrangle. "One of our hotel's five-star customers."

The tramp, pinned against the wall by the blade of light, had thrown up an arm to protect his eyes. He was skeleton-thin, fragile enough to be blown away by the first puff of wind.

"Let's have a look at you," said Brannigan. He climbed out of the car. The tramp slowly lowered his arm.

"Why, if it isn't Percy!" said Wrangle.

The tramp smiled nervously.

"You know him?"

"One of our regulars."

"What are you up to, Percy?"

"Just taking a little walk, Sergeant."

Brannigan checked for a moment. It was the voice that stopped him. The voice and intonation of an educated man. Then he said, "You've got no right to be hanging round at this time of night. I've a good mind to run you in."

"You can't do that," said the tramp. "I have the wherewithal for a night's lodgings."

He held out one hand, palm upwards, with a shining fifty-penny piece in it.

Brannigan knocked his hand up, and the coin went spinning into the gutter. The tramp dropped on his knees, whining like a child, and clutched at it before it disappeared down the grating. Then he got to his feet, swaying slightly.

"You hit me," he said. "You had no right to do that."

"Don't you tell me what I've got the right to do and what I haven't got the right to do. People like you, I've got the right to do anything I like with. You're rubbish. You're nothing."

He stretched out his big hands, caught the tramp by the

3

lapels of his coat and lifted him. He weighed no more than a child. He held him for a moment, his face a few inches from his own. He could see the tears of weakness and fury trickling down the caved-in cheeks.

"I'm a citizen," said the tramp. "I've the right of every citizen to be treated fairly."

Brannigan put him down on the pavement with a thump, turned about and climbed back into the car.

"Does he always carry on like that?"

"Only when he's lit," said Wrangle.

"Is that right?"

"Hopped to the eyebrows."

"Where the hell would a man like that get the money to buy dope?"

"I expect there's money in the family," said Wrangle. "Must have been. You can see he's been educated."

"Hasn't done him much good, has it?"

As the car moved off he looked back. The tramp had sunk back into the shadows and become part of them.

"It's funny to think," said Wrangle, who was feeling philosophical, "that when Percy was a kid his old man sends him to Eton and Harrow and all that caper and thinks, one day my son may be prime minister."

"It's mothers think about their daughters that way now," said Brannigan sourly. He was a male radical.

For a full five minutes after the car had gone the tramp stayed still, like an animal that has been frightened. When he moved he kept close to the fence. As he walked his lips were working. He seemed to be counting. Two lamp standards and six paces later he stopped again.

At this point a plane tree on the far side of the paling had grown to such a height that it was already well clear of the top. Its strong roots, growing outwards, had undermined the footing of that particular plank and had worked it loose. Over the years the parasites which feed on wood had followed the roots down and completed the job. The plank looked secure enough, but in fact it was held in position only by the three lines of metal strip. The first and the third lines had been carefully severed, so that when the tramp pressed on the bottom of the plank it swung inwards, pivoting on the center strip. The tramp went down onto hands and knees and wriggled through without difficulty, pushing the plank back into position behind him.

Once he was inside, it was clear that he was following an established track. After climbing over a low railing he came out onto a cinder path which wound its way for a hundred yards or more between piles of abandoned and rusting machinery, skirted a pit full of oily water and ended at a solid-looking pair of wooden gates. The moon had come out from behind the clouds, and there was enough light to read the name painted in faded white letters: Hendrixsons, Shipping Agents and Chandlers.

The tramp bypassed the gates quite simply by squeezing through one of the many gaps in the corrugated-iron fence. Inside there was a concrete yard. The left-hand side was open shed. The back and the third side, which had once been a smart office block, was now a sad parody of itself. There was a rusty grill over the front door, fastened with a chain. The windows were barred. There were gaps in the roof, and every grime-smeared pane of glass had been shattered, as though by shrapnel.

The tramp made for the open shed. A flight of wooden steps at the back led up to the first story. This was full of every sort of debris and refuse. There were broken packing cases, cardboard cartons, the straw skirts which careful packers put round bottles, heaps of rags, piles of sacking and hundreds upon hundreds of old newspapers. It was a rats' nest, enlarged to human proportions.

There were human rats in it. As the tramp climbed the steps he heard them stirring. He hoped that no one had trespassed into his favorite bedroom. This was a man-sized carton in the far corner, which had once been used for the transport of an electrical generator. It was lying on one side and was half full of newspaper and straw. It was empty. Good.

The tramp crawled into it and wriggled down among the debris. As he was doing so, he paused and sniffed. Someone, not far away, had been smoking a cigarette. He twisted round and poked his head out of the doorway of his cardboard room.

A voice from the darkness said, "Watcheer, Percy."

The tramp grunted. He recognized the voice. It was a middle-aged lay-about called Irish Mick. He said, "If you go on smoking, Mick, one fine night we'll all go up in flames."

"Sure, and some night we'll all die any road. What's the odds?"

Other voices were muttering in the darkness. Conversations interrupted by the new arrival were starting up again. Whispered, husky, confidential colloquies which sometimes went on through the April night as the homeless men confided their meaningless secrets to each other.

— 2 —

"It's a dump," said David Rhys Morgan. "It's as old-fashioned as my Auntie Tamsin's knickers. But not so attractive."

The building which carried the brass plate of Martindale, Mantegna and Lyon, Chartered Accountants, had once been the rectory of the Church of St. Martin-at-Hill. The church had fallen out of use many years before and had been opened to the sky by Göring's bombers. Somehow the rectory, tucked away in a cul-de-sac, had survived bombs and developers. It was totally unsuited to be an office. It had no lift. Its hot water and heating system was subject to unscheduled stoppages. Its windows were so overshadowed by neighboring giants that electric light was needed in most of the rooms for most hours of the day.

"A nineteenth-century dump," said Morgan. "Straight out of the pages of Charles bloody Dickens."

He was talking to himself. It was a quarter to two, and everyone else was out at lunch. He had had his own lunch from the bottle in the bottom drawer of his desk, and he was now wasting an agreeable half hour snooping into other people's rooms.

Samuel Lyon, the senior partner, had locked his door.

"Suspicious old bugger," said Morgan.

7

The room next door belonged to one of the junior partners, Gerald Hopkirk. It was a nodding acquaintance with Gerald that had got Morgan his job in the firm. He had been there for three months now. He was already fed up with it.

"My old da was right," he said. "Never stay in one job too long. It's the bird that hops from bough to bough that gets the pick of the fruit."

Hopkirk's door was unlocked. Morgan went in and seated himself behind the desk. Close to his right hand was a filing cabinet. He opened the drawer labeled A–K, picked out a handful of files from the middle and spread them on the desk. One of them seemed to interest him. It was an old file and had seen a lot of service. It was labeled "Argon Finance—PAYE and National Insurance." There was a newspaper cutting, already yellowing with age, stapled onto the inside of the cover. Morgan tipped his chair onto its back legs and started to read.

Tragedy on Highgate Hill

The torrential rain which burst over London yesterday was the direct cause of a tragedy which claimed three lives. Julius Mantegna, a partner in the well-known firm of City Accountants, Martindale, Mantegna and Lyon, was driving to a business appointment in North London, accompanied by a client, Lt. Colonel Ian Paterson, and his secretary, Miss Phyllis Blamey. As they approached Highgate Archway a lorry and trailer, driven by Alfred Birch, which was coming down the hill, struck a patch of flood water and skidded. The lorry and trailer jackknifed across the road and hit the car head on. All three of the occupants were killed instantly. The driver of the lorry was taken to the Whittington Hospital suffering from shock, but was released later. The lorry belongs to the McCorkindale Transport Company. Mr. Fergus McCorkindale said, "This was a terrible thing. Alf Birch has been driving for us for thirty years, and this is the first accident he has ever had."

The file was full of PAYE returns and letters from and to the Inspector of Taxes. Among them was a single communication from the client himself. It was on good paper, headed "Argon Finance and Investment Limited," over a small and rather well-designed logo of a ship under sail. The directors were named as Randall Blackett, C.A., and Ian Paterson, D.S.O. The registered office was a 513 Anstey House, Theobalds Road.

"Fifth floor of a big block," diagnosed Morgan. "Sounds O.K. but could have been a crummy little joint."

The letter said: "Dear Julius, Get after the tax man with a big stick. He doesn't seem to have read the last Finance Act. Yours, Randall."

The "Randall" had been written in thick black ink with firm strokes of the pen. The signature of a man who knew his own mind and did not suffer fools gladly.

"Why, Mr. Morgan," said Miss Crawley, "whatever are you doing in here?"

She had opened the door softly and was standing peering round it. "Like a startled but indignant hen," said Morgan.

"*What* did you say?"

"I said, Miss Crawley, that I was looking for file nine hundred and ten."

Miss Crawley advanced cautiously into the room and peered over his shoulder. She said, "You oughtn't to come into partners' rooms without asking. And that isn't file nine hundred and ten."

"I didn't say I'd found it, sweetheart. I said I was looking for it."

"That's a very old file."

"None the worse for that." Morgan tipped his chair forward, stretched out one hand and placed a finger on Miss Crawley's high-necked old-fashioned blouse. Miss Crawley gave a squeak of alarm and reversed towards the door. She said, "What are you doing, Mr. Morgan?"

"It was a ladybird," said Morgan. "It had alighted just above your right breast. I thought it kind to remove it before it came to any harm."

"Oh!"

9

"Ladybird, ladybird, fly away home, Your house is on fire and your children have gone."

"I believe you've been drinking."

"In moderation."

Miss Crawley whisked out and slammed the door. Her feet went pattering off down the passage. Morgan grinned and returned to a study of the file. He seemed interested in the newspaper cutting and read it again.

Heavy and deliberate footsteps in the passage announced the arrival of the owner of the room.

"What have you been doing to Miss Crawley?" said Gerald Hopkirk. "She looked like a bird that's had its tail feathers pulled."

"Is it not odd how everyone not only resembles a bird or an animal, but behaves like one. You are a big cuddly teddy bear, fond of honey and nuts."

"Don't change the subject."

"Then again, some people look like fishes. There's something very turbot-like about our Mr. Platt, don't you think?"

"What were you doing to Miss Crawley?"

"A ladybird had alighted on her bosom. I assisted it to escape."

"And what were you doing in my room?"

"Working, Gerald bach, toiling. Whilst the rest of the staff were feasting and drinking in the wine bars and the grill rooms of the City, I was applying myself to my daily task."

"What's an old file of PAYE returns got to do with your daily task?"

"It caught my eye. It had my reference on it, you see."

"*Your* reference? You've only been here a few months, and this file—oh, yes. D.R.M. Quite a coincidence. That was poor Moule."

"Mole?"

"Pronounced Mole. Spelt Moule."

"Like Cholmondeley or Leveson-Gower."

"Yes. But not very like. There was nothing county about Dennis Moule."

"Why was he poor?"

"It was a tragedy, really. When he came here he was quite a promising young accountant. He was engaged to old Mantegna's secretary."

"A sound ploy. Many a professional man has got his feet under the Board Room table by marrying the boss's secretary."

"He didn't get round to marrying her. She was killed."

"On Highgate Hill, in a rain storm."

"How—?"

"I was reading the cutting."

"I see. Yes. They got the name wrong, incidentally. Phyllis Blaney, not Blamey. A nice girl. The best secretary he ever had, Julius used to say. It broke poor old Dennis up. He took to drink. Became quite impossible. They had to get rid of him."

"It seems odd to me," said Morgan, "that people should need an *excuse* for drinking. I've always found it quite easy to do it without any reason except that I like it. Which reminds me. You're coming to dinner with us tonight."

"Thank you."

"Susan is a perfectionist. Her masterpieces of the culinary art never appear on the table before nine o'clock. So we shall have time for a drink beforehand. Or possibly for two drinks. Do you know the Coat and Badge?"

"No. What is it? Another of your pubs?"

"How can you speak so lightly about that great, that immortal, that unique institution, the English tavern? Suppose the Mermaid Tavern had never existed. Should we have had the plays of Shakespeare and Ben Jonson?"

"All right," said Hopkirk resignedly. "I'll buy it. Where and what is the Coat and Badge?"

"No mere description can do justice to it. You shall see it for yourself."

"Not bad," said Hopkirk. "How did you find it?"

"I have a nose for such places. I was walking past, in the street, when instinct awoke. It said, David, there's something

11

down that passage that you ought to investigate. And the instinct was sound."

The Coat and Badge was tucked away at the foot of one of the alleys which runs down from Lower Thames Street to the river. It had a small public bar, a smaller private bar and a very small garden, with an iron table and some iron chairs in it.

They took their second pints into the garden, where they drank for some time in silence, looking across the river at the back cloth of wharves and spidery cranes on the South Bank.

Morgan said, "Blackett. Randall Blackett. He's a large slice of our cake, isn't he?"

"Sixty-two companies. It might be sixty-four. They grow so fast you can hardly keep count of them."

"And it was his partner, Colonel Paterson, who got killed in that accident."

"That's right. Why the sudden interest?"

"I always take an interest in my work. Are we accountants and auditors of all Blackett's companies?"

"As far as I know."

"Have you ever met him?"

"I've talked to him on the telephone. I don't think I've ever seen him. Sam Lyon does most of his stuff. I expect he has to meet him from time to time."

"A Napoleon of finance," said Morgan. "A Genghis Kahn of the business world. A king tiger in the jungle of industry. And I'll bet his wife bullies him."

"He's a bachelor."

"Ah! A man of good sense." Morgan got up, went into the building and reappeared with a tray containing two further pints of beer and two glasses of whisky.

"The old Scottish custom of the chaser," he said. "It improves both the beer and the whisky."

"Steady on," said Hopkirk. "We don't want to turn up stinking."

"What a truly horrible expression. In the days of the Regency, if a man happened to have consumed rather more alcoholic liquor than was wise, he was said to be glorious. 'Stinking,' indeed. How we have debased the language of drinking. You'll be talking about 'blotto' next."

He swallowed the whole of the whisky and half the beer. Gerald Hopkirk followed suit, but more slowly.

"Stop looking at your watch," said Morgan. "We've lots of time. . . . April weather. I'm getting cold. Let's have a last one inside."

The public bar had a dozen customers now. A dozen made it seem crowded. Three men in executive suits, two middle-aged and one young, were occupying the three stools at the bar.

"The three bears," said Morgan. "Father Bear, Mother Bear and Baby Bear."

This was unkind, especially to Mother Bear.

"Were you talking about us?" said Father Bear.

"I was talking to myself," said Morgan. "It's a terrible weakness I have. Two more of the same, please, Sidney."

"I think you were being bloody rude," said Mother Bear.

Baby Bear said, "He's just a bloody Welshman."

"That's right," said Morgan, "a bloody Welshman." He sounded pleased. "There's just one thing wrong with this country, boyo. Thanks, Sidney. Have one for yourself."

"You were saying?" said Father Bear.

"I was saying," said Morgan, taking a pull at his drink, "that there's one thing wrong with England. It's full of Englishmen." He roared with laughter.

"He's drunk," said Baby Bear. "Don't pay any attention to him, Tom."

"I'm not drunk, I'm happy," said Morgan. "Another drink for each of my ursine friends."

There was no fight. Three reciprocal rounds later, Morgan and Hopkirk were walking up Lower Thames Street in search of a taxi. No taxis appeared.

13

"We'd better take the Underground," said Morgan.

"We're going to be late," said Hopkirk.

"Never do things by halves," said Morgan. "If we're going to be late, let's be thoroughly late. I know a sweet little place, just down here to the left—"

"No," said Hopkirk.

—— 3 ——

They were very late, and Susan was very angry. She said, "You might have telephoned. The soup's boiled over twice, and the meat will be like old leather."

"Nothing that you have cooked could possibly be like old leather."

"I suppose you've been on a pub-crawl. Take your hands off me and wash them."

"I'm terribly sorry," said Hopkirk. "I tried to get him back in reasonable time, but it was a losing battle."

Susan was not placated. She said, "Just because David is a selfish pig, there's no need to play up to him."

After an uncomfortable meal, at which most of the conversation was supplied by David, Susan went out to the kitchen to make the coffee, and Gerald said, "I think I won't wait for coffee. I'll be buzzing off now."

"Don't be a rat. You can't push off and leave me."

"I think I must."

"Have your coffee first. The worst is over."

David was wrong. When Susan came back, the banked-up fires burst into yellow flame. She said, addressing her remarks pointedly to Gerald, "Did you have a very tiring day at the office? Sugar? Milk?"

"Fairly tiring. Sugar, thank you. No milk." Gerald stirred his coffee energetically.

"I expect you like getting home in the evening and relaxing."

"Yes. Yes, I do."

"You have a service flat, I believe. With its own restaurant. That must be very convenient."

"Oh, it is. Very."

"So you can please yourself what time you get in."

"Within reason."

"I see." Susan looked out of the corner of her eye at David, who was also stirring his coffee. "So if you rolled in drunk at nine thirty, you'd still get something to eat?"

"I expect they'd scratch up some sort of meal."

"But then, it's different when you're living somewhere on a commercial basis. I mean, when you're paying your way."

"That's right. I think I ought to be moving along now."

Susan ignored this. She said, "You'd suppose, Gerald, that someone who was living somewhere at someone else's expense would be even more considerate, don't you think?"

"Well—"

"If you mean me," said David, "why not say so. Someone! Somewhere! Someone else! For Christ's sake, stop wrapping it up. What you're saying is that I scrounge on you."

He had gone very red.

"Since I pay the rent of this flat and the rates and the cleaning woman and the electricity and the gas, and you occasionally chip in for the groceries, yes, I suppose you could put it that way."

"I'm an incumbrance. And you want to get rid of me. Is that right?"

"I didn't say so. I was simply stating some facts. More coffee, Gerald?"

"No, really—"

"You don't have to say it twice," said David, "you've made your meaning quite plain. I can take a hint as well as the next man."

He got out of his chair, upsetting his coffee cup as he did so, stumped across to the door and went out. Gerald said, "Let me mop that up before it ruins the table," and shot out into the kitchen to fetch a cloth. When he came back with it, Susan was standing beside the table.

She said, "Thank you, Gerald. I'll do that." Her face was rather white, but otherwise she seemed unmoved. She mopped up the spilt coffee, poured herself out another cup and said to Gerald, "You might as well have one. You can't go now."

They could hear David bumping round in the bedroom.

"What's he going to do?"

"He's packing."

"He really means it, then."

"Means what?"

"Means to go."

"He always means to go. The last time—let me see, that was about six months ago—he stayed away for a whole month. A very useful month as far as I was concerned. I got the flat spring-cleaned, chair covers, curtains and all."

David reappeared. He was carrying a bulging kit bag. He said, "If you'll be good enough to pack up my other things, I'll send round for them."

Gerald half expected her to say, "Don't be silly," but anger still seemed to be bubbling underneath. She said, "Certainly. If you'll let me know where to send them."

David turned his back on her and said to Gerald, "Are you coming?"

"Well—I think—perhaps—" said Gerald unhappily, torn between the desire to get away and an effort not to be rude to his hostess.

"If you're thinking of staying the night, Susan prefers to sleep on the right-hand side of the bed."

"Really, David!"

Susan said, "He's only being bitchy. I shouldn't take any notice. If you're going, David, just clear out quick."

"It couldn't be too quick as far as I'm concerned."

17

"And don't forget to leave your keys behind."

David put his hand in his pocket, extracted a latch key and an outer-door key from his ring and threw them both onto the table. They slid off onto the floor between him and Susan. Neither of them looked down.

David shouldered his kit bag and marched out. They heard the front door slam.

Susan said, "Are you sure you wouldn't like another cup of coffee? I could easily heat it up."

"No, no," said Gerald. "I really must be going. Thank you for the supper."

"A pleasure," said Susan.

—— 4 ——

"Not one of our better evenings," said David. His eyes were red-rimmed, and the slur in his speech suggested that he had had little sleep; or maybe had already taken a stiffener to see him through the day. "I'm sorry I dragged you into it."

"That's all right," said Gerald. "Does that sort of thing happen often?"

"From time to time. She gets over it."

"I hope so, for your sake."

"I'm not sure. There are advantages and disadvantages. Pros and cons, as you might say."

"I should have thought it was all pro. A lovely pad and a lovely girl."

"Do you think she's lovely?"

"I certainly do. So, I should imagine, does every other chap who sets eyes on her."

"She's all right, I suppose. I mean, considered as a girl."

"For God's sake," said Gerald. "Some people simply don't know when they're well off. If you don't want her, I—"

"No," said David quickly. "Don't even think about it. I was only joking last night. It wouldn't do. You're not her sort. You're much too serious."

"All I was going to say," said Gerald stiffly, "was that I imagined there would be no shortage of candidates to take your place."

"What Susan needs is someone she can fight with. It's her French ancestry. The Perronet-Condés were Huguenots. Of course they've been over here for a long time now, but you can see that look in her eye every now and then. St. Bartholomew's Eve and all that."

"The Huguenots didn't kill the Catholics on St. Bartholomew's Eve. It was the other way round. The Catholics killed them."

"You mustn't believe all you read in the history books, boyo. Slanted stuff. Up with the big nations, down with the small ones. Tell me one history book that's fair to the Welsh!"

"The only people who are ever fair to the Welsh," said Gerald, "are the Welsh. If you haven't got any work to do, I have. Yes! Who is it? Come in, Rowley. What can I do for you?"

"I was looking for Mr. Morgan. I thought I heard his voice."

Fred Rowley had been a sergeant in the Royal Horse Artillery and was the office manager. Morgan and he had tested each other's drinking capacity in a number of stiff bouts, and neither being able to put the other down they had declared a state of friendly neutrality.

"What's up, Fred?"

"Mr. Lyon wants you."

"To give me the good news, perhaps, that he intends to increase my inadequate remuneration."

"I wouldn't bank on it." As they moved out into the passage he lowered his voice and said, "I saw Miss Crawley coming out of his room."

"Creepy Crawley," said Morgan. "Thank you, Fred, forewarned is forearmed."

He knocked at the door and went in without waiting for an answer. Samuel Lyon was seated behind his impressive twin-pedestal desk pretending to sort through his morning post. He said, "Oh, Morgan—"

"You were wanting to speak to me," said Morgan, seating himself uninvited in the clients' chair beside the desk.

Mr. Lyon said, "Yes—um. I did. Yes, I wanted a word with you." He was fat, flabby and fifty. He looked as though a little less for lunch each day and a little gentle exercise in the evening might, though it was probably too late, stave off the heart attack which he was going to have when he was sixty.

He said, "I've just had Miss Crawley in here. She was complaining—that is, she told me that you had been intimate with her."

Morgan opened his eyes so wide that his eyebrows almost seemed to merge with his hairline.

Lyon said hastily, "Don't misunderstand me. I wasn't implying intimacy in the—er—police court sense of the word."

"I'm glad you don't mean that," said Morgan comfortably. "Because if you had, I should have been bound to wonder whether she was mad or I was. What exactly has she accused me of doing? Undressing her with my eyes, perhaps. Even that would take courage."

"She says that you touched her."

"Touched her?"

"On her, um, breast."

"Where did this act of gallantry take place?"

"In Mr. Hopkirk's room, in the lunch hour, yesterday."

Morgan reflected for a moment and then said, "Of course. It was the ladybird. Did she tell you about the ladybird?"

"No."

"Coming from I know not where, flying through the open window, it alighted on Miss Crawley's blouse. Possibly it mistook the pattern of green and brown leaves for the thicket where it had abandoned its children. I thought it kind to remove it."

"And that was all?"

"If Miss Crawley has led you to believe that anything of an improper nature took place, then I am afraid that she has allowed an overvivid imagination to run away with her." He leaned forward in the chair and said, more seriously, "We both know how women—of a certain age—" He let the sentence hang.

Mr. Lyon said, "Yes, well, it's a possible explanation." He seemed glad to leave the topic and move onto firmer ground. "That wasn't the only thing I wanted to talk to you about. Your attendance record is far from good. Two days ago I wanted to look at one of your files and was told that you had not arrived. That was after ten o'clock."

"A holdup on the Underground. We were kept waiting for twenty-five minutes between Chancery Lane and St. Paul's. Several women fainted. You may have read about it in the papers."

"I see," said Mr. Lyon drily. "As long as these holdups don't occur too often. In an office like this, time is money."

The events of the evening before, which had left their mark on David Morgan, did not seem to have affected Susan Perronet-Condé. She arrived at the office of M. N. Harmond Ltd. on the stroke of nine, looking her usual fresh, cheerful and composed self, and had been working for half an hour by the time Toby Harmond breezed in.

Toby was the great-grandson of the Michael Naysmith Harmond who had founded the firm midway through the reign of Queen Victoria, at a time when private enterprise had not yet learned to be ashamed of itself. The firm dealt in all varieties of printers' ink. Its continuing prosperity had been based on the hard work and application of Francis Naysmith Harmond, Toby's grandfather, and Edward Naysmith Harmond, Toby's father.

By the fourth generation some of the enthusiasm had worn thin. Toby had played racquets and rugby football for Wellington and had recently discovered the joys of squash, at which he had become more than proficient. He had tried to lure Susan onto the court with him, so far without success.

She said, "I don't see why I should sweat about retrieving

impossible shots and losing every game nine–nil."

"Good for your figure."

"What's wrong with my figure?"

"Nothing," said Toby with enthusiasm. "Nothing at all. Suppose we give it a try this evening."

"Give *what* a try?"

"Squash. We could have dinner afterwards."

"After half an hour on the court with you, I should be flat on my back."

"An excellent idea," said Toby. "You could come and lie flat on your back on my sofa whilst I cooked the supper."

"This is no time for frivolity," said Susan sternly. "The six-monthly report and marketing analysis is due." She indicated a large buff envelope on the desk. Toby looked at it with distaste. He said, "We've just done one."

"Six months ago."

"It seems like yesterday."

Two years before Toby had given up the struggle to remain independent. The technical processes of ink manufacture, which had been simple in the days of Queen Victoria, had now become sophisticated and expensive. It was a sharply competitive market. To fall behind meant disaster. To keep up involved an increasing expenditure of capital which he did not possess. It was at this point that Martin Brandreth had arrived.

Toby knew Martin as the managing director of Sayborn Art Printers, one of the main purchasers of their inks. Brandreth had laid his proposition on the line without preamble. He said, "You're undercapitalized. If you don't do something about it your company will lose money again this year. As you have for the last two years, only more so. You can survive for another year or so on your reserves. After that, it'll be a creditors' liquidation."

"That's a lot of nonsense," Toby had said. "You know nothing about it, and anyway what business is it of yours?"

"I know about it because I've read your published accounts.

It's my business because I've got a proposition for you. I can introduce you to a man who will buy a fifty-one percent stake in your company. He can also find the money you need for new machinery."

The only thing which had made Toby hesitate had been that he neither liked nor trusted Brandreth. He said, "Who's the fairy godmother?"

"Randall Blackett."

It was already a name of power in the City.

Brandreth had added, "If it's any comfort to you, you might like to know that he took us over a couple of years ago."

"What's in it for Blackett?"

"If he makes the same arrangement with you as he did with us, he won't even ask for a seat on the Board. He'll sign himself up as a consultant to your company. At a good fee."

"And absorb all our profits."

"Wait for it. The arrangement is that he doesn't get a penny of fee until he has at least doubled your turnover *and* your profit."

Toby had known that he was going to have to say yes. The decision was a simple one. Whether to remain captain of a sinking ship or sign on as first mate of a ship which had a prospect of staying afloat. The deciding factor had been that if Harmonds did go down, his father's pension would go with it. His father was enjoying his retirement, down in Hampshire, in a farmhouse which had some fishing rights. He caught few fish, but was very happy.

In the event, it had not turned out as badly as Toby had feared. The dreaded Blackett had intervened very little, so far, in the running of the company, and all his interventions had been helpful. For the most part they had consisted of suggesting new outlets for Harmond products. Outlets, Toby suspected, in which Blackett also held a partial or a controlling interest. The only feature of the new regime which he found oppressive was the half-yearly report.

This was an extensive document, covering every aspect of the company's business. The factual bits he could fill in easily enough with the assistance of his chief accountant. It was the two blank pages at the end which baffled him. One was headed "Prospects," the other "Ideas." On the first occasion he had written, "Prospects good. Ideas—none," and had been tersely informed, by Blackett in person, that this was not good enough.

The two blank pages began to haunt him. He had never been good at expressing himself on paper and had never troubled to analyze the *rationale* of his business. Now he had to do both and had to do it every six months.

"You're a girl with ideas," he said to Susan. "Why don't you do it?"

"It's not my job."

"Just for this once."

"You've been at this all your working life. I've been here exactly three months."

"Exactly. You'll be bringing a fresh mind to it. Come out to lunch and we'll talk about it."

Over lunch they talked about it. And about other things. Susan had suspected for some time that Toby was working up to a proposal of marriage. He was not a young man who concealed his feelings. She hoped he never got into a game of high-stakes poker.

The eating place he had chosen had those tall wooden pews which were a pain in the neck for the waiters, but gave diners a lot of privacy. They had been late starters and by the time they reached the coffee stage the place was nearly empty. For some minutes now Toby had been wearing the determined look of an infantryman about to go over the top.

He said, "Susan."

"Yes, Mr. Harmond."

"We're not in the office now, remember."

"Yes, Toby."

"There's something I want to ask you."

"There's something I want to ask you, first."

Toby looked deflated. It was as though the attack had been called off at the last moment.

"What's that?"

"Why are you scared of Blackett?"

This had the hoped-for effect. Toby said, "Scared? I'm not scared of him. Who said I was scared of him?"

"Then why do you look like a dog threatened with a bath when this half-yearly report form arrives?"

Come to think of it, he was almost exactly like a golden Labrador they had had when she was young: large, friendly and without an ounce of guile.

"It's a bore," said Toby. "I can never think of anything new to say." At least, his mind seemed to be veering away from proposals of marriage. "I can put in all the guff in the first part. It's the Prospects and Ideas bit which buffaloes me. I think you might lend a hand with it. After all, you are my secretary."

"I might be able to work out what Blackett wants if I had any idea what sort of man he was."

Toby took a lump of sugar out of the bowl and ate it to assist thought. He said, "I don't really know a lot about him. Everyone says he's a wonderful chap, and they must be right when you think what he's done. He's a sort of water diviner. He goes round with his hazel rod looking for money. When the rod gives a twitch, he knows he's onto something worth backing and he backs it for all he's worth."

"With money?"

"Money and connections and advice."

Susan caught the waiter's eye, and he refilled their coffee cups. Toby was safe for the next ten minutes. She said, "How did he start? Do you know?"

"Only what I've heard Brandreth talking about. He did a lot of different things immediately after the war. That was when he qualified as an accountant. And I think he spent some time in America. Then he started his own outfit, Argon Investments. He had a piece of the action in a property company run by a man called Woolf. Woolf died, and he bought out the widow. That's when he really took off."

"When was this?"

26

"About ten years ago."

"I seem to remember that a lot of people lost a lot of money about then."

"Not Blackett. He saw the crash in the property market coming and sold out before it happened. That's what gave him his reputation in the City."

"A wizard *and* a water diviner," said Susan. "I do see that your essay on Prospects and Ideas would have to be something rather special."

"You will lend a hand with it, won't you?"

"I'll think about it," said Susan. "We shan't get anything done by sitting here."

— 5 —

"Have you found somewhere to live?" said Gerald.

"After one night spent walking the streets and a second night on a bench on the Embankment, in the shadow of Cleopatra's Needle, inadequately covered by copies of the *Daily Telegraph*—"

"Stop talking nonsense. If you really haven't anywhere to go, I could fix you a bed in my place."

"You're a true friend," said David. "But I'm all right. I've organized myself a room in a small hotel not far from the Cromwell Road. I've got a pull with the landlady. I once saved her from a fate worse than death. I advised her not to cash a check for a respectable Scotsman who had been staying in the hotel. Her gratitude was immense and well deserved."

"You talk so much nonsense," said Gerald, "that I never really know whether to believe what you say or not."

"It's a form of self-protection practiced by all oppressed minorities."

"For God's sake, don't start talking about the Welsh again. Haven't you got *any* work to do?"

"There is always work to do," said David with a sigh. "I see it stretching ahead of me, mile after mile, a barren desert of toil. Every day, a long hot march, with the faint hope of an oasis at the end of it. Talking of which," he added more cheerfully, "what about coming out for a drink this evening?"

"Certainly not. You're totally irresponsible. You nearly got into a fight last time. And do you know who that man you insulted was?"

"Father Bear or Mother Bear?"

"The fat one on the left. It was Tom Porteous."

"I feel certain I should fall on my knees and beat my forehead three times on the floor at the mere mention of his name. Who is he?"

"He's the senior partner in Ancrum, Porteous and Byfold. And he happens to be one of Sam Lyon's pet clients. And an old friend into the bargain."

"It's a beautiful friendship, I'm sure. Based on bills regularly presented and regularly paid. If you won't come out with me I'll have to try and lead Fred Rowley astray."

"You'll have your work cut out."

"Fortunately we both drink off the same handicap."

The Reference Section of the Hammersmith Public Library, one of the best in London, stayed open late on certain weekdays. By hurrying home, Susan could rely on getting a full hour among its shelves of reference works, treatises, blue books and Government Reports. She made occasional notes, reading more than she wrote. From her French forebears she had inherited a hard analytical mind. She preferred facts to theories. She thought of facts as small, easily handled bricks. With them you could construct buildings: square, reliable buildings, with foundations which would carry the weight of their own superstructures without crumbling or cracking.

When the assistant, who knew her, said, "It's past half past seven, Miss Condy," she looked up in surprise.

"Goodness," she said, "how time disappears when you're interested in what you're doing."

"I don't know what you can see in all that stuff," said the assistant. "It looks dull to me."

"It is dull," said Susan. "Terribly dull. But terribly interesting, too, if you know what I mean."

As the assistant was putting the books away, she examined the titles. They seemed to be mostly concerned with the printing trade.

She said to the supervisor, "You'd think a girl with her looks would have something better to do in the evenings than bury herself in this stuff."

The supervisor, who was an amateur psychologist and a student of the columns in the papers which prescribe for other people's troubles, said, "I expect she's had a tiff with her boy-friend and is striving to forget."

"Singles tonight," said Fred Rowley. "And no hanging about."

"You're not feeling well?"

"I'm feeling fine. But I'm saving up to buy a new car."

"I could introduce you to a man who'd sell you any new car you name for three-quarters of the list price."

"Uninsured, unlicensed and stolen the week before."

"That's unworthy of you, Fred," said David. "Just because you've a devious mind you mustn't suppose that everyone else is on the fiddle."

They were in the saloon bar of the Green Man, a much larger house than the Coat and Badge, with a mixed clientele. The bar was crowded, but by a bit of elbow work they had got themselves a table.

Rowley said, "What did Uncle Sambo want to see you about?"

"Our Miss Crawley reported that I had made an assault on her virgin fortress."

"If you were brave enough to climb the wall, you'd find the garrison anxious to surrender, I guess."

"Exactly what I told Sam. Repressed spinster. Vivid imagination."

"You want to be careful, all the same. It was Crawley who got one of your predecessors the boot."

"Which one?"

"Chap called Dennis Moule. Five or six years ago."

"*He* didn't make a pass at her, surely."

"No. This was drink. Took to drink when his fiancée was killed."

"On Highgate Hill in a rain storm."

"Right. How come—?"

"I read it. In a newspaper cutting inside an old file I was looking at. I happened to notice his initials on it. D.R.M. Same as mine. I didn't know you were here when that happened."

"Was I not? It was the sort of day you don't forget in a hurry. February fourteenth, St. Valentine's Day. It started raining at nine in the morning and it never bloody stopped. Low black clouds, like the end of the world was coming and not just raining. Pouring, solid, like someone up there had pulled the plug and was emptying a bath over you. I'd seen something like it in Burma before. Never in England."

"Keep my seat and I'll get another drink. Thinking about all that water—very depressing—you need something to cheer you up."

He fought his way to the bar and returned, managing to carry two glasses of whisky in one hand and two pints of beer in the other. Some of the beer failed to survive the journey.

"Go on," he said. "What happened next?"

"What are you talking about?"

"The St. Valentine's Day massacre."

"Oh, ah, that." Fred lowered half his beer and said, "There was a lot of fuss going on all day. Something to do with one of our spot customers. Mr. Mantegna looked after him. A man called Blackett."

"Randall Blackett?"

"That's right. You can't hardly open a paper nowadays without seeing he's bought up some other outfit. Seems to collect 'em like cigarette cards. Not that he was much then, but I'm talking about some years ago. Well, like I was saying, there was some panic on. Mr. Mantegna said we *must* get hold of him. Had all of us telephoning round. I tried his partner, in the property business, Harry Woolf. He was away ill. Died a few months later, I seem to remember. Then Miss Blaney, his secretary, got through to another director, Colonel Paterson. Found him at his club. He said he thought Blackett was up in North London, visiting different people. If it was all that urgent, he said, he'd bring his car round and pick up Mr. Mantegna, and they'd go after him. No chance of a taxi in that weather. Have you noticed? As soon as it starts raining and you need a taxi, they all disappear."

"I've noticed it," said David patiently. "What happened next?"

"The next thing was the Colonel turned up, looking big and red and cheerful. Not drunk, mind you. He'd had a good long lunch and one or two afterwards to top it up. You notice a lot of people who'd been in Jap prison camps were like that. As if they felt they'd got three or four years of drinking time to make up. Anyway, there he was with his car, and he said why didn't Miss Blaney come with them? She lived up Highgate way, and the weather being what it was, of course she said yes. Funny how making a little decision like that turns out the way it does."

Fred lowered the other half of the beer whilst he considered the philosophy of cause and effect.

David said, "Just how do you mean, exactly?"

"What I mean is, if she hadn't gone she wouldn't have been killed, and if she hadn't been killed she'd have married Dennis Moule and she'd have kept him on the straight and narrow, and he'd still be working for the old firm. Might be a partner by now."

"What *did* happen to him?"

"Search me. I remember we got him a job as cashier with a firm that ran Continental tours. Office in Bloomsbury. I'm off. Buy the first round next time."

The crowd was thinner now. David had noticed the white-faced girl standing at the end of the bar. She had been talking to a group of men, but they seemed to have abandoned her. He caught her eye and made a very slight gesture of invitation. She came slowly over. David shifted the empty chair towards her, and she sat herself in it. She said, "Your friend left you?"

Her voice was exactly what David had expected.

He said, "That's right. Left me all alone and sorrowing. I shall be crying in a moment."

"Like me to lend you a hankie?"

David looked at her closely and said, "I've got a better idea than that. Let's find somewhere to eat."

"Let's do that thing."

They found a Wimpy Bar that was open. The girl crammed food into herself as though she had eaten nothing for a week. When she had finished a second helping and a third cup of coffee she started to talk. Just as he had known what her voice would be like, he knew what her story would be. Born and bred in Liverpool. Parents in the awkward no-man's-land between lower class and lower middle class. Job in a mill. No prospects. Bored stiff. Came to London. Couldn't land a job. Hanging round ever since.

David seemed hardly to be listening to what she was saying. He gave her a cigarette and noticed the look in her eye. He said, "Keep the packet."

She smoked nervously and quickly, one eye on her watch. When she had finished the cigarette she said, "We'd better be getting along. I've got an arrangement with the girl I share my room with. We get there at nine o'clock we shall have an hour."

"And what would we need an hour for?" said David innocently. "It can't be another cup of coffee, surely to goodness. You've had three already."

They found a taxi, and it took them ten minutes to reach the girl's place. It was a house in the egg box of streets behind Liverpool Street Station, which seemed, from the long line of names and numbers in the dark hallway, to be divided into about thirty privately owned apartments.

33

Forty minutes later they were lying beside each other on the divan bed which almost filled the tiny room. They were both smoking.

The girl said, "You're an odd person, David. First, you haven't even asked me my name."

"What is your name?"

"Marlene."

"I don't believe it."

The girl giggled. She said, "You're quite a performer. I mean, you were good. But you didn't seem to be giving more'n half your mind to it."

"When you've got a mind like mine," said David, "half of it is enough for most jobs."

"I believe the truth is your own girl's turned you down, and you're just doing this so you can forget about her for a bit."

The tinkle of the electric bell behind the door saved David the trouble of answering.

"Deuxième service," he said. "I'd better get my trousers on."

—— 6 ——

Susan was early at the office next day. She wanted an undis-
turbed hour to sort out her thoughts on the future of the printing ink industry. She had a little room to herself on the other
side of the passage from Toby Harmond's office. She swept
all unnecessary papers off her desk, selected a new pad of paper
and a sharp pencil and started to write.

Every now and then she referred to a sheaf of notes which
she had brought with her. She was disturbed twice. Once when
the old-age pensioner who looked after the post room pottered
in with the morning mail and said, "Hard at it, miss. That's
the stuff." Once when the office cat came in and tried to scratch
a hole in her stockings.

She had covered three pages in her neat, unfussy handwriting
and was starting on the fourth when the telephone rang. It
was the outside line, with the unlisted number, and she hesitated before answering it. Normally all calls on that line were
switched straight through, on his extension, to Toby. She looked
at the clock. Nine fifty. The telephone continued to ring. She
picked up the receiver. A bland voice at the other end said,
"Splendid. Someone is awake. Would you put me through to
Mr. Harmond."

At that moment Susan heard Toby's step in the hall. Without

losing hold of the receiver, which fortunately had a long flex, she slid out from behind her desk, opened the door of her room and said, "Who shall I say wants him?"

Toby said, "What's all this?"

The man at the other end of the line said, "Am I talking to Mr. Harmond's secretary?"

"That's right."

"How many people use this number?"

"Three, I believe."

"Then you should know all their voices by now."

"Would you be Mr. Blackett?"

"I would."

She was unable to tell whether the voice was angry or amused. Toby had bolted into his office.

She said, "I'll put you straight through, Mr. Blackett."

Ten minutes later her bell rang. She gathered up the pages she had written and went into Toby's office. He seemed to be still sweating. He said, "That was a narrow shave. What would you have done if I hadn't turned up?"

"I should have said you were at the dentist."

"The dentist?"

"It always sounds more convincing than saying you're at a meeting. It invokes a little sympathy, too."

"You're a remarkable girl."

"Did Mr. Blackett want anything in particular?"

"He wanted to know how my half-yearly report was getting on. Apparently it's the only one he hasn't had yet."

"He gets them from *all* his companies?"

"Every one. And reads them."

"Would you like to cast an eye over this? It's only a draft. But you might get some ideas out of it."

Toby looked at the four pages of neat script as a shipwrecked mariner might view a sail on the horizon.

He said, "Gosh, you are a girl, Susan."

She said, "Read them before you thank me."

"Don't go away."

She sat down and watched him as he read. He was good-looking, clean and easy. He had everything except brains and drive. He was a born subordinate. Randall Blackett supplied the brains and drive. She was still unable to make up her mind whether she liked his voice or not.

When Toby had finished reading he said, "Gosh," again. And then, "Where on earth did you get all this stuff about Japanese manufacturing methods?"

"From a book in the library."

"Well, type it out, and we'll bung it in."

Susan said, doubtfully, "It was meant to be just a basis for your report."

"I think it's absolutely marvelous," said Toby. "I'll stand you the best lunch London can buy."

"Not today," said Susan. "I'm having lunch with my uncle."

"You're late again, Mr. Morgan."

"I fear so, Miss Crawley."

"Another holdup on the Central Line?"

"Between Bond Street and Tottenham Court Road this time."

"It's a funny thing that I have been traveling by that line for the last five years and have never been held up once."

"Some people are born lucky, Miss Crawley. Others are born beautiful. But we mustn't stand here gossiping all day. I have work to do."

Miss Crawley snorted. Gerald Hopkirk, arriving at this moment, said, "Good morning, Miss Crawley," and got a second snort in reply.

He said, "What have you been doing to her now?"

"Miss Crawley and I are like oil and water," said David. "Try as we will, we don't mix."

"You want to watch it," said Gerald. "I've told you. She's a dangerous woman."

Mr. Raymond Perronet-Condé was a large, untidy man who bought expensive suits and shoes and ruined them with great speed. He lost an umbrella every fortnight, was apt to leave his briefcase in trains and sometimes arrived at his office in the Stock Exchange Building wearing odd socks. None of these habits seemed to prevent him from being a successful bill broker.

He had a secretary who loved him and organized his life for him. She had procured him a table in one of the three City Lunch Clubs to which he belonged and had dispatched him to it, with a fresh rose in his buttonhole, in plenty of time to be there when Susan arrived.

He was fond enough of his niece to take some care in ordering the meal. During it, he entertained her with a number of scandalous stories about his clients. When they arrived at the sorbet, he cocked his head on one side and said, "What are you up to?"

"Up to, Raymond?"

"You didn't invite yourself to lunch with me to listen to City gossip."

"Not entirely," said Susan with a smile.

"Out with it, minx. What do you want to know?"

"I want to know about companies."

Mr. Perronet-Condé said, "It's a large subject." He signaled to the waiter and ordered coffee, a glass of kümmel for his niece and a large vintage port for himself. "Any companies in particular, or a lecture on company law?"

"What I wanted to know was, if a man has half the shares in a company, but he isn't a director, can he boss the company? I mean, can he tell the directors what to do and sack them if they don't do it?"

"Half the shares?"

"A fraction over half. Say, fifty-one percent."

"Ah! It's that last one percent that makes all the difference. If your chap has got over half—even one share over half—he can remove all the existing directors of the company and put himself and his nominees on the Board. So the answer is Yes. He can, *if* he chooses, boss the company."

"But suppose he was just acting as an adviser to the company.

Until he did what you just said—sacked the directors and took over—he wouldn't actually be in command."

"Correct."

Susan thought about it. Her uncle said, "Is this a 'Mr. A, Mr. B' problem, or am I to be allowed to know who we're talking about?"

The arrival of the coffee gave Susan time to think about this. Although her uncle gave a general impression of being a disorganized teddy bear, he was, in fact, both shrewd and discreet. She said, "The company's the one I'm working for now. You wouldn't have heard of it. It's a tiny affair called M. N. Harmond. It makes all sorts of inks. It's been in the same family for four generations."

"And this man who controls the company, but doesn't actually run it?"

"Randall Blackett."

Mr. Perronet-Condé said, "I see. It's one of his group, is it?"

"Has he got a lot of companies?"

"Fifty or sixty. The same arrangement with each of them, so I understand. He has a controlling shareholding and acts as consultant, for a fee. They do a lot of intertrading. There's some tax wangle in it. It's no good asking me about that. Tax is mumbo-jumbo as far as I'm concerned. A crazy system run by crazy people. If you try to understand it, all you succeed in doing is driving yourself crazy as well."

"Then how do you deal with your own tax?"

Mr. Perronet-Condé said, with a grin, "I pay a very good accountant to do it for me. I'd no more fill out my own tax return than I'd cut my own hair." As they were finishing their coffee he said, "You're not getting out of your depth, by any chance?"

"Not me personally, no. Why?"

"Blackett's big league."

"He's not a crook, is he?"

Mr. Perronet-Condé took his time over this one. In the end

he said, "I shouldn't think so. I don't think he could afford to be. I'd rate him as a very clever operator, who sails within five points of the wind, but knows too much about the game to get pooped."

By seven o'clock that evening the last of the staff had left the offices of Martindale, Mantegna and Lyon. By eight the cleaners had performed their ritual functions. By half past nine the City, so crowded and clamorous by day, was peaceful and empty and the cul-de-sac of St. Martin-at-Hill was a badly lighted ravine between the cliffs of silent buildings.

A patter of feet on the pavement announced the arrival of a newcomer. Miss Crawley was not moving furtively. Why should she? Was she not a law-abiding citizen, going about her business? As a long-serving employee she had been entrusted with a key to the office door. Had she not a perfect right to return there, to recover some papers which she had left behind?

Nevertheless, when, as she was coming out of Cannon Street Underground, she had spotted a patroling policeman, she had drawn back into the station entrance to allow him to get clear before she proceeded on her way.

The old rectory had a semibasement, two main floors and an attic. The basement was occupied by cashiers, telephonists and other creatures of the subworld. The plum offices were on the ground floor. Miss Crawley's den was on the first floor, immediately at the top of the stairs. She opened the front door, walked along the entrance hall and started up the stairs. She hadn't imagined that the office could be so different by night. It was full of noises which she had never consciously heard before. The muttering of the old-fashioned water-heating apparatus in the basement; the ticking of the clock in the general office. Somewhere a tap was dripping.

When she reached the top of the stairs she seemed to be short of breath and had to stop to steady herself and consider what to do next.

First she must go into her own room and recover the papers which were the excuse for her visit. The electric light had been turned off at the main by the cleaners when they left, but she had provided herself with a torch.

She found the papers, crammed them into her large handbag and went out again into the passage.

David Morgan's place of work was at the other side of the stair head—a tiny room, in the original arrangement of the house probably a maid's bedroom.

The door had no lock. Miss Crawley went in and shone her torch on the old-fashioned desk that took up most of the floor space. One of the larger drawers at the bottom would be the most likely. Feeling remarkably like a burglar, she dropped onto her knees and tugged at the right-hand drawer.

It was not locked and held nothing but old files. She tried the left-hand drawer. This contained a pullover, a set of hair-brushes, a towel and—yes—surely this was what she had come to find. She could feel it, tucked away under the towel. Its shape was unmistakable.

Not wanting to disturb anything unnecessarily, she lifted one corner of the towel and shone the torch down into the drawer. Its light was reflected back from the glass bottle. Lifting the towel a little farther she could read the label. The bottle was half full.

Miss Crawley closed the drawer gently and sat back on her heels. Anyone who could have seen her at that moment would have been shocked by the look of savage satisfaction on her normally expressionless face.

"Right, Mr. Morgan," she said. "That fixes you."

It was at this precise moment that she heard the sound. Her heart seemed to turn right over. Someone was moving on the floor below.

She switched off her torch and knelt, in the dark, her heart bumping so hard that she felt it must be audible. She said to herself, "Don't be stupid. You've a perfect right to be here. More right than he has, probably." She felt certain the intruder was a man. She could hear him more clearly now. He was walking along the passage which led to the partners' rooms.

That gave her a breathing space. She climbed to her feet and made her way out onto the landing, shutting the door gently behind her.

Her heartbeats were steadying now. Curiosity was replacing alarm. Standing at the top of the stairs she could see right down the passage. The man was at the far end of it and seemed to be crouching down. She heard a click. And then the door of the end room, which was Mr. Lyon's office, swung open, letting in a glow of light from the big window at the far end.

So it was a burglar, and he was forcing his way into the senior partner's room—a room which, as she knew, was always kept locked. A curious burglary. So far as she knew there was nothing of value in the room. She seemed to remember that clocks were often stolen, but Mr. Lyon had an electric wall clock. Any money would be in his pocket or at the bank.

Could she telephone the police? In the silence of the office the sound might be heard. The risk was too great.

Miss Crawley came to a decision which combined courage and discretion.

She tiptoed down the stairs and paused to listen. She could hear the sound of one of the filing cabinets in Mr. Lyon's room being opened. Even more curious, but reassuring. The intruder had left the front door unlocked. She opened it quietly and slipped out. Three broad steps led down to the pavement. From there another, narrower, flight served the area in front of the basement rooms. The only lamp in the street was almost directly opposite the steps.

Miss Crawley descended into the basement and concealed herself at a point where she could get a clear view of the intruder as he left.

There were moments during the next interminable hour when she regretted her impulse. Had she known he was going to be so long she could easily have summoned help. She felt cramped and cold, but she stuck to her post.

Eleven was striking from all the City clocks when her patience was rewarded. She heard the front door open and shut. A key grated in the lock, and the intruder came down the steps and walked away up the road.

He was whistling to himself and sounded relaxed and cheerful.

Miss Crawley had no difficulty in recognizing him.

— 7 —

From her window in the office, Susan saw the dark blue
S-class Mercedes 450 draw up to the curb and stop. The driver,
a big, light-haired boy with a solemn Slav face, held the car
door open.

She picked up the intercom and said, "I think the boss has
arrived."

She heard Toby make a sound, halfway between a grunt
and a gasp, like the noise driven from the body when it plunges
into cold water. She opened the door of her own room in time
to hear Randall Blackett announce himself to the girl in the
outer office, who seemed so overcome that she could do nothing
but open and shut her mouth.

Susan emerged and said, "I expect you want Mr. Harmond,
Mr. Blackett. Can I show you the way?"

The man swung round and looked at her. It was a brief
but all-inclusive inspection. He said, "You are Mr. Harmond's
secretary. We spoke on the telephone yesterday. I recognize
your voice."

"Correct," said Susan with a smile. "The room's along here
on the left. Although I expect you've been here before."

Blackett did not move. He said, "No. This is my first visit.
Might I know your name?"

44

"It's French and rather difficult. Perronet-Condé."

"Acute accent on the *e?*"

"Correct."

"Like the prince of that name in the sixteenth century?"

"Correct."

Blackett seemed to be tabulating these facts. Then he said, "Lead on."

Susan walked in front of him to the door of Toby's room, held it open, saw Toby jump to his feet and shut the door on them, then went back to her own office and sat down.

Impressive. No doubt about that. It was nothing to do with his clothes, which were regulation tycoon. It was the combination of arrogant face, soft voice and controlled, muscular movement. A brigand. Violence, cloaked under the trappings of civilization. Or was she reading too much into the short encounter? Making the mistake of building a character on the basis of what she knew he had done? Her reading in the library had widened lately. She knew a good deal about the Blackett empire now.

The bell on her desk rang. She picked up her shorthand book and made her way sedately across the passage.

Toby was looking uncomfortable. Blackett was smiling. He said, "I was questioning Mr. Harmond about the background of the really remarkable essay which accompanied his half-yearly report."

The tiger was purring.

"The statistics, which were new to me, of Japanese production and the three-stage method they employ. He seemed doubtful about the origin of these facts. And, indeed, of much else in the essay. Do I gather that you helped him with it?"

"She didn't help me," said Toby, red in the face and looking like a schoolboy owning up to a breach of school rules. "She did it all herself."

"Ah," said Blackett.

45

Susan said to Toby, "You rang for me. Did you want me?"

"*I* wanted you," said Blackett. "I wanted to congratulate you."

Susan said, "Thank you." There seemed to be nothing else. She departed, closing the door softly behind her.

"First," said Mr. Lyon, ticking off the indictments on one podgy finger at a time, "you go out of your way to be rude to one of our oldest and most valued clients."

"Unwittingly," said David.

"Possibly. Had it been an isolated instance, I should have taken no notice of it. Secondly, and contrary to my express instructions, you bring drink into the office."

He waited for David to ask him how he knew, but David seemed disinclined to oblige him. He said, "On doctor's orders."

"Indeed. And what is this remarkable complaint that has to be attended to by regular doses of Scotch whisky?"

"Hypothermia."

"I think you're making it up."

"Indeed I am not. The symptoms are very distressing."

"Might I ask what the symptoms are?"

"A sudden unassuageable thirst."

Mr. Lyon's face was pink already. It slowly turned to a dark red. "Just like my old schoolmaster," said David to Gerald afterwards. "When he was making up his mind to whop you and you said to yourself, boyo, one more crack like that and it's your head under the desk."

"I suppose you think that's funny," said Mr. Lyon at last. "I'm afraid I don't. And now perhaps you'll be good enough to explain what you were doing in the office at ten o'clock last night?"

"Some work I had to finish."

"Very creditable. But how, exactly, did you get in?"

"Most keys fit most locks. I happened to have one by me that fitted the office door."

"And another one that happened to fit the door of my office?"

David looked surprised. He said, "What makes you think that I—"

"It's no good lying about it. My informant tells me that you not only had the impertinence to break into my room, but that you spent nearly an hour in here. I think I'm entitled to a serious explanation of that, not another of your silly jokes."

"Well, now," said David thoughtfully. "I think perhaps you are. To tell you the truth, it was what you might call a matter of insurance."

"I imagine you'll condescend to explain in your own good time."

"I am doing my best," said David with dignity. "It has not escaped me that I am not the most popular of your employees. I derived from that the further thought that the time might come when you would wish our ways to part."

"It *has* come."

"Exactly," said David, in the tones of one who has scored a valuable debating point. "Exactly. And when that time did come, I wished to be certain that our parting would be without acrimony. In short, that you would give me a glowing testimonial, recommending me to my next employer and a modest sum of money—I had in mind no more than five hundred pounds—to soothe our mutual sorrow at my departure."

Mr. Lyon stared at him for a moment, seeming to sense a threat that had not been uttered. Then he said, "And what makes you think that I should do either of these improbable things?"

"It would be very much in your interests. An Industrial Tribunal can offer me ten times that amount for unfair dismissal."

"Unfair? You've brought it on yourself three times over."

"I'm entitled, I think, to proper warning. Two warnings at least, I understand. In writing."

Mr. Lyon said, contemptuously, "Try it on, if you like. Tribunals aren't fools."

"Indeed not. They have enough sense, I don't doubt, to understand me when I say that the real reason you are getting rid of me is because I was not prepared to co-operate in some of your more doubtful practices."

"What are you talking about?"

"As a law-abiding citizen and a taxpayer, it pained me to see the Inland Revenue being defrauded."

Mr. Lyon said, in a choked voice, "Would you kindly explain this nonsense and then get out."

"For instance, in a letter to our mutual acquaintance, Mr. Porteous, on"—David whisked a notebook out of his inner pocket—"on March twentieth last you said, 'I see no point in going out of your way to draw the attention of the Revenue to that particular payment. If they challenge it, we shall have to deal with it.' Was that not a little underhand? Then, in another letter, to Mrs. Porteous, you said, 'We may be asked to prove strictly that your husband was employing you as his secretary. I don't suppose any salary passed, but you should arrange for entries in your bank accounts.' Was that quite honest?"

The silence that followed was painful.

David said helpfully, "I have copies of these letters. And of several others in which little devices are suggested to our clients."

"You filthy little blackmailer!" The words were forced out of Mr. Lyon's mouth. They tumbled out, chasing and tripping over each other. "You filthy Welsh spy."

"Insults are charged at fifty pounds a time," said David, making a note in his book. "My price has now gone up to six hundred."

"I didn't know that"—he was going to say "scum," but seeing David's eye on his book he changed his mind at the last moment. "I didn't know that people like you existed."

"We learn a new fact every day of our lives, boyo. I am quite prepared to go ahead with this if you wish. I can give you two minutes to make up your mind."

There was a further bursting silence. Then Mr. Lyon said,

"How can I possibly recommend you to one of our clients?"

It was capitulation.

"Six hundred of the best," David said to Gerald. "A month's salary in lieu of notice and a glowing reference designed to secure me a post with Rayhome Tours Limited."

"Wasn't that the place Moule went to?"

"Was it, indeed? I seem to be following him downhill."

"You won't meet him there. I believe he ran into a bit of trouble and got booted out."

"Poor Moule," said David. "Perhaps he was one of those people who are destined to descend. Like me."

"You? You go round asking for trouble."

"True," said David with a sigh. "And trouble rarely refuses the invitation. However, we must not be downhearted. I am planning a pluperfect piss-up for tonight. I shall drink mathematically. Seven different drinks at seven different pubs. I shall start at the Coat and Badge, where I may have a further opportunity for being rude to Mr. Porteous. I hope you'll come with me."

"I shall do nothing of the sort," said Gerald.

— 8 —

"You seem to have made the biggest possible hit with the boss," said Toby.

Susan said, "Oh?"

"He's having your paper assessed by his Merchant Bankers. If it stands up, it will mean installing a lot of new machinery here and doubling or trebling the whole output."

"That's splendid, isn't it?"

"Splendid, yes."

"Then why are you looking like a wet Monday at Clacton?"

"Was I?" said Toby. He tried out a light laugh. It was not a success.

"What's the catch?"

"The catch is that I'm losing you."

"I should have thought that was something for you to decide. You hired me. You can fire me."

"In theory that's right. But you know how things are here. I'm managing director. But if I step out of line, I'll be out on my ear tomorrow."

Susan said, "That's nonsense. Blackett couldn't get rid of you just because you refused to sack your secretary."

"It isn't a question of sacking. You're moving up the ladder.

Into the next division. You're to work for Martin Brandreth, at Sayborn Art Printers."

"You've got this all wrong," said Susan. "You seem to imagine that we're back in the Middle Ages, when peasants belonged to the lord of the manor and could be shifted around his estates as the fancy took him. Wake up, Rip van Winkle. This is the twentieth century. I work for exactly who I want to work for."

"Of course," said Toby. "You're a free agent. It's me who's the peasant."

"Are you serious?"

"Absolutely."

"You mean, if I didn't agree to work for Mr. Brandreth, Blackett would take it out of you?"

"Without thinking twice about it. I'd be sorry to go. This business was founded by my great-grandfather and built up by my grandfather and father. I'd hate to see it fall to pieces because of me. Of course, I'm just being selfish."

"You're not being selfish at all. You're being rather nice."

This was a mistake. Toby came round his desk quickly, grabbed Susan and said, "Will you marry me?"

Disengaging herself without difficulty, Susan said, "No, Toby, I won't."

"Why not?"

"We shouldn't deal well together."

"You mean you're too good for me?"

"I don't mean anything of the sort. It's a question of genes and hormones and miscibility."

"I thought it was simpler than that," said Toby gloomily. "I thought two people just had to love each other."

"That's the icing on the cake. Now sit down and be sensible. We've got to think this thing out. Do you really mean that if I refused the job he's offering me he'd take it out of you?"

"Certainly."

"He must be mad."

"Not mad. Just touchy. There was a chap called Phil Edmunds in one of his other third-line companies. He pulled

Blackett's leg in public about wearing a Guards' tie, which he certainly wasn't entitled to, because as far as I know he was in the ack-ack. He blasted Phil out of his job and took a lot of trouble to see he didn't get another one."

"What a filthy thing to do."

"Mind you, that's one side of him. If he likes you, and believes in you, he backs you all the way. And he can be very easy to get along with."

Susan said, "Oh." It seemed to be one of her favorite remarks. Sometimes it was cold, sometimes noncommittal. On this occasion there seemed to be a hint of interest in it.

"Why don't you give it a run? Martin's all right, in his own way. And Sayborn Art Printers is a much bigger show than this."

"I'll think about it," said Susan.

She was still thinking at eleven o'clock that night. If she was not thinking about Toby and Martin Brandreth and Blackett she must have been thinking about something, because she had been sitting for half an hour, in an armchair, in front of a blank television screen.

When the telephone on the low table beside the chair rang, she hesitated. Then she picked up the receiver.

David said, "It's me."

Susan said, "Oh!" Ten degrees below zero.

"I've got something important to say to you."

"You're drunk."

"Certainly I'm drunk. If you'd had eight pints of beer and eight whiskies in eight different pubs you'd be drunk too."

"I'd be unconscious," said Susan resignedly. "But if you really have got something to say, say it. I'm tired. I want to go to bed."

"Look," said David. He spoke with the gravity of a statesman delivering an ultimatum. "You think that I'm just a good for nothing stupid clapped out boozed up Welsh wolf. Chase any tart with big boobs and dyed hair who'll give me a ride for ten quid a bang. You're a million lightyears out of date. All right. Some years ago I might have been. But that's all finished."

"And was that all you wanted to say?"

"All I wanted to say. All finished."

"Go to bed," said Susan and replaced the receiver.

Then she stretched out her hand again, this time to switch off the tape recorder.

— 9 —

Rayhome Tours operated from a building near the British Museum. The ground floor was an art bookshop. A narrow staircase, with its own entrance door, on the left of the shop led up to the second and third storys, which were all Rayhome.

"It's not much to look at," said Paula, the well-built blonde who presided over Reception. "But then, we don't see a lot of our customers. Most of our business is done by post. It's you who deals with the customers, Mr. Morgan."

"David."

"David, then."

David looked at the plaque on the desk which said, "Miss Welham." He said, "And I'm sure you've got another name, too."

"Suppose I have."

"I shall have to know it, shan't I."

"Why?"

"How do you think I can take you out for a drink this evening if I don't know your first name? Have a port and lemon, Miss Welham. It doesn't sound right."

"Do you always ask a girl out for a drink the first day you meet her?"

"Only the beautiful ones."

"Go on with you."

A telephone buzzer sounded beside the reception desk. Paula said, "Yes, Mr. Cheverton. He's here. I'll send him along." And to David, "It's the second door on the left."

David seemed in no hurry. He said, "There are two Mr. Chevertons. Which one was that?"

"That's Bob. He's the younger brother. They're neither of them all that young, really."

"The years pass," said David. "Our hair gets thinner, our teeth fewer, our breath shorter."

"You'll be short of a job if you don't hurry."

Both Mr. Chevertons were in the large front office. As Paula had said, they were past their first youth, but still impressive figures—thick-set, muscular, with the confidence which comes from running a successful business in a highly competitive market.

Bob Cheverton said, "Sit down. This is my brother Ronald."

"Pleased to meet you," said David politely.

The older Cheverton smiled bleakly, but said nothing.

"We'll explain the job to you. If you don't like the sound of it, it's not too late to back out."

"Tell me the worst, then."

"You'll find it easy enough. Once you get the hang of it. We run regular twelve-day tours. Leave on Thursday morning, back first thing Monday. You get Monday, Tuesday and Wednesday off. Three days every fortnight. Then you start again. France and Italy alternately. We used to do Germany, but the exchange rate killed it. Do you speak French?"

"Enough to order a drink."

"Let's hear you do it," said Ronald Cheverton.

"Donnez-moi, s'il vous plaît, un whisky avec un peu de glace et un Gordon's avec Martini."

"Now you're in Italy."

"Per favore, un po' di vino."

Bob Cheverton said. "O.K. You should get past. We've got our own coaches. Two of them. Custom-built for the job. A third one for emergencies or extra tours. Collings, he's our regular driver—can do any talking at the garage. He's been doing the job for years and is very reliable. So listen to what he says."

"His words shall be as gospel to me."

Ronald Cheverton said, "You're Welsh, aren't you? That means you've the gift of the gab. See you use it. The people you'll be looking after are mostly middle-class and respectable. Maybe the first time they've ever been abroad. They like being talked to."

"Perhaps a funny story, every now and then."

"As long as it's funny," said Bob.

"And clean," said Ronald.

"Next thing. We've got the routine for the paperwork lined up. All you have to do is follow the rules." He indicated a bag standing beside the desk. David had noticed it when he came in. It was made of black leather, a solid, heavy job with a steel locking bar along the top and two handles.

"That's your baby. You don't let it out of your sight by day and lock it up in your room at night. It carries all the passports, all the tickets and reservations and a float of exactly a hundred quid in cash for emergencies. Also, it's got your log book. Every day you write down in it how the trip's gone. Notes about the accommodation. Notes of complaints. Things like that. You get me?"

"I get you."

"When you arrive back after a trip, you come straight in here, as soon as you get off the coach, and you hand in that bag."

"So you can see the cash is still there," said David with a grin.

"So we can see everything's there," said Bob unsmiling. "The cash is the least important. You lose someone's passport, and there'll be hell to pay. All right. Any questions so far?"

"When do I get paid?"

"You get two weeks' pay when you get back."

"When do I start?"

"Tomorrow. At nine o'clock."

David stopped on the way out to have a word with Paula. He said, "I've got the job. That calls for a celebration."

"Meaning you and me?"

"Who else, lovely. When do you get away?"

"Half past five."

"Meet you at Henekeys, in High Holborn, at six."

"I might be there," said Paula.

"That's the girl."

"Just look at those cows," said Mrs. Fairbrass. Being French cows, they were different and, even after three days of travel, were still exciting.

"What do you suppose that building on the hill up there is?" said Miss Prothero. "It looks as if it ought to be a church, but isn't it an odd shape!"

The bus was negotiating the twisting road which skirts the northern foothills of the Pyrenees.

"That, ladies, is a Mormon chapel," said David.

"Mormons," said Miss Prothero. "What an idea. I don't believe they allow Mormons in France. Do they, Mr. Collings?"

Collings was concentrating on his driving. He was a middle-aged man with a face like an on-course bookmaker and a useful pair of shoulders on him. He grunted and said that they allowed anything in France.

"Indeed, France is very tolerant of strange religions," said David. "You'll find more chapels and tabernacles and meeting houses in a French village than you will in a village in Wales. And, believe me, ladies, that's saying something."

"What sort of religions?" said Miss Prothero suspiciously.

"Anabaptists, Second Adventists, White Mohammedans, Fifth Monarchy Men, Druids."

"Now really, Mr. Morgan," said Mrs. Fairbrass. "The others

I might swallow, but I can't swallow Druids. He's not telling the truth, is he, Mr. Collings?"

"All Welshmen are liars," said Collings.

It had been an agreeable trip so far, starting with a smooth Channel crossing and two days of sunshine. Rayhome Tours believed in taking things easy. Late starts, short runs, good meals. From David's point of view the only difficulty he could foresee was how he was going to fill in his spare time.

He expressed this thought to Collings that evening in a hotel in the outskirts of Pau. They were sharing a double bedroom, as they always did.

"Depends what you want," said Collings. He had been shaving and was now dabbing after-shave lotion onto his chin and neck. "Me, I usually go and find a woman."

"In a respectable town like this?"

"You can find a woman anywhere if you know where to look. Cost you about a hundred francs."

"I'll have to wait till I get paid before I go in for anything like that."

Collings completed his toilet and paused at the door to say, "Watch that bag. Better lock it in that cupboard *and* lock the door when you go out."

David regarded the bag with disfavor. He said, "What I'd have done would be hand it over to the hotel office and forget about it."

"Orders are, don't let it out of your sight by day. Lock it up in your room at night. Don't trust hotel safes. First place a thief would make for."

Standing at the window, David watched Collings padding off down the street. He thought that if he was a girl he wouldn't fancy a bout with Collings. There was a dangerous and disturbing animal quality about him.

"Well, da, it's not you who's got to share his attentions," he said. "Now let's have a look at you." He unlocked the black bag and tipped the contents out onto the bed. Passports, tickets, a thick folder of correspondence with hotels and a number of brochures. The log book in which he had not yet got round to making an entry. An unsealed brown envelope which contained bank notes.

David took them out and counted them. They were new notes and tended to stick together, making counting difficult. It took him two recounts to confirm that what he had was not a hundred pounds, but one hundred ten. He looked thoughtfully at the money before returning it all to the envelope.

He went across to his own case and took out, from underneath the clothes, a finely graduated steel rule and the sort of spring balance with a hook on the bottom that fishermen use for weighing their catch. Placing the black bag empty on the chest of drawers, he first weighed it carefully. Then he measured its depth, inside and outside, and repeated the process, measuring it across, in two places, from side to side.

"Tried and acquitted on all counts," said David. He had been suspicious of the bag from the moment he saw it and would not have been surprised to find that it had a false bottom or double sides with concealed pockets in them. Apparently not so.

He replaced the contents, relocked the bag, locked it in the wall cupboard, pocketed both keys and went out, locking the door behind him.

At Grasse Mrs. Fairbrass and Miss Prothero, who had struck up a holiday friendship with her, were discussing their new courier.

"Nicer than the last one," said Miss Prothero.

This was undeniable. His predecessor, David gathered, a man called Watterson, had been morose, monosyllabic and, by the end of the trip, almost permanently drunk.

"I think he's very nice," said Mrs. Fairbrass. "My late husband came from Dolgelly. It's a pleasure to hear a Welsh voice."

"He certainly does a lot of talking."

"And those stories he tells."

"A bit near the knuckle, some of them. That one about the Baptist minister and the budgerigar."

"You laughed as loudly as anyone."

"It was funny, the way he told it."

"I think he's a most unusual man," said Mrs. Fairbrass. "There's something about him. It's difficult to explain. As though there's more in him than meets the eye."

"Depths within depths."

"I'll tell you what. Why don't we ask him out to dinner to-night?"

"Go to a restaurant, you mean," said Miss Prothero, mentally counting her spare cash.

"I'll pay," said Mrs. Fairbrass. "I've brought plenty of money."

"All right. Let's ask him. It'll be a change from the hotel."

Mr. Morgan expressed himself as charmed by the invitation, and the three of them spent a very pleasant evening. By the end of it he knew a lot about them and had given them an interesting account of his own youth in the valleys. It appeared that his father had been a miner and that he, David, had succeeded, due to the coaching of a devoted schoolmistress, in winning a scholarship to Oxford.

"How did it go?" said Bob Cheverton.

"All right," said Collings. "He was a great hit with the pussies."

"In other ways, I mean."

"O.K. so far. At least he's honest. I gave him every chance to help himself to a couple of fivers."

"That's something, I suppose. And he seems to have written up his log all right." He was flicking through the book, page after page covered by Morgan's scrawling writing. "What's all this about trouble at Dijon?"

"That was on the way back. They tried to overcharge us. They tried to land us with the full tariff, when they'd agreed to demi-pension."

Collings, who was no French scholar, pronounced this last word as though it was something his employers were going to pay him when he retired.

"But you sorted it out."

"Morgan sorted it out. He told the proprietor exactly where he got off."

"In English or French?" said Ronald Cheverton, looking up for the first time from some papers he was studying.

"Oh, in French."

"Pretty fluent, I suppose."

"The proprietor seemed to understand it all right."

Ronald Cheverton said, "Hmm," and returned to his reading.

"He'll be waiting for his pay packet," said Bob. "Do we keep on with him?"

"Yes, I think so," said Ronald. "We'll give him a dry run to Italy and make our minds up after the next French trip."

Later that evening, in Henekeys bar, David said, "Big celebration tonight. We'll have a couple of drinks here and then go on and have a slap-up dinner."

"They must pay you better than they do me," said Paula.

"It's not the pay. It's the perks."

"What perks?"

"They liked their courier so much they had a whip-round at the end. Forty-five pounds. Ten of them from Mrs. Fairbrass, bless her old heart. Who said Yorkshire people were close with their brass?"

They had two drinks and then one more and went to a restaurant in Soho and had a couple of drinks while waiting for their meal. Paula had a hard head, for a girl, but she was loosening up by the time they were halfway through a large flask of Val Policella.

"It's all right for us wage slaves," said David, "but I'm damned if I know how Ronald and Bob do it."

"Do what?"

"Make a living out of it. I know what the customers paid for this trip and I know what the accommodation cost. Add in the petrol for the coach and the cross-Channel tickets and pay for me and Collings and there can hardly be twopence left for them."

"I expect they get a rake-off from the hotels."

"Could be. I know someone who gets a rake-off and that's Mike Collings. He chooses the places we stop for our midday meal. Must be worth a tenner a time to him."

"He gives me the creeps," said Paula. "He's like one of those people on the telly. As soon as he comes on, the music goes 'twang' and you know he's a baddy."

But her mind wasn't on Collings. It was fully engaged in the tantalizing problem that David Rhys Morgan presented. He was a grand talker. Was he also a doer? In short, was she going to end the evening alone in her bed, or with him in his?

She need not have worried.

—— 10 ——

"And this," said Martin Brandreth, "is the print shop. You won't have anything to do with it, not directly, but it's a good thing for my secretary to know what goes on at the sharp end."

It was a huge room, lit from above and on three sides by big windows. It was full of a bewildering variety of machinery which Susan later identified as the Roland Parva, the Roland Ultra and the Roland Favorit, the Kords, the Smart Densitometer, the Muller-Martini Trimmer Stitcher and the Krause-Wohlenberg Guillotine.

"We're one of the best-equipped outfits in the South of England. We can tackle anything from a pocket-sized brochure to a six-by-eight poster. Basic red, black, yellow and blue, but any number of combinations and shades. The client chooses the exact mix. Just like when you buy clothes in a shop. You pick out the colors you want before they start designing the dress."

He led the way through the clattering room to an apparatus of gleaming steel and blue glass. Susan was doing her best to take in the information which was being tossed at her, but was really more interested, at that moment, in the people who were operating the machines.

Her father, who had been a soldier, had once said to her,

"If you want to find out whether it's a good regiment, watch the men when the Colonel goes on a tour of inspection."

Judged by this, it did not seem to be an entirely happy outfit. The men answered up when Brandreth spoke to them, but they proffered no information, and she had yet to see one of them smile.

The young man who seemed to be in charge of this particular machine stood back as they approached. He had carroty hair, worn rather long, and the pale, freckled face which goes with hair of that color.

Brandreth said to him, "Well, Simon. How is it going?" and turned away as he said it, giving the impression that he either anticipated a routine response or was not really interested in what it turned out to be.

When the young man said nothing at all, Brandreth swung round on him. He said, "Something up?"

"I'd rather you talked to Mr. Lambie about it, sir."

The "sir" came after an interval long enough to make it sound not only reluctant, but offensive.

Susan had noticed a white-haired man hovering near the machine, who took this as a cue to advance.

"Something wrong, Lambie?"

"I'd prefer to discuss it in the office."

"As you like."

When Susan hesitated, he said, "You'd better come along too. Lambie is the father of the Chapel. He's the most important man here. Much more important than me. I'm just the mug who signs the pay checks."

He led the way out of the print shop and up to the next floor. The works had been built on a sloping piece of ground, and when they had climbed the stairs and made their way to the front of the building they were still on street level.

The front office was busy with clacking typewriters. Brandreth's suite of offices was at the far end. A conference room, a small outer room for Susan, then Brandreth's private sanctum. It was like a self-contained flat. There was even a tiny bathroom.

Brandreth paused in the conference room, as if making up his mind whether to go any farther. Then he pulled back the chair at the head of the table, plumped himself down in it and gestured to Susan and Mr. Lambie to be seated. Everything he did, Susan decided, was based on the idea of how a top man ought to act. It would have been more convincing if it had been less self-conscious.

"Well, Lambie," he said. "What is it?"

"It's Simon Wales."

"That much I did grasp. What does he want? More money?"

"No, sir. He wants an assistant."

There was a thick, red-covered, thumb-indexed book on the table. Lambie had a copy of the same book with him. Both men opened their books together and found the place they were looking for. Just as though they were going to sing a duet, thought Susan.

"He's within his rights, you know," said Lambie. "That machine rates two operators."

"I can read," said Brandreth. "If it rates an assistant, why hasn't he got one?"

"He did have. Young Ward. Went off to join his father in a newsagent's business end of last month. You remember?"

"I thought we'd got a replacement."

"We advertised for one. But the earliest anyone could come was beginning of June."

"Well, O.K. Tell him he'll have his assistant. In three weeks' time."

"He says he wants him now."

"For God's sake!" said Brandreth, losing all hold of a temper which had been slipping for some minutes. "What is this place? A bloody nursery. Does everyone want their hand held by someone else? He can have an assistant in three weeks' time. Until then he's got to work the bloody machine by himself."

"He won't do it, sir."

"Then put someone on the machine who will."

"If we start moving people from their jobs onto other jobs, we really shall be in for trouble. Like as not, they'll all walk out."

"Then shut that machine down for three weeks and send Wales on holiday."

"What about the Golden Apple job?"

There was a long and brittle silence.

Finally Brandreth jerked back his chair, jumped to his feet and started to walk up and down. Someone had left a box-file on the floor beside the table. Brandreth kicked it so hard that it flew open and all the papers spilled out onto the carpet. Mr. Lambie watched him impassively. When the exercise had worked some of the steam out of him, Brandreth sat down again and said, "Suppose you make a helpful suggestion for a change. You're meant to be impartial."

"It's difficult. We might offer him a large bonus. On the grounds that he'll be doing two people's work for the next three weeks."

"Blackmail."

"In a way."

"And another thing." Brandreth was leafing through the book on the table which Susan was now able to see was called the *Printing Industries Annual.* "There are three other machines where the rules say that the operator *may* have an assistant *if* the work justifies it. You can bet your bottom dollar, if those three lads hear that Wales has been paid a bonus, they'll all ask for an assistant, or a large bonus if they don't get one."

"It's more than likely," said Mr. Lambie stolidly.

Susan watched Brandreth curiously. He was up against a brick wall, and no one was going to help him to climb it. He seemed to realize this, because he sat back and said, "All right, Lambie. I'll have to think about it. Tell Wales I'll give him an answer by the end of the week. He can carry on for three days, surely."

"I expect he'll do that," said Mr. Lambie.

When he had gone Susan said, "What are you going to do about it? It seems quite a problem."

"I'm going to have a word with Blackett," said Brandreth. "He's solved worse problems than that. Let's get on with the work in hand. Come inside."

They went into the inner office, and Brandreth picked up the top letter from his in tray and started dictating an answer, rather fast. Susan kept up with him, her shorthand moving smoothly over the page. A lot of the letters were about the Holmes and Holmes order. It seemed to be a major operation and one that was being carried out against the clock. She began to understand why no breakdowns or delays in the print shop were wanted at that particular moment. It seemed that Holmes and Holmes were mounting an advertising campaign for a new sparkling nonalcoholic drink under the name of Golden Apple. It invigorated and refreshed, stimulated your mental and physical powers and had remarkable rejuvenating properties. Susan thought it sounded the sort of drink she would go a long way to avoid and smiled in the middle of taking down a letter to the marketing manager.

Brandreth said, "What's the joke?"

"Sorry," said Susan. "Just a thought. I was wondering what a Welsh ex-boyfriend of mine would have said if you'd offered him a glass of Golden Apple."

"Filthy muck, I imagine. But that doesn't alter the fact that it's one of the biggest orders we've had for some time. Posters, shop-window displays, tear-out leaflets and brochures. And it's a race."

"Against whom?"

Brandreth smiled and looked almost human for the first time that morning. He said, "I've never had a secretary before who'd say 'whom.' It's a race against Peppo. That, you may be surprised to hear, is a remarkable new sparkling nonalcoholic drink which inspires, refreshes and rejuvenates. It's being put out by the U.K. subsidiary of an American firm, and Merry and Merry are doing the advertising. With all these new products it's the early bird that catches the worm. A fortnight's start—even a week—can make all the difference."

"And we're running neck and neck."

"I should say we're ahead at the moment. But Merry's get all their printing done in Belgium—where they don't have strikes and go-slows and work to rules and bloody twerps like Simon Wales gumming up the whole show to screw a few more pounds for himself, and old women like Lambie sitting on their bottoms and not lifting a hand to help. Next letter—"

That was on Tuesday.

On Thursday Brandreth suspended his morning's dictation to say, "I've had an idea."

"Yes," said Susan cautiously.

"There are a lot of points about our organization that I haven't been able to explain to you. Mainly because I haven't been able to spare the time. Why don't you come down at the weekend, to my cottage in the country. We'd have plenty of time then. No disturbances. I could put you fully into the picture, give you a real idea of the organization."

"It sounds an excellent idea," said Susan. "There's just one thing. I take it your cottage is equipped with a resident chaperone?"

"Good gracious! You don't imagine—what a very old-fashioned idea."

"I'm an old-fashioned girl," said Susan. "Anyway, it wouldn't be possible this weekend. I'm spending it at Salisbury."

"Oh?"

"With my grandmother. She lives in the Close. She ranks next to the Dean's wife in order of unofficial precedence."

"It sounds like a weekend of mad gaiety. Then perhaps one of the following weekends? I will install my sister as chaperone specially for you. She will bring an Alsatian bitch and two Skye terriers."

"That sounds reasonably safe," said Susan.

11

Mrs. Perronet-Condé would have been a remarkable character in any setting. After only ten years she was, as Susan had observed, the Second Lady of the Close.

She welcomed her granddaughter affectionately, said, "I'm afraid you'll find it very dull," and proceeded to organize her weekend for her.

"There are several people I want you to meet. General Wheeler was a great friend of your father's. They went out to North Africa in the same convoy in 1940. You won't mind talking about him?"

"Not a bit," said Susan, with a smile. "It's long enough ago, now, not to mind."

Her father, having survived an adventurous war, first in the desert and afterwards in Burma, had fallen dead, under the shower-bath, after a not particularly strenuous game of squash. Susan had been fifteen years old at the time. She had loved her father very much, and it had taken her a long time to get over it, but she could think about him and even talk about him now without the cold, knotted-up feeling in her inside.

"If we call on him at twelve o'clock," said her grandmother, he will be able to offer us a glass of sherry, and our own luncheon will be an excuse to get away at a quarter to one.

There'll be tennis in the afternoon at the West Canonry. You've brought your racquet? And proper tennis clothes? Good. In the evening we are having drinks with the Dean. On Sunday morning, after Morning Service, we all congregate in the Chapter House for a cup of coffee. You'll be able to meet everyone else then."

"Everyone?"

"Everyone you would wish to meet."

"Including Mrs. Woolf?"

"I didn't know that you knew Rebecca Woolf."

"I've never met her, but I want to. I'd like the chance of a talk with her."

"What a curious idea. You realize that she has only one topic of conversation? Her late husband. He was what people call 'Something in the City.' Such an odd expression. Almost as though he was an animal in the zoo."

"In the wolf house."

"In property, actually, I believe. He died years ago, and she still speaks of him as if it was the day before yesterday. Rather an affectation, I'm afraid. I'm wrong about her only having one interest. She has a collection of Meissen china which she claims to know something about."

Her grandmother did not ask her why she wanted to meet Mrs. Woolf. Susan had reckoned on this. Her grandmother had been properly brought up and did not ask people why they wanted to do things. She usually found out in the end, though.

Breakfast was at eight, and by a quarter to nine Susan was in her car, heading for Winchester. She found the shop she wanted at the third attempt and purchased a cylindrical spill box. At Smith's bookshop she was able to pick up a book about china.

The tennis in the afternoon was rained off. Susan tucked herself away in her grandmother's drawing room and imbibed a good deal of information about the products of the Meissen factories at Dresden and their later competitors.

After service next morning she followed her grandmother

through the door in the north transept, out into the cloisters and through the slype. It was a slow progress. Her grandmother knew everybody, and most of them had something to say to her. Finally, they reached the Chapter House and joined the queue for coffee. It was as they were coming away, cup in hand, that her grandmother spotted a wrinkled lady, dressed in black, talking to one of the minor canons. She descended on her, cut out the minor canon and said, "Rebecca. This is my granddaughter, Susan. She very much wanted to meet you."

Mrs. Woolf looked surprised, but gratified. Susan got the impression that it was not often that people wanted very much to meet Mrs. Woolf. She said, "I believe you're an expert on Meissen china. I happened to pick up a small piece in Winchester yesterday and would welcome your opinion on it."

She caught a flash from her grandmother's eyes which said as clearly as words, what's the girl up to now?

Mrs. Woolf said, "I'd hardly call myself an expert. I have a few little pieces. Most of them were acquired by my late husband. I have added a number from time to time. If you'd care to bring it round, I'd be delighted to see it. Let me think. Would you be free about four o'clock? Then we could have a cup of tea."

"That would be very nice."

"I have a cottage near the High Street Gate. Your grandmother will show you where it is."

"Lovely."

As they walked back for lunch Mrs. Perronet-Condé looked as though she was going to ask questions; but breeding won.

Mrs. Woolf's collection of Meissen china turned out to be an impressive one, occupying two display cabinets and a long dresser. If Susan had been afraid that the gaps in her newly acquired knowledge would give her away, she need not have worried. Mrs. Woolf did the talking. Susan's part was confined to making appreciative noises and occasionally turning a piece over to identify the different designs of crossed batons on the underside.

By the time the tea was on the table they had moved, without effort on Susan's part, onto the second of Mrs. Woolf's preoccupations.

"Harry was a most unusual person," she said. "There are men who have a head for business and men who have an eye for beauty. Harry had both. It was a question, I suppose, of instinct. He could detect, at a glance, the difference between something that was genuine and something that was fraudulent, whether it was a piece of china or a property deal."

"I'd always understood that he was an expert in property," said Susan. "Wasn't he the founder of that company that everyone talks about nowadays—Blackford, or some name like that?"

"Blackbird Enterprises. He founded it when he came out of the army in 1945. He put his gratuity and all his savings into it, and I was able to help him with a little money I got from my mother when she died. It was a tiny thing to start with, but it grew." Mrs. Woolf separated her hand gradually, to demonstrate the growth of Blackbird Enterprises. "He used to buy things that are called options. You will understand that better than I do, I expect. He used to say about his options that they were like eggs. Sometimes they went bad, but sometimes they hatched out the most beautiful chickens. Let me cut you a slice of cake. I'm afraid this is terribly boring for you."

"It isn't boring at all," said Susan truthfully.

"Are you a businesswoman?"

"That's as good a description as any. I read Economics at London University and did my accountancy training afterwards. I've always been interested in how people make money. I think it can be one of the most fascinating subjects in the world."

"I should have thought a young girl like you would have had other interests," said Mrs. Woolf archly.

"From time to time. But don't let's bother about me. Tell me the rest of the Blackbird story."

"Harry and I had all the shares, and we were both directors.

We used to have directors' meetings in our drawing room. Once, when he suddenly remembered that we ought to have had one, do you know"—Mrs. Woolf gave an almost girlish giggle—"we held the meeting in bed. I sat up beside him and read out the minutes of the last meeting. It was all quite formal. Harry said, 'Those in favor,' and we both held up our hands. What fun it all was. Then we got bigger and bigger. More options and more properties. And then Blackett came along. Of course, things changed then."

"I imagine so," said Susan. She spoke almost in a whisper.

"After that, meetings were held at the office. And accountants got involved."

"How did Blackett get in?"

"Harry saw that it was getting too big for him to handle alone. And we wanted more money for one particular deal, and Blackett offered to buy some of our shares. He was in the same sort of business and had his own company, called Argon. I think it was Argon."

"Argon Investments Limited."

"That's right. You see a lot about it in the papers these days. It's a big affair now, I believe. But then it was only just starting. Blackett had been in the army too. He'd been a prisoner of war, and Harry was sorry for him because of that. I don't think he really liked him, though."

"When you said he bought some of your shares, you don't mean that he took over the company?"

"Oh, no. Harry would never have allowed that. I seem to remember it was thirty percent he bought. Fifteen from me and fifteen from Harry. And, of course, he became a director. And soon afterwards—well—that was when it happened."

There was a long silence, which Susan hardly liked to break.

"It was cancer," said Mrs. Woolf. "Cancer of the stomach. Nothing to be done about it. He came home early from the office one day, in the middle of January, and sat down in his armchair beside the fire and told me all about it. He wasn't worried for himself at all. It was me he was thinking about, all the time. He said, 'I've made Blackett an offer. He can have the rest of the shares, yours and mine, for one hundred thousand pounds. I've given him a month to make up his mind. If he doesn't, I'll put the shares on the market. We'll get the money, all right. It'll buy you an annuity, which will look after you quite comfortably.' That was the sort of man he was."

For a moment Susan saw, through the wrinkles of long widowhood, the real Rebecca Woolf, the wife who had held a Board meeting in bed with her husband. She said, "If Blackett was only just beginning, I wonder how he raised a hundred thousand?"

"He very nearly didn't. It was only a few days before the month which Harry had given him was up. It must have been just before February fourteenth, because Harry came back, with all the annuity documents in a large envelope, and he'd put a Valentine card in with them. It's there on the mantelpiece. My dear, I don't know why I'm telling you all this. I've never talked to anyone quite like that before. It must be your pretty face."

When Susan got back her grandmother said, "Well, I hope you had a good time."

"I thought she was an interesting woman."

"I have a great respect for your judgment," said her grandmother drily. "I must add her to my visiting list."

What she meant was that she would go round and try to find out what Susan and Mrs. Woolf had been talking about and unearth from this the object of her granddaughter's peculiar behavior.

Susan doubted whether she would be successful.

— 12 —

The first Italian tour and the second French tour went off smoothly enough. Collings was the only fly in the ointment. It had not taken David long to realize that he had two jobs. One was to drive the coach. The other was to see that David stayed in line. He was obliged to share a bedroom with Collings. His personal habits did not make him an ideal companion. Apart from this minor inconvenience, he had no complaints.

The Chevertons seemed to have accepted him as a regular member of the Rayhome team. It was after the second French trip, when he was being paid off, that Bob Cheverton said to him, "In August and September, with the bookings coming in as they are, we have to squeeze in additional tours. Don't worry, they won't affect you. You go on with the regular ones. We'll probably get Watterson back, on a part-time basis."

"I've heard people speak of him," said David.

"Nothing complimentary, I imagine. He wasn't really satisfactory. But he did the job for three years and he knows the ropes. By the way, he can use your bag. It's getting a bit scruffy. We like our regulars to have the best kit. Order yourself a new one. That's the man who makes them for us." He showed David a card which had the name "Egbert Smiles" printed on it, followed by an address in Leather Lane. "If you go straight down now, he'll have it ready for you by Thursday morning. He makes them for us specially. He's a real old-fashioned craftsman. You'll have to pay him in cash. They cost one hundred twenty pounds, and we add a fiver for him." He took an envelope out of the desk drawer and pushed this across. "The money's in there. Bring back the receipt."

Egbert Smiles took some finding. There was no sign of his shop in Leather Lane, but David finally located his card, tacked up beside a door in one of the tiny streets which lie behind the Lane, relics of gas-lit Victorian days. The premises were in darkness, and the door was locked.

David rang the bell, waited patiently and rang it again. He had just concluded that Mr. Smiles must be out when there was the sound of approaching steps, the light went on and the door was unlocked and opened.

The room, two steps down from the street, was a shop of sorts, with a collection of sandals, belts and handbags, arranged on shelves and looking as though they had been there for some time. Egbert Smiles was a small, bent man with a white beard. Six more like him, thought David, and he wouldn't be surprised to find Snow White asleep on a couch at the back.

"I've come about the bag," he said. "The bags you make for Rayhome Tours."

"That's right," said the old man. "I've made a lot of them."

"They want another."

"Satisfied customers, eh?"

"Highly satisfied. There's a bit of hurry about this one. I've got to pick it up on Wednesday evening."

"No problem. I have the pieces ready-cut. Just a matter of sewing them together. Might I know your name?"

"The name's Morgan. David Morgan."

The old man had produced an order book. It looked newer and more business-like than anything else in the shop. There was fresh carbon paper between the pages. Mr. Smiles pressed heavily on a stub of pencil as he wrote, "One special courier's bag, ordered by Mr. David Morgan. For delivery Wednesday evening." He pushed the book across to David, who signed it. He then tore out the top copy, handed it over to David and seemed to be waiting for something.

David said, "Do I pay you now or when I collect the bag?"

"Usual thing is, you pay me now. I'll give you a receipt."

"If that's the arrangement." David got out the envelope which Bob Cheverton had given him and handed it across. Mr. Smiles counted the money twice. When he had satisfied himself that there were twelve ten-pound notes and one fiver, he recovered the copy of the order form which he had given David and scribbled on it, under David's signature, "Paid cash £120 E Smiles." This seemed to conclude the transaction. As David left he heard the sound of the door being locked behind him.

Making his way back, on foot, towards the British Museum he thought about Egbert Smiles. There had been something offbeat about the whole scene. It was difficult to put a finger on it. He stowed it away in his memory as one more oddity about Rayhome Tours—which he was beginning to think was rather an odd outfit altogether.

Back at the office he handed over the receipt to Bob Cheverton. "Odd sort of cove, Mr. Smiles," he said. "Does he do anything except make bags for our couriers?"

"One or two other jobs, I imagine. Special orders. That sort of thing. He's a fine workman."

"He does a good job," agreed David. On his way out he met a middle-aged man, with a sour face and a cavalry moustache, propped up against the reception desk.

"Meet your predecessor," said Paula. "Bill Watterson. He had three years of it and still comes back for more."

"You the new boy?"

"The very latest thing," said David. "If you're not doing anything at this very moment, why don't we go out and have a small drink? Then you can tell me all the snags. The ones I haven't encountered already, that is."

Watterson looked at his watch and seemed to be debating

which of a number of important engagements he would have to postpone. "Just a quick one, then," he said.

The quick ones started at noon in a public house in New Oxford Street and were still going strong at four o'clock in a small club behind the British Museum which was patronized by ladies with crew cuts and artists with beards. It was not clear whether Watterson was a member, but he seemed to be on Christian name terms with the proprietor.

"Don't touch the gin," he said. "Dan makes it in his bath. The Scotch and the vodka are good."

They drank the Scotch and the vodka alternately. Watterson was showing all the signs of a man who is not an alcoholic, but is only one stop short of it. He put down his first few drinks at a galloping pace, fiercely and with no apparent pleasure. Now he was slowing down. Although he had taken three drinks to David's two, without appearing to note the discrepancy, he was not drunk. Possibly, thought David, the concentration of ethyl alcohol in his bloodstream was already so high that adding enough to it to put a moderate drinker under the table made little appreciable difference. "Which makes nonsense of breathalysers and blood tests," said David.

"Pardon?"

"Just a passing thought."

"You're an odd character. I knew that as soon as I set eyes on you. What are you doing in this setup?"

"Turning an honest penny."

Watterson seemed to be having a fit. David prepared to administer first aid and realized that what was convulsing his drinking companion was laughter. When he had recovered his power of speech, Watterson said, "Honest? You did say honest, didn't you? Yes. I thought you said honest."

"It looks straight enough to me."

"Straight. Straight as a corkscrew. Straight as a spiral staircase. Straight as—" Here Watterson's imagination failed him.

"Where's the twist?"

"I don't know exactly what they're up to. But stands to reason

78

they must be up to something, doesn't it? They couldn't buy tram tickets with the money they make out of those tours. They give the customers five-star treatment at one-star prices. That's why they're so bloody popular."

"Then what's the sideline? Some sort of smuggling, I suppose."

For a moment Watterson looked wholly sober. He said, "I'll give you some advice, son. If you want to keep the job, don't ask questions. Keep your mouth shut, and it's a good job. I ought to know. I had it for three years, and they still want me back when there's a rush on. The chap who had it before me, man called Moule—"

"Mole?"

"Right. Like the little creature who digs down under your lawn, only spelt with a *u*. He started digging. They put the hard boys onto him. End of Moule."

"What did they do to him?"

"They made faces and said, 'Boo,' and he scuttled off down the nearest hole. Poor little Moule."

"He doesn't sound like a very heroic person."

"Mind you, I think he'd started main-lining by then, and that's not something that builds up the character. The only time I saw him since then—he was coming out of a doctor's surgery, down near the Surrey Docks. Dr. Ram Jam something-or-other. One of the people you could get to prescribe the hard stuff. If you were prepared to pay. He'd have done better if he'd stuck to drink. Drink in moderation never hurt anyone."

David took the hint and had both glasses recharged. At that point one of the crew-cut ladies took a swing at a bearded artist. By the time peace had been declared the room was a lot emptier, and David brought the drinks over to a table in the corner.

He said, "Let's sit down for a bit. I want to hear about Moule."

"Why?"

"He did the job before. If he ran into trouble, I'd like to know about it, then I can dodge it."

79

"Nothing much to tell you about him. He did the job all right, for a bit. Then he started on drugs. Reefers to start with, I'd guess. He was an educated man. Bit of money behind him, too. I believe he used to be an accountant with quite a good firm."

"Not really a big firm. But an old, established one. Martindale, Mantegna and Lyon, in the City."

"If you never met Moule, how do you know that?"

"The long arm of coincidence. I worked in the same firm for a time. That's how I got this job. Rayhome are one of their clients. Only in a small way. Most of their work is done for Blackett and his group of companies."

Watterson put down his half-empty glass on the table. His face, normally red, had become mottled. He said, "Are you talking about Randall Blackett, by any chance?"

"That's the one. Do you know him?"

For a moment David thought that Watterson wasn't going to answer him. His eyes had a fixed look, as though he was staring at something a long way off. Then he said, "Certainly I know Blackett. Not like people know him nowadays, with Saville Row suits and a big car and a chauffeur and everyone saying, 'Yes, sir. No, sir.' I've seen him without his smart clothes on. Almost, you might say, with no clothes on at all."

He swallowed the rest of the drink and sat silent. David said nothing.

"The first time I saw him, he was wearing a strip of sacking round his beautiful young body and a big smile on his beautiful young face. The sacking was the normal dress in a Japanese working camp. The smile was unusual. Why was Lance-Bombardier Blackett smiling? He was smiling because it was his nineteenth birthday and he'd had a lovely birthday present. A special meal of rice and real meat with a glass of saké to top it off. The Commandant gave it to him. Blackett had paid for it by selling him his lovely white body."

On the last word Watterson fell forward. His head hit the table with a thump. Dan came out from behind the bar and propped him up. Watterson's face was red and sweating. His mouth was wide open, and his eyes were shut.

"Seen them go like that before," said Dan. "Nineteen drinks and sober as an archdeacon. Number twenty and they go out flat. You got a car here?"

"I'm afraid not."

"Never mind. I'll get a cab. I know where he lives. I'll look after him."

"That's very kind of you. I'd better pay for the cab."

"Don't bother," said Dan. "I'll get it out of him next time he comes."

The second Italian trip started on the same lines as the first one. The Rayhome coach, every seat full, made its leisurely way through France and Switzerland, crossed the frontier at Domodossola and spent a night at Bologna before crossing the Apennines by the beautiful Via Stradale and descending on Florence. Here the party was due to stay for five days.

David could not decide whether there really was something different about Collings's attitude or whether he was imagining things based on the suggestions put into his mind by Watterson. He was no more offensive than usual, but seemed to be more tense and to be watching David more closely than on previous trips.

The situation became clearer on the third night in Florence. The party was staying at a large pensione in the Via Solferino behind the Opera. As usual, David had been allotted a room with Collings. He was sitting on his bed, watching Collings prepare himself for an evening foray. He had shaved for the second time that day and was now rubbing on some powerful after-shave lotion. When he had finished he said, "Any objection if we make it a twosome tonight?"

"A twosome?"

"Look round the town together. You speak a bloody sight better Italian than I do. Seems, from something you said to one of the pussies, you've been here before. Is that right?"

"Once or twice," said David cautiously. "But I would imagine that you have been here many more times than I have. Is it not one of your regular stopping places?"

"Maybe. But not speaking the lingo you don't get round to what you might call knowing the people. You pick up a girl and all she says is 'Ten thousand lire' when you meet her and 'Ta-ta' when you go."

"Hardly an intellectual conversation," agreed David. "If we both go out together would it not be better, do you think, to leave the bag in the hotel safe?"

"It's right enough where it is," said Collings. He indicated the corner cupboard which was a solid construction. "I've got the key. No one's going to bother to break that down."

"All right, then. Let's have an evening on the tiles together. Have you any idea of where to start?"

"There's a place behind the Market. You can usually get what you want there."

"Depending on what you want."

"That's right," said Collings with a grin.

They went on foot, through the small dark streets that led to Central Station and across the piazza in front of it, dodging the scurrying taxis. Collings seemed, for once, to be in a talkative mood. He said, "Tell you the truth, Morgan, this place gives me the creeps. Very picturesque, no doubt. But look at those houses. And those bloody great wooden doors you never see open. What's behind them?"

"The Middle Ages," said David.

"You're dead right. You put your finger on it. They're still living like they were five hundred years ago. Daggers and poison and Borgias and things like that. I bloody near got done myself in one of those rat-holes. Mind you, that was over a girl. When I was going away, her ponce turned up and tried to double the price. When I told him what he could do, he pulled a knife."

"What did you do?"

"Kicked him in the crutch and scarpered."

"Sound tactics," said David.

At the far side of the piazza was the Via S. Antonio, full of bakeries and sweet shops, still open although it was after nine o'clock.

The place they were making for was on the north side of the market and was a surprise. David had imagined that, if it suited Collings's objectives, which would be drink, more drink and girls, it would be a fairly sordid place. In fact, the Toscanella turned out to be well lighted and cheerful. There was one large and noisy party in the corner by the bar, but most of the tables were occupied by couples drinking red and green liquids out of long glasses and minding their own business.

Collings ordered a bottle of Pernod and a jug of iced water, and they started to drink, not rapidly, but steadily. Between drinks, Collings continued to talk. He was not a practiced conversationalist and soon started to repeat himself. David prodded him along with an occasional question and wondered what it was all in aid of.

They had got a long way down the Pernod when Collings noticed the girl. David had seen her some time before. She had light hair, more red than blonde, unusual in a city of black-haired girls. She was not young, nearer thirty than twenty, David guessed, and undeniably attractive.

"Quite a dish," said Collings. His voice had suddenly got thicker.

"I think she's waiting for someone."

"She's waiting for me."

"Do you know her?"

"I know her type."

"She doesn't look like a tart to me."

"I know more about tarts than you've forgotten," said Collings. He lurched to his feet and swaggered across to the girl.

She was too far away for David to hear what Collings said to her, but the meaning of her answer would have been clear at any distance. Collings sat down in the empty chair, put his

83

elbows on the table and said something else. The girl gave him a look which would have stopped a charging buffalo. Collings grinned, leaned forward and grabbed her wrist. The girl wrenched herself free and scrambled to her feet.

By this time the noise and clatter in the room had died down, and attention was concentrating on Collings and the girl. She said in clear but clipped Italian, "Take your hands off me, you filthy, drunken pig."

A big man with curly black hair had detached himself from the party in the corner. He reached Collings in three quick strides, said, "English filth. Leave our girls alone," and smacked his face.

Collings jumped up, grabbed the chair he had been sitting on and hit the man with it. A second man from the party surged across the room. Collings swung the chair again, lifted it too high and brought down the light above the table, and in doing so fused all the table lamps.

By this time the proprietor had reached the street door, just ahead of half a dozen customers who had decided to get out and were now blocking the exit.

David had kept his eye on the girl. She had backed away from the fight and was standing against the wall. David moved across, touched her on the shoulder and said, "Come with me."

He pushed her ahead of him, through the door which led into the kitchen. He walked quickly through, ignoring a protesting lady in a black dress and a frightened-looking youth in a chef's hat, opened a door at the far end, crossed a cluttered courtyard and found himself in an alley full of dustbins.

As they came out, they heard the wah-wah of a police car approaching the front of the restaurant.

"Down here," said David, "and let's hope it leads somewhere."

The alley led to another alley, then to a third. David remembered Collings's description of rat-holes and daggers and was glad to see lights ahead. They emerged from under an archway and out into the Via Guelfa.

David said, in his best Italian, "Might I perhaps get hold of a taxi to take you home?"

"It's very kind of you," said the girl, in perfect and upper-class English. "It's hardly worth a taxi. We live in the Via Zanobi. The second turning across the road."

"Then let me escort you as far as there."

"You got us out of that place very skilfully."

"The first thing I do in any strange restaurant, I locate the way out through the kitchen."

"It sounds as though you have a very adventurous life."

"Not at all. It's just that I'm an expert at running away."

By this time they had reached the front of a tall, gaunt house in the Via Zanobi. A stone staircase led into upper darkness.

"You've got to come up and meet my husband, Carlo. He'll want to thank you."

"Are you sure?"

"Certain. He is an architect and a very fine one. Some day the name Carlo Aldini will be known through the whole of Italy. Through the world, perhaps. I'm afraid there's no lift."

"*Excelsior*," said David.

On the third landing they stopped again. The girl said, "I warn you. He will be repentant. Violently repentant. Carlo does nothing by halves."

"Repentant for what?"

"He was to have met me at the Toscanella. We were going to have a drink there and a late supper at Piero's. He is engaged in an important project and will have forgotten all about it. You'll see."

They reached the fourth floor. The girl inserted the key in the lock and opened the door. Immediately, from the room at the far end of the hallway, came a sound halfway between a roar and a scream. It reminded David of the mating call of a gorilla. The door was flung open, and a young man with a mop of black hair hurled himself out, fell on his knees in front of the girl and clasped her round the ankles.

"Carlo, get up at once," said the girl. "This is—"

"David," said David.

"He rescued me from a very embarrassing situation."

"Caused by my atrocious, my criminal forgetfulness."

He jumped to his feet and pumped David energetically by the hand.

In ten minutes David had found out all about them. The girl was Clarissa Hope-Masters. He remembered the name. It was something to do with merchant banking. He guessed that it was her money that was supporting the household whilst Carlo made his way. Carlo showed him some of his work. He knew too little about architecture to do more than make appreciative noises. They had a drink and then another one. It was nearly midnight when David said good-bye. They seemed genuinely sorry to see him go.

When he was leaving, Clarissa said. "If ever you're in difficulties about somewhere to stay, we've got a spare bedroom. Our telephone number isn't in the book yet. I've written it down for you." Carlo seconded the invitation. They sounded as though they meant it.

As David walked home through the streets, empty of pedestrians but still plagued by the unwearying, unceasing motor traffic, he was thinking about his hosts. He had known a number of Anglo-Italian marriages, some successful, some not. He had liked both the young people and wished them well.

When he reached the pensione, the entrance hall was deserted and the night porter was not at the reception desk. Also, the key of his room was missing from its hook.

His room was on the third floor. There was a lift, but David decided to use the stairs. From the point where they emerged on the third-floor landing he could see the door of his room. There was a strip of light showing under the door. He stood at the head of the stairway and thought about it. He could not believe that Collings had succeeded in disentangling himself from the situation at the Toscanella and got back to the hotel by midnight. He remembered turning the light out before they had left. It was not the sort of hotel where maids came in and turned down beds.

He heard the click of the handle and saw the bedroom door opening. He took a step back to the stairhead.

He had a clear view of the two men who came out. They turned out the light, closed the door and locked it. Their movements were unhurried. The taller of the men had a long, sad face topped by a bush of hair and a chin so deeply cleft that it might have been cut by a sword. The second man was smaller and rounder and had square, executive-type glasses. Both wore dark suits and might have passed in the street for businessmen; but not in that deserted corridor, and not at that hour of the night.

After a moment's hesitation, which brought David's heart into his mouth, the men turned to the left and made for the lift. He stayed where he was, listening to the whine of the lift going down, the clang of the gate opening, footsteps on the tessellated pavement of the hall and the sound of the front door shutting. Only then did he make his way down the stairs. His room key was back on its hook, but there was still no sign of the night porter.

David studied the row of hooks. Most of those for the first and second floors were empty of their keys. These would be the rooms of the Rayhome contingent, energetic sightseers and early bedders. A few of the third-floor keys were on their hooks. David's room was 317. The next two rooms, 318 and 319, were, he thought, empty. He pocketed his own key and key 318 and was turning to go, when a door behind the reception desk opened and the night porter appeared.

"I thought I heard someone," he said.

"You were right," said David. "It was me, but it might have been a thief."

"We are not much troubled with thieves."

"No? Did you see the two men who went out just now?"

The porter blinked his red-rimmed eyes and seemed to be debating the question. Then he said, "No, sir. What men? I saw no one."

"One tall, one short and stout with glasses."

"They would be visitors to the hotel, perhaps."

"Perhaps," said David. "Good night."

"Good night, sir."

When he got back to the third floor, David went along to room 318 and opened the door cautiously. The bed had been stripped down, and the room was plainly unoccupied. There was a key in the corner cupboard. David extracted it and returned to his own room. As he had hoped, the key from 318 worked equally well in his own corner cupboard. He took out the black bag, unlocked it and tipped out the contents onto the bed.

"Now, friend of my travels," he said, "let us see how well Italian food suits you." He got out the fisherman's scale, put the hook round the handle of the bag and held the dial up to the light. "A diet of spaghetti and pasta is said to be fattening. And Jesus, so it has been! You have gained more than a kilo since I weighed you last. My goodness, you will have to watch your waistline!"

He put away the scale, took out his ruler and made some careful measurements.

The right side of the bag was the interesting one. He pressed it gently and listened.

"So! Now what is the way in? It can only be by the top."

The lips of the bag were formed by thick strips of steel. The strip on the left held the bag's locking apparatus. The one on the right, the slot into which the tongue of the lock fitted. It did not take him long to discover the catch which controlled the right-hand strip and enabled it to slide. Inside the cavity formed by the outer and inner walls of the bag were six flat cellophane envelopes. David opened one of them, tipped a few of the tiny crystals onto the palm of his hand and touched them with the tip of his tongue. Then he tipped the grains equally carefully back into the bag, resealed the envelope, replaced it, closed the cavity, relocked the bag and put it back in the corner cupboard, being careful to position it exactly as he had found it.

When he had relocked the cupboard, he returned the key

to room 318, relocked that door and, after considering the matter carefully, left the key in the lock. He hoped that anyone finding it there would assume that the last person using the room had left it there by mistake.

Then he went back to his own room, undressed, put on his pyjamas and opened the window. Collings had not encouraged this practice, not being a believer in fresh air, but Collings would be sleeping somewhere else that night.

He leaned on the windowsill and looked out. The sky was full of stars. He could hear the traffic on the Lungarno, far enough away to be a soothing background to his thoughts.

A number of things were becoming clearer.

Small wonder that the Chevertons had not worried about the profit on their coach tours. Two pounds of pure, high-grade heroin would net them twelve thousand pounds. The retailers, at curb-side prices, would make twice as much. Pull that off once a month, and you were doing all right. There was little risk. Rayhome Tours were a well-known and respected outfit. Their coaches had been crossing to the Continent for years, coming back crowded with happy, middle-class passengers clasping souvenirs from France and Italy. And suppose they had been searched. First, the searchers would have had to be clever enough to find the carefully concealed pocket in the courier's bag. *And if they had found it?*

David was suddenly conscious of a cold feeling. He had just grasped the meaning of the transaction with Egbert Smiles. He had himself signed an order for a "special" bag. He had paid for it himself in cash. The receipt had gone back to the Chevertons. There was not a scrap of evidence that David had not ordered the bag with the hidden pocket to indulge in a little private smuggling on his own. Smiles was working with the Chevertons and was no doubt handsomely paid to keep his mouth shut.

"Sod the lot of them," said David. He got into bed and lay awake for some time, thinking. One thing was clear. They did not mean him to be caught, and it was very unlikely he would be caught. With that comforting thought he went to sleep.

Collings arrived back after breakfast the next morning. David was in the front hall when he was driven up in a smart car. The chauffeur was a tall man with a bush of hair and a deeply cleft chin. The man sitting at the back with Collings wore square executive glasses. Collings had a small bruise on the left side of his chin, and his hair was combed forward, possibly to hide a cut on his forehead. Otherwise he looked his normal surly self.

He said to David, "You made yourself scarce, I noticed."

"No point in both of us getting involved. What happened to you?"

"The caribs picked me up."

"And let you go?"

"I've got friends. They fixed it."

"Friends are always useful," said David.

The next day the party left for England. There was no trouble at the French customs and none at Dover. The coach rolled sedately home through the fields of Kent. The arrangement was that the passengers were dropped at various points in London, and by the time they drew up at the Rayhome office it was nearly dark and David and Collings were alone in the coach.

The normal routine was observed. Collings took charge of the leather bag and disappeared with it into the Chevertons' office. David parked himself in the small room at the end of the passage and waited.

It was ten minutes before Bob Cheverton appeared. He was smiling. He said, "That seems to have been a successful trip. We've already had one pair on the blower, telling us how much they enjoyed it. We're adding a small bonus to your pay." He pushed across an envelope.

"Well, ta very much," said David. "I enjoyed it myself."

When he counted the money later that evening, he found that the small bonus was fifty pounds.

——— 13 ———

When Susan arrived at the office of Sayborn Art Printers at
nine o'clock on the Monday after her Salisbury visit, it seemed
to her that there was an unusual air of activity in the place.
Martin Brandreth, who was not normally on view until ten
o'clock, had evidently arrived early for once, and she could
hear his voice from the inner office. He was delivering a ha-
rangue.

Presently the door opened, and the red-haired Simon appeared. His face was whiter than usual, and he seemed to be
walking in his sleep. The bell on Susan's desk rang, and she
picked up her shorthand notebook and went in.

Brandreth was standing with his back to the window, looking
pleased with himself. He said, "Apparently we shan't be having
any more trouble with young Mr. Simon Wales. Which is a
good thing, because we shall be working against time for the
next few weeks. I spent most of Sunday with Blackett. It ap-
pears that Merry and Merry have been getting their skates
on. It's going to be a close finish. They're planning to put forward the opening of the Peppo campaign by four days, which
gives us four days less to produce the goods."

"I'm sure we'll manage it," said Susan.

"We shall have to reorganize the whole of the printing schedule. I've called a meeting of the department heads for eleven o'clock. We'll draw up a co-ordinated program for each of the machines. It'll mean overtime working, and we shall have to agree on special rates for that. I'll have a word with Lambie as soon as we've got the outline arrangements sorted out. Ready?"

He started dictating. Susan admired the clarity of his thoughts and the precision of his language. No doubt this was what working under Blackett's whip did for you.

It was a busy morning. At half past one the pace slackened sufficiently for her to be able to think about getting something to eat.

The normal lunch break was at one o'clock. She was surprised to find one of the girls still at her desk in the outer office. As Susan appeared she got up and said, hesitantly, "If you're going out to lunch, would you mind very much if I came with you?"

"Of course not," said Susan. The girl was called Eileen, and she knew her vaguely. She had once caught her reading Lyne on economic fallacies and suspected her of going to night classes.

They fought their way into an overcrowded restaurant in the High Street and were lucky enough to find two stools round the far end of the lunch counter, where their nearest neighbor was a stout man who was ingesting oxtail soup into a cavity under a walrus moustache.

Under cover of the noise he was making, Eileen said, "I didn't know who to talk to about it, but I had to talk to someone."

"Try me," said Susan agreeably.

"It's about Simon. We're—well, we're not exactly. But you know what I mean."

"An unofficial arrangement."

"That's right. Well, it was what happened on Saturday. He was going to the dogs." Eileen smiled and suddenly looked less intellectual but a lot more attractive. "I mean the races. The afternoon program at Dagenham. I don't really care for that sort of thing, so we arranged we'd meet at my place for a concert we were going to that evening. He didn't turn up. He's usually very conscientious about things like that. I telephoned his house. He lives with his mother. He hadn't come home. She was terribly worried, and we wondered if we ought to tell the police, only it sounded so silly. Well, anyway, we thought we'd wait. I telephoned about an hour later, and his mother said, yes, he'd come home, but wasn't at all well. He was in bed. So I said, fine, I'm glad he's back. I'll look him up tomorrow. She didn't seem keen on the idea at all. She said, leave him till Monday. So I said, all right, I'd do that. And this morning—well you saw him. He's not himself at all. But when I asked him about it, he said I wasn't to ask questions. Just like that. Don't ask questions. He needs help. I'm sure of it. But I can't help him unless I can find out what it's all about. I wondered if you—it's a lot to ask, I know."

Susan said, "All I really know—and that's no secret—is that he was refusing to operate his machine without an assistant and now he's changed his mind, much to Mr. Brandreth's relief."

"But what *made* him change his mind? Something happened to him on Saturday afternoon. I'm sure of it."

"Dog tracks are rough places. Suppose he got involved in some sort of trouble. He looked to me as if he might be suffering from delayed shock."

"Is that something he ought to see a doctor about?"

"I shouldn't think so. Time's the best cure. Look, why don't you give him a day or two, and he'll probably be himself again."

But not quite himself, thought Susan. Someone who's been badly frightened never quite gets over it. There's a lesion, deep down. Like a scar which gives you a twinge in the cold weather.

"I would like to find out what happened. I really would."

Susan said, "If I were you, I'd leave it alone. I mean that."

"If you think that would be best."

She seemed relieved that someone else had made the decision. They walked back to the office together. The first thing Susan noticed was the dark blue S-class Mercedes 450 which was sneering at the other cars in the car park. The next was the large, light-haired boy in the driving seat who caught her eye and winked at her.

Susan went inside thoughtfully and sat down behind her desk. She could hear the voices from the private office. Presently the door opened, and Blackett came out, followed by Brandreth. She thought that Blackett was going to ignore her, but he swung round at the last moment, came back and stood in front of her desk, balancing forward on both feet like a swimmer on the edge of the high board.

He said, "Mr. Brandreth will have told you that we're in for a race."

"Golden Apple versus Peppo."

"Right. And it's going to be a closer thing than I thought. Merry's have cut another three days out of their printing schedule. What would you suggest we do about that?"

He seemed to be asking her opinion seriously, so she thought about it. She said. "There's not much slack in our new schedule. If the bus and Underground posters are the important thing, we could get them out first and fast. It would mean all-night working, but it could be done."

"There's an alternative. We might buy up Merry and Merry."

"Suppose they aren't for sale?"

"Most things are for sale if you offer the right price. I'm going to see my accountants about it now. Talking of which, I understand we have something in common."

"Oh?"

"I qualified as an accountant in 1950. When did you take your finals?"

Susan nearly said, "How did you know that?" but realized it would be stupid and said, "Three years ago."

"But never practiced?"

"I thought I'd have a shot at a business career first."

"Very sensible. I thought I'd have a shot at it, too. I've been shooting ever since."

94

Brandreth was fidgeting, but Blackett showed no signs of wanting to depart. He said, "Accountancy training is like legal training. Once you've been through it, it conditions your thinking. I knew you were an accountant as soon as I read that report you did for young Harmond. It stood out a mile."

He swung round and stalked out. Brandreth trotted after him. When they reached the car park, the chauffeur already had the door open. Blackett waved to Brandreth to get in beside him.

He said, "If you employ that girl as a shorthand typist you'll be wasting her. She's got an organizational brain."

"I'd realized that. I think she'll be very useful."

"You can keep her as long as you use her properly. No longer."

"It's a mystery to me why she's in the job at all. She must be around thirty. With a brain like hers and her looks, I'd have thought she'd have been married long ago."

"Any sign of a boyfriend?"

"She did mention once—I can't remember quite how it came up—that she had a Welsh ex-boyfriend."

"You're sure she said 'ex'?"

"Yes. And said it pretty firmly."

"That's the snag about having all the talents. You have to find someone to match up to you. It isn't always possible."

This seemed to be the end of the conversation. Brandreth got out, and the car drove off.

"I told you at the time he was no good," said Miss Crawley triumphantly. "I saw him coming out of this public house with a common girl on his arm. He was drunk. He was always drunk."

"I shouldn't wonder," said Gerald Hopkirk. He was tired of Miss Crawley and wanted to get on with his work.

"It passes my comprehension why Mr. Lyon gave him a reference, as well as all that money."

"How did you know what he gave him?"

"I knew because Mr. Morgan told me. With a nasty smirk.

I said, if I'd been Mr. Lyon—if I'd found you nosing round among my private papers—I'd have booted you straight out. What would our clients have said if they'd known that he was snooping into their private affairs? What would Mr. Blackett have said if he'd known you'd caught him looking into his files?"

"What indeed?" said Blackett.

The Sergeant had opened the door for him, and he was half-way into the room. Miss Crawley gave a squeak of agitation, and Gerald jumped to his feet.

"I understand that Lyon is still not back from his lunch." Blackett looked pointedly at his wristwatch as he said this. "Perhaps I could explain to you a simple matter that I wanted looked into, and you could pass it on to him. The matter is urgent, or I wouldn't have bothered you."

"Of course," said Gerald, Miss Crawley fluttered out, followed by the Sergeant. "I'm sure Mr. Lyon won't be long. But please sit down."

"And who was the unsatisfactory character you had to get rid of?"

"A chap called Morgan. He wasn't a bad sort, really. But he didn't quite fit into an accountant's office."

"I think I remember seeing him. A Welshman, medium height, thick-set."

"That's him."

"And which of my files was he interested in?"

Gerald remembered, with a feeling of relief, that it had been an innocuous collection of PAYE returns. He said, "I think it was a genuine mistake. He was looking for another file and happened to notice his own initials on this one." Gerald picked the file out of the open drawer beside him and put it on the desk. "You see. D.R.M. It wasn't really his initials, of course. They belonged to another chap who used to work here. Dennis Moule."

"I remember him well," said Blackett. "He was Julius Mantegna's number-one boy. What happened to him?"

"I'm afraid he went downhill a bit."

"And Morgan's going downhill after him? This office must have a demoralizing effect on its assistants. Hullo! You've still got that."

It was the newspaper cutting, stapled onto the inside cover of the file. Blackett read it through carefully, his face quite expressionless. Gerald had never been entirely at ease with Blackett. He gave off the disturbing radiation of power and money, but there was more to it than that. He had known other rich and powerful men and had been quite easy in their company. He was relieved when Sam Lyon came bustling in. Blackett said, "I gather you've been having a good lunch."

"A boring lunch, followed by an equally boring meeting," said Lyon. "Shall we go along to my room?"

Blackett took a last look at the file on the desk, as though he was committing something to memory, and then said, "Let's do that."

It was nearly an hour later when Blackett left the office. He said to the chauffeur, who was holding the door open, "I want you to do something for me, Harald. Find our friend, Mr. Trombo. He should be in his shop at this hour. Tell him I'll expect a call at five o'clock exactly. A public box, the usual procedure. You can take the car. I'll go on by taxi."

When Harald had driven off, Blackett stood for a moment, unmoving. Miss Crawley, from her upper window, thought, "What a terrible man. Doesn't he look splendid. An emperor." She followed him with her eyes as he moved off down the street.

At the nearest telephone kiosk, Blackett dialed a number and spoke briefly. He said, "David Rhys Morgan. He used to work for my accountants, Martindale, Mantegna and Lyon. When they sacked him he got a job with Rayhome Tours. I want you to find out all about him. No action, just information. Where he lives. Girl friends, present and past. Other connections. Right?"

"Right," said the voice at the other end.

— 14 —

The next French trip went off so quietly, and Collings was so relaxed, that it confirmed David's guess. The heroin traffic was confined to Italy. This was logical. He knew that base opium was manufactured in Turkey and Afghanistan and was converted in small factories in Greece and Albania, first into morphine hydrochloride and then into the infinitely more valuable diacetyl morphine, popularly known as heroin. It would cross the Adriatic in fishing boats and be sold to distributing agents in Italy. This part of the organization was a Mafia monopoly. The end market was Great Britain, where the sale of heroin was doubling every year.

"And here am I," said David, "a humble link in this profitable chain, and wondering whether I can keep a wee piece of the profit for myself. Does not the Bible tell us that it is lawful to spoil the Egyptians? Yes, indeed."

He was under no illusions about the risk he was running, and he made his preparations with corresponding care. He was staying at the time in a small hotel in a street on the Pimlico side of Victoria Station. Half the people there were more or less permanent residents; the other half were one-night stop-overs, traveling to or from the Continent. The proprietor was a genial Barbadian with one leg.

David's first job on the Tuesday morning following the French trip was to get rid of the man in jeans and a mock-leather windcheater who seemed to be interested in his movements. He accomplished this by waiting in Theobald's Road until there was only one taxi in sight, hailing it and driving off.

He dismissed the taxi at Bond Street Underground Station, took a bus to Piccadilly and walked down St. James's Street. At the chemist's shop halfway down on the left he presented the formula which he had scribbled on the back of an envelope. The assistant said, "Going in for home photography, sir?"

"Indeed, yes," said David. "An old-fashioned camera and an old-fashioned darkroom. None of your instant snapshots."

At a second chemist's shop in Pall Mall he bought a large box of antihistamine tablets ("a sovereign remedy for all catarrhal afflictions").

"You want to be a bit careful with those jiggers," said the young man who sold them to him. "Lay off alcohol when you take them, and lay off driving too, if you can. They make you very sleepy."

"Fortunately," said David, "I am a rigid teetotaller and I possess no car."

At the next shop, which dealt in fishing accessories, he bought half a dozen plastic bags of the type used for live bait. A tube of clear adhesive from a stationer's in Lower Regent Street completed his shopping, all of which went into his capacious briefcase. This, in turn, was deposited in the Left Luggage Office at Leicester Square Underground Station. After which he had a drink, a sandwich and several more drinks at the Chandos and spent the afternoon in a cinema which advertised French Fantasy Films—the "Ultimate in Erotic Titillation." He fell asleep halfway through the first film and woke up at six o'clock, stared blearily at the screen, then at his watch, and remembered that he had a date with Paula and was already late for it.

Paula had to be placated with drink and food. Towards the

end of the meal, in one of the smaller Soho restaurants, he said, "You remember Moule?"

"Dennis Moule. Yes. He got the push soon after I came."

"Do you know why?"

"Well, he was getting ever so queer. People said it was drugs."

"Poor Moule. He had a brilliant mind."

"Did you know him?"

"We were at school together."

"He wasn't Welsh."

"I didn't go to school in Wales. My father wouldn't hear of it. He said, 'Before we know where we are, they'll be teaching you to speak Welsh.' So I was packed off to an English public school. That was where I met Dennis. He was my first and best friend. We spent hours in the school workshop turning pieces of metal."

"Whatever for?"

"We made them just the right size and weight to fit a slot machine in the town that sold packets of cigarettes. We used to smoke them in a lonely barn. We had to stop when the farmer turned up unexpectedly and Dennis dropped his lighted cigarette into the straw. What a bonfire that was!"

"And you were both expelled?"

"Nothing of the sort. We slipped out at the back without being caught. Even at that age I had a talent for avoiding trouble. Since then I've developed it into a fine art."

"You're a terrible liar. I don't believe you knew Dennis at all."

"Certainly I did. And when I met him the other day, we recognized each other immediately."

"You met Dennis? I thought he'd be dead by now."

"What makes you say that?"

"He was on drugs. People on drugs don't last long."

"You surprise me. He looked quite fit, I thought. A bit thin. Maybe he'd taken a cure."

"He didn't seem to me the sort of man who'd have the guts

to do that," said Paula. "But you never can tell. What's he doing these days?"

"He's got a job selling encyclopedias. And he asked me to do something for him. He said that letters or parcels might be coming to the Rayhome office addressed to him. I didn't absolutely follow it. Something about not having been able to give his own address to some people. I said, if anything did turn up I was sure you'd forward it. Send it care of Poste Restante, Burnt Oak."

"Poste Restante, Burnt Oak," said Paula agreeably. "O.K. There doesn't seem to be a lot left in that bottle."

"The deficiency shall be remedied at once."

On Wednesday morning, David saw the same young man propping up a lamp post outside the hotel. He looked dispirited. David put him down as a junior and not very experienced employee from a private enquiry agency and wondered who was interesting themselves in his movements. The most likely solution was that his Rayhome bosses were checking up on how he spent the intervals between trips. It would have been a sensible precaution.

David used the back door of the hotel. It seemed to be unguarded, but he was taking no chances. There was a large supermarket in Wilton Road. He went in at the front, through and out at the back, boarded the first bus that came along, left it at a traffic light and nipped quickly down a side road. No one else got off the bus and no one followed him.

He walked to the nearest Underground station, took the Central Line to Bethnal Green, changed onto the East London Section and got out at Surrey Docks Station.

It was a beautiful morning, and even the desolate little streets and weed-grown wasteland seemed to be warmed and cheered by the genial sun. David had an out-of-date street map, but by asking his way of a number of children, who answered him in the almost unintelligible dockland twang, he eventually located Pipe Street.

Unlike most South London streets, where houses seem to

have been poured into a mold and turned out to cool, the houses in Pipe Street had been designed with flair. One had turrets, another had battlements, a third had a chimney shaped like the funnel of a ship. Number seven had a front garden the size of a billiard table, which was so crammed with models that the front path had some difficulty in finding its way between them. There were dwarfs, gnomes, windmills, castles, lighthouses, and helter-skelters; in a place of honor, a full-scale representation of the Mad Hatter's tea party.

David picked his way up to the door and rang the bell. The door was opened by an elderly man with a brown face and white hair. Leonard Mullion had started life in the Docks Police, had retired early and was now the park keeper in charge of the smallest of the three Rotherhithe parks. He seemed to be expecting David and waved him into the front room. On the table was a peacock, cast in iron. Mr. Mullion was decorating its tail, using a dozen little pots of paint of the type used for touching up the bodywork of motorcars.

He said, "I got the room ready when I heard you might be coming in. At the back, nice and quiet."

"That's just the ticket, Len. I don't quite know when I'll be needing it, but I guess it might be any day now. So what I'm going to do is pay you four weeks in advance and collect a key. When I do come, I might come in a bit of a hurry."

"Suit yourself," said Mr. Mullion. "But if you turn up after dark, mind where you put your feet. The last man who had that room—he was a crane driver—he came home pissed one night and trod on the Mad Hatter."

"I'm a sober citizen," said David. "I can only remember being drunk once in my whole life."

"That's half the trouble. People *don't* remember it."

"I was fourteen at the time. My da took me on a choir outing, and I was sick over the leading tenor's boots. That's not a thing you forget in a hurry, I can tell you."

When he got back to the hotel he went in again by the back door. The watcher was still standing about in the street in front. "He'll get picked up for loitering if he doesn't watch it," said David. He did a good deal of talking to himself when there was no one else to talk to.

"He did what?" said the head of Gowers Enquiry Agency.
"Stayed in his room all day. Never came out once."
"How do you know he didn't come out the back way?"
"Not being able to be in two places at once," said the young man aggressively, "how would I know if he came out the back way or not?"

His feet were hurting him.

"Something in that," agreed Mr. Gowers. It had been presented to him as a routine job, of no particular urgency. All the same, Randall Blackett was a man who preferred results to excuses.

"If he really stays in his room all day," he said, "he must do most of his business on the telephone."

"There's no telephone in his room. He'd have to use one in the cabinet in the front hall."

"All right. We'll see if we can lean on the nig who runs the place to get us a tap on it. There'll be an extension in his office."

"Then I'd better spend the day sitting in his office," said the young man hopefully.

"No point in that. Tomorrow's Thursday. He'll be off on one of his Continental coach trips. We'll get it set up for when he comes back."

The routine was by now so well established that David began to feel that he had been doing it all his life. He even recognized two members of his first contingent, a silent married couple called Longmore, who had come back for a second helping.

On this occasion their progress was even more leisurely. A night at Amboise, two days' sight-seeing round the castles of the Loire, a night south of Poitiers and a third stop near Grasse. As August turned to September, the weather became wet and cold, but when David suggested that they ought to lose no time getting south of the Alps, Collings disagreed.

It was plain that he was working to a carefully timed program.

It was not until the evening of the seventh day that they reached Florence. They were booked in to a large, modern hotel overlooking the Filippo Strozzi Park. The bedrooms had in-house television sets, drink cabinets ("Rings a bell downstairs every time you open it," said Collings sourly) and a secure-looking built-in wall cupboard. It did not look the sort of thing which could be opened by any old key. Collings observed it with pleasure. He took charge of the black bag, locked it in and pocketed the key.

"I guess you'll be glad to forget about it for a bit," he said.

David agreed. He was finding that he could read Collings like a barometer. On the first two days in Florence the pressure was low and the weather was set fair. On the afternoon of the third day the needle began to creep up. He was not a bit surprised when, that evening, Collings suggested a night out together.

David affected to think about it. He said, "All right. As long as you behave yourself this time."

Considered as a social event, it was not a wild success. Collings had clearly got orders to keep them both away from the hotel until after midnight. On two occasions, when David yawned and suggested that they might go home, Collings called for more drinks.

"If this was his technique with my predecessors," thought David, "no wonder they smelled a rat. Perhaps he simply explained the whole plot to them and cut them in for a share of the loot. Watterson might have agreed. Maybe Moule, too. Come to think of it, that was probably what started him on the downward path."

By the time they finally got back to the hotel, it was one o'clock, and Collings, in spite of his surprising capacity for absorbing alcohol, was as nearly drunk as David had seen him.

He sat down on the end of his bed and started to take his shoes off. David said, "What about a nightcap?"

"If you touch that bloody drink cabinet, you'll have to pay for every bloody bottle in it."

"I wasn't going to touch it," said David.

He opened his own traveling bag and extracted a half-empty bottle of Highland Malt whisky. Collings eyed it with approval.

"That's better," he said. "We've had enough of that Italian muck. A glass of the old and bold. Just what the doctor ordered." He took off his coat, removed his collar and tie, loosened his belt and belched.

David fetched two glasses from the bathroom annex, poured a generous portion into one of them and gave it to Collings, and a rather more modest one into the other.

He said, "Water with it?"

"Never insult a good whisky with water," said Collings. He took a gulp and smacked his lips. "There are times," he said, "when I think you're a Welsh bastard. There are other times when I love you."

David grinned. He said, "I hope that's not a proposal of marriage," and went out to put some water into his own drink. He was a minute or two doing this. When he came back Collings's empty glass was on the floor, and Collings was flat on his back on the bed. His face was bright red and his mouth was wide open.

David looked at him anxiously. He was making a noise like a man who was fighting for breath and trying to snore at the same time.

"I hope I haven't overdone it," said David.

He slipped the braces off Collings's shoulders and pulled off his trousers. Collings in underpants, shirt and socks was not an attractive sight. David covered him with a blanket and put a pillow under his head. He then extracted the keys he wanted from Collings's trouser pocket, opened the cupboard, took out the black bag and set to work.

By the time he had finished, Collings had rolled onto one

side, and his face was a more normal color. Three o'clock was striking as David undressed, turned out the light and climbed into bed. Even Collings's snores failed to keep him awake.

"Christ almighty!" said Collings. "What the hell did we drink?"

"A bottle of lousy grappa, half a bottle of lousier ouzo, and a glass each of my good malt whisky."

"It can't have been the whisky."

"You're dead right it wasn't the whisky. I've been drinking it for years. It was the mixture."

"I've got a head like a bloody dynamo." Collings peered at him with bloodshot eyes which bulged from a face with a yellowish tinge. "You're looking too bloody cheerful."

"I have a very peculiar constitution," said David. "My microcosm synthesizes with alcohol. I'll have to be getting along now. I promised to conduct a party of our clients round the Uffizi."

Collings said, "Ugh," and then, "I'm going back to bed."

That was their last full day in Florence. David noted with interest the care which Collings now exercised over the safety of the black bag. When they finally departed, he took it out of the cupboard and carried it down himself to the coach and placed it beside the driver's seat, where it would be under his eye. At Calais and again at Dover, when David had to open the bag to get out the tickets and the passports, he could feel Collings breathing down his neck. He almost said something about it, but refrained. The charade was now so open, and he was so much a part of it, that any comment would have been superfluous.

Their crossing had been a later one than usual, and it was dusk when they reached London and dark by the time they pulled up outside the Rayhome office. Collings carried the bag upstairs. The reception desk was empty, but David could see a line of light under the door of the Chevertons' room and could hear the rumble of voices.

As Collings carried the bag in, David caught a glimpse of both the Chevertons and a third man, someone he had not seen before. He got an impression of a belted raincoat and a broad pair of shoulders before the door shut. He walked slowly along the passage and sat himself down in the small waiting room at the end.

Time passed. David looked at his watch. More than thirty minutes. He got up and moved across to the door. He had heard no sound, but it seemed to be locked.

David examined the window. It was unbarred and opened easily, but it gave onto a sheer drop of nearly twenty feet into a small, enclosed courtyard.

"If this was a bedroom," he said, "I could knot three sheets together and be off. Even a pair of curtains might do the trick. But no curtains."

He was regretting the lack of soft furnishings when the door opened and Bob Cheverton came in. He was smiling. He said, "Sorry to keep you waiting, David. We had a couple of telephone calls to attend to. Another successful trip, I gather."

"Did you have to lock me in?"

"Lock you in? We didn't lock you in. Why should we? There isn't a lock on the door. It jams sometimes."

"My mistake," said David. "I suffer terribly from claustrophobia. It started when my mother locked me in the airing cupboard at the age of six and forgot about me. I was there seventeen hours."

Cheverton was still smiling. He said, "One thing all our clients tell me about you is that you have a wonderful imagination. Here's your bonus. Same as last time. Now you're getting into your stride, we should be able to make it a regular one." He handed David an envelope. "No need to bother the tax man about it, eh?"

"One of the prime objects in my life is to save the tax man bother," agreed David. They were out in the passage by now. A quick backward glance showed him that there was a bolt right at the top of the door.

As he passed the Chevertons' room he could see Ronald Cheverton sitting at his desk. Belted raincoat had gone. David shouted out, "Good night." Ronald raised his head for a moment and looked at him with dead, dispassionate eyes.

David went out into the street.

He was thinking hard.

It was possible that the door had, in fact, been jammed and not bolted; but he did not believe it. It was possible that the Chevertons and the stranger had examined the bag and not detected the substitution he had made. He did not believe this either. In which case, the needle had swung round to Storm Warning. Force Twelve on the Beaufort Scale.

It was neatly done.

A girl was coming towards him along the pavement. She seemed to be drunk and was tacking gently from side to side, talking to herself. As she reached David she veered towards the roadway. David naturally veered inwards. The man stationed in the doorway at that point hit him, once, with a silk stocking full of wet sand.

"Nothing," said the man in the belted raincoat. His name was McVee, and his nickname, used only by privileged friends, was Monkey. He had a nose shaped like a little boot, which had been squashed down, in some fight or accident, onto his upper lip. This may have accounted for the nickname.

"You're sure?" said Bob Cheverton. He was trying to keep his voice level and not succeeding very well.

"Sure? Of course I'm sure. If he'd had half an ounce of tobacco on him we'd have found it."

"So what's he done with it?"

Collings said, with a truculence which failed to conceal his own nervousness, "One thing's bloody certain. He didn't get bloody nothing out of that bag from the time we left Calais. I'm not saying he mightn't have picked a lock and got it out one night on the trip. Like I've told you before, I can't stay awake all night. It's not reasonable. But *if* he got the stuff out of the bag, it's still in Italy. That's for sure."

"What do you mean?" said Bob. *"If* he got it out. Who else could have got it out? Apart from you."

Collings said, "I'm not taking that from you or anyone," and lumbered to his feet.

There was a fifth man in the room, a plump character, without much hair on his head. His tanned face, neat dark suit, silk shirt and discreet gold cuff links suggested a businessman who spent his holidays in the Bahamas or the South of France. His voice, when he spoke, matched his appearance. There was authority in it. He said, "Don't be stupid, Collings. Just relax. No one's accused you of anything, yet."

"He said—"

"It doesn't matter what he *said.* All he was doing was examining certain possibilities. For myself, I can see two and two only. Either Morgan filched the stuff one night, in the way you've suggested, or it was never there at all."

The four men considered the second possibility.

Bob Cheverton said, "I can't see the sense in it, Trombo. We've played straight with them on twenty consignments or more. We've paid them their money. Why should they cheat on this one?"

"I didn't say they *were* cheating. I said they might have been. Myself, I don't believe it. They're businessmen. How would it pay them to shortchange us? Very well. So let us look at the alternative. Your new man, Morgan, removed the real stuff and put in this substitute. I do not blame Collings. One man couldn't keep an eye on another man all the time, day and night. If he was clever with keys and had his wits about him, he *could* have lifted this consignment. Next point. We know that it did not come back to England with him. So what did he do with it?"

Bob Cheverton said, "He might have had an accomplice. Someone on the Continent he passed it to."

"I don't believe it," said Ronald. "He's a loner."

"I don't believe it for another reason," said the man called

Trombo. "The market for the stuff is *here,* in London. He has hidden it. Somewhere in or around Florence. When the heat is off, he'll go back for it. He can afford to wait. We can't. So we must find it. Or buy another package. *And buy it quickly.*"

There was silence in the room. Everyone there knew what he was talking about. Their consignments went to half a dozen doctors whose dubious medical ethics allowed them to sell it on, at exorbitant prices, to the addicts who craved it, begged for it, lived for it. If they could not satisfy their patients, they could be in trouble. A man or woman, screaming and raving, who thought the doctor was holding out for a higher price. A patient who was capable of killing the doctor and wrecking his surgery in a mad search for the white crystals that meant the difference between temporary happiness and intolerable misery.

Bob said, "Buying a package in London will be very expensive. Perhaps impossible, in the time available."

"Right," said Trombo. He awarded him the bright smile which a teacher gives to an intelligent member of the class. "In that case, the answer must be that we find the original package. Yes?"

"Somewhere round Florence," said Ronald. "What a chance!"

"You forget something," said Trombo. "What does the proverb say? He who hides can find—or can be made to find. Well?"

The four men looked at him. In an emergency there was no doubt who was leader.

"We could ask Mr. Morgan to tell us what he has done with our property. If we asked him in the appropriate way, I think he would tell us. The disadvantage of that method is that it would be slow. He might give us information which subsequently proved to be misleading. This would not, ultimately, do him any good, but it would cause undesirable delay. Or we can send him to look for it. You will ask him to conduct the additional tour to Italy. The one Watterson was going to take."

"Won't that make him suspicious?"

"Not if Watterson is unable to take it himself. You can arrange that, surely?"

Ronald had already started dialing. Bob said, "It's no good. You won't find him at home. Not at this time of night. He'll be out on the booze."

But the telephone was answered. They could hear that it was a woman's voice. Ronald was saying, "Oh, I am sorry. When?" And after a long explanation, "I see. It must have been a great shock. You've got our number. If there's anything we can do to help, just give us a buzz."

He rang off and said, "That was his sister. Watterson had a stroke. Luckily she was on the spot and got him into hospital."

"Lucky in lots of ways," said Bob. "Now we don't need any excuses."

Trombo said, "When does your next trip leave?"

"In two days' time."

"Very well. When he gets to Italy he will be under professional observation. Either he will lead the observers to the hiding place. He will be given every possible chance to do so. Or if, by the end of the trip, he has not done so, then our Italian colleagues will remove him to a quiet place and will persuade him to divulge the necessary information."

"Suppose he won't tell them?"

"Why suppose anything so stupid? Do you want me to explain to you the methods by which they will cripple him?"

"No," said Bob thickly. "I expect you're right."

Ronald Cheverton said, in his gravelly voice, "And suppose he refuses the trip. He's done his six trips. He's due a fortnight off."

"Invite him round tomorrow. He should by that time have got over the effects of the unfortunate experience he suffered when leaving your office. Indeed, it will have left him short of cash. You will be sympathetic. Offer him a substantial bonus if he will take this extra trip."

"And if he still refuses?"

"When you make the offer, McVee and two of his friends will be on the premises. If he refuses, you can immediately adopt the alternative solution. Our friends may not have the finesse of the Italians, but they are not inexpert in extracting information."

McVee's small mouth opened, and he uttered a sound like a gentle kiss.

David was not unconscious for more than a minute. As the lightning flashes in front of his eyes slowed down and the mist cleared a little, he realized that he was being handled by at least two men. They had taken his coat right off and were now pulling down his trousers. He wondered vaguely about this and decided to let it ride. There was very little he could do about it.

Hands slid inside his open shirt and felt his body. He grunted and tried to roll over. Other hands pinned his shoulders to the ground. The floor was cold against bare skin. Hands were sliding down now, inside his legs. His shoes and socks had already been pulled off. He wanted to be sick, but realized that if he showed any signs of coming back to life he would be hit again.

He decided not to be sick. He contented himself with groaning.

There was a muttering of voices which went on for a long time. Then his coat and trousers were dumped on top of him, and there was the tip-tap of footsteps going away.

Three men, he thought.

He sat up cautiously. His head was opening and shutting like a frenzied oyster, but the lightning flashes had died away. He had been concussed often enough on the rugby field to recognize the familiar symptoms.

Either you were going to be sick or you weren't. You weren't. All right. What about trying to get dressed before you die of cold? The trouble was that his coat and trousers seemed to have been turned inside out. It took him several minutes to overcome this minor difficulty. Socks and shoes next, but don't bend forward too far or too suddenly.

Now try standing up. Hold onto that door handle whilst the floor stops rocking.

He had been dragged into the open entrance hall which served a block of offices. A notice, inches from his eyes, said, "Happy-Go-Lucky Food Products." A fine time to talk about food.

His wallet had gone, but there were coins still in one of his trouser pockets. Enough for a train fare, if he could walk as far as the station.

Stop being feeble, Morgan. Of course you can walk.

The exercise seemed to do him good. By the time he reached Holborn Kingsway Underground Station he was able to buy his ticket and get past the barrier without causing any comment. The back of his neck was stiff and sore, and his head was still throbbing, but the rhythm was slowing down. Perhaps he hadn't got concussion after all. Perhaps it was just a stiff neck. He repeated this to himself a number of times.

"An important point, David, bach. A vital point."

He was still saying it as he opened the door of his hotel room. The point was that if he was concussed, he ought not to drink spirits. If he wasn't, a stiff whisky was exactly what any reasonable doctor would have ordered.

He poured himself out a stiff whisky, sat down in the shabby armchair in front of the gas fire and drank it. It seemed to do him no harm. He poured out another, but did not drink it at once.

He wanted to think.

He knew, of course, why he had been slugged and searched. He knew that the taking of his wallet was the merest blind. He wondered what would happen next.

What he really needed was comfort. Someone to hold his hand.

Susan was on the point of going to bed when the telephone rang. She said, "Yes. Who is it?" in her senior-secretarial voice.

"It's me."

"Oh, God! Not again. What do you want now?"

"What I want, love, is someone intelligent. Someone to hold an intellectual conversation with."

"Don't you ever give up?"

"This is only the second time I've telephoned you this month."

"Only the second? It seemed like a lot more often. What do you want?"

David appeared to be considering the question. Then he said, "I need help. Help and comfort, in great therapeutic doses."

"Why don't you get it from that dishy blonde you've been seen going round all the Holborn bars with. Who is she, anyway?"

"No names, no pack drill. As we used to say when I was in the army."

"When were you in the army? And where?"

"Out East. The gorgeous East—palm trees, palanquins, Pepsi-Cola."

"If you enjoyed it all that much, I can't think why you troubled to come back."

"The end of that chapter in my life is a sad one. It was the Colonel's daughter. A beautiful girl of no more than eighteen years with a taste for romance."

"Then a liar like you should have suited her down to the ground." There was a long pause. "I say, are you all right? You sound a bit funny."

"Three doctors have advised on my case, all men of experience. They all advised whisky."

"My advice, which I give you for nothing, is that you should go to bed."

"But who with?"

"Alone, for once in a way."

"Big deal."

"Look, David. You're fun to talk to, sometimes, when you're

sober. When you're tight, which I think you are now, you're just a dead bore."

"A hard woman. Harder than rock. Harder than chilled steel. A soothsayer at Portmadoc once warned me to beware of hard women."

"Stuff and nonsense."

"What's stuff and nonsense?"

"What you've been talking for the last five minutes. I'm tired. I've got a lot of work to do tomorrow."

"In that case," said David with dignity, "I shall terminate our conversation forthwith. If you wish to renew it, you can do so through the usual channels."

"*Good* night."

"Good night."

David replaced the receiver. He still looked sad, but not as sad as he had been. In fact, he looked rather pleased with himself.

"My dear fellow," said Bob Cheverton, "of course you must report it to the police."

"A useless and troublesome exercise," said David. "I know exactly what they'll say. 'Can you describe your assailants, sir?' And when I confess that I never even saw them, they'll say, 'Of course, that makes it very difficult, sir. We'll do what we can.' And then they'll do damn all."

"But they got all your money."

"They were kind enough to leave me enough to get home by Underground."

"Naturally, we'll help out. An advance against your next bonus or a loan. Just as you like."

"That's very kind of you."

"The least we can do. Particularly as you're helping us out."

David had agreed, with surprisingly little demur, to take the forthcoming Italian trip.

"Poor old Watterson," he said. "I only met him on that one occasion, but I can't say I'm greatly surprised. It wasn't simply the amount of alcohol he consumed. It was the speed with which he put it down. Like a desert sucking up rainwater after a long drought."

"Sad," said Bob. "Very sad. Well, if you're quite sure you're up to it, we'll look forward to seeing you here tomorrow morning. We've a full coach load for you."

"It should be a most interesting trip," said David.

— 15 —

It was at about this time that Susan received two letters, both of them with the Salisbury postmark.

"My dear Susan," wrote her grandmother. "I so much enjoyed your last visit—all too short—and hope you will soon be coming down again. A number of the people you met have spoken kindly of you. You seem to have made a great impression on old General Wheeler and an even greater one on young Mr. Preston, our most recently joined vicar-choral."

Susan vaguely remembered a tall, serious young man with unruly elbows and knees.

"I called yesterday on Rebecca Woolf, who must also be counted as one of your admirers. She seems to regard you as a great expert on Meissen china—surely a *new* departure for you? I had no idea you were a collector. I did my best with her, but I am afraid I still find her an excessively dull conversationalist. I learned nothing about her husband that I had not heard many times before. You said you found her interesting. I wonder what you found to talk about."

In other words, said Susan, you tried to pump her, and she was too clever for you.

"The weather remains hot. What a pity that our one wet

afternoon should have spoiled your tennis for you. Your loving grandmother.

"P.S. You left behind in your room an elementary guide to the collection of china. You must remember to pick it up next time you come. I won't bother to post it to you, since I imagine that, as a collector, you must have a large library of more advanced works."

"Cat," said Susan.

The second letter was from Rebecca Woolf. After a number of opening comments on the weather, a Meissen cup and saucer which she had picked up for a fraction of its real price and the Series Three Communion Service, which had just been introduced in the cathedral and of which she disapproved ("a sort of *conversazione* with the Almighty"), she continued:

"Yesterday, I had a state visit from your grandmother. It was not actually preceded by trumpeters on horseback, but I felt that her calling on me raised me quite a number of steps up the social ladder. We did not have a very interesting conversation. However, after she had gone a thought occurred to me. You were kind enough to be genuinely interested in my late husband . . ."

So she realized that I hadn't come to talk about china.

". . . and a name came into my head which I had totally forgotten until that moment. At about the time when my husband died, Randall Blackett was becoming very friendly with a rather terrible little man called Arnie Wiseman. An appropriate name, I thought, on the only occasion that I met him, because he looked as though he knew every shortcut in the world of finance. I had wondered whether Blackett was planning to bring him into the company, but I knew that it would never do, because my husband could not have tolerated him. However, soon afterwards my husband died, and Blackett bought our shares, as I told you, and took over the whole company, so that my feelings about the odious Mr. Wiseman did not arise. Then the most extraordinary thing happened. Mr. Wiseman disappeared! One day he was there and the next day he wasn't. It made a great sensation at the time and was in all the newspapers. Of course it all happened years ago, and I expect most people have forgotten about it, though some of your friends in business circles may remember it. I suspected myself that he might have gone a bit far in one of his shady deals and thought it prudent to remove himself to South America. Enough of such ancient gossip. Do come and see me again next time you are down here."

As Susan folded the letter up and locked it away in her desk, she was thinking that Rebecca Woolf was a lot shrewder than people gave her credit for.

On the day that Susan received these letters, Randall Blackett was driven into London from his house at Virginia Water. He dismissed his chauffeur, Harald, and the car in Queen Street and walked through the lanes and passages which lie behind Cheapside, finally arriving at the inconspicuous offices of Messrs. Gowers and Tring, Private Enquiry Agents and Process Servers. He was evidently expected and was shown straight into the offices of Wing Commander Gowers, the head of the agency. The Wing Commander had a typed document of three pages which he handed to Blackett, keeping a photocopy of the same document on the desk in front of himself.

Blackett read in silence for some minutes. He had a thin silver pencil in his hand and marked two of the passages. When he had finished, he said, "Is Dixon one of your most experienced men?"

"He has been with me for a year or two."

"He doesn't seem to have discovered a great deal that we didn't know already."

"He has discovered that Morgan is a slippery customer."

Blackett said, "Yes," and studied the report for a further minute in silence. "What about this girl friend?"

"An ex–girl friend, I understand. You know that we managed to make an arrangement to listen to Morgan's outgoing calls.

He rang her up once and had a rambling conversation, but she soon choked him off."

Blackett said, "It's not good enough. I'm becoming very interested in that young man. I want you to put three of your best men onto him."

"We shall have to wait for a bit. He's off tomorrow morning on one of those Rayhome tours."

"Rayhome, yes." Blackett seemed to be about to say something and then changed his mind. He said, "When he does get back, I want to have any telephone calls he makes from that hotel taped. I want to know exactly what he does say."

"Even to ex–girl friends?"

"Particularly to ex–girl friends," said Blackett.

"And why do you want to know that?" said Raymond Perronet-Condé.

"Simple feminine curiosity," said Susan. "What a lovely room this is."

"When my club did finally decide, after two hundred years of male chauvinism, to admit females for luncheon, they naturally devoted time and thought to producing a suitable ambience. And don't change the subject. Why are you interested in the late Arnie Wiseman?"

"Is he really late?"

"After seven years have gone by without a man being heard of, I believe that even lawyers are prepared to assume that he has passed on to a better—or a worse—world. In Arnie Wiseman's case a worse one, I should guess."

"Was he a crook?"

"I seem to remember that the last time we lunched together you asked me the same question about Randall Blackett. The answer's the same. Wiseman has never, to my knowledge, been convicted of any criminal offence. But if you're asking me whether I, personally, would have trusted him with a penny of my money, then the answer's no. He had at one time, I believe, been a solicitor, specializing in commercial work. He

120

was reputed to know a great deal about the Companies Act and all the ways of slipping through its meshes. In the end he tried to be a bit too clever, and the Law Society clamped down. He wasn't struck off. Warned, I think. Gave up private practice, went into the City and managed to make quite a lot of money one way and another. He used some of it to buy into Blackett's company, Blackbird. The rumor was that he'd loaned Blackett some money when he needed it in a hurry."

"Of course," said Susan. "That makes sense. Harry Woolf."

"Harry who?"

"Woolf. He was dying of cancer. He offered Blackett his own and his wife's shares in his Blackbird Property Company, for one hundred thousand pounds. He gave him a month to close the deal. Blackett made it only a day or two before the deadline. He must have borrowed the money from Wiseman and given him a fat slice of his own company in exchange."

"Very possibly. It was early days for Blackett. He wouldn't have found it easy to raise money like that on the open market."

"And then Wiseman disappeared."

"Post hoc, but not necessarily propter hoc?"

"If I'd paid more attention in Latin class I might have some idea what you're talking about."

"I mean," said her uncle, "that Wiseman certainly disappeared *after* he had become a director in Argon and a sharer in its fortunes. Are you suggesting that he disappeared *because* he had done so?"

"That's just what I'd like to find out."

"It's not easy to disappear nowadays. Not in this world of telephones and telexes and international press coverage. A man might manage it, I suppose, by joining a lamasery in Tibet or becoming adopted by an aboriginal tribe in the Papuan jungle, but, sooner or later, one can't help feeling a television reporter would roll up to get the exclusive inside story."

"I can't really imagine Arnie as a monk or an aborigine, can you?"

"On balance," agreed her uncle, cutting himself a slice of the famous club Stilton, "I think it is much more likely that he is a small heap of whitening bones."

"Could you find out if anyone has any ideas about that?"

"How do you suggest I would set about it?"

"Dear Uncle Raymond," said his niece, gazing at him with her candid grey eyes, "I know all about you. I mean, about the other job you do when you go on those business trips to the Middle East. You must have some contacts in official circles. Couldn't you ask them?"

"I might," said her uncle cautiously, "if I could give them some plausible reason for wanting to know. I don't think it would wash if I told them it was simple feminine curiosity."

"I suppose not," said Susan.

Mr. Perronet-Condé thought about it. He said, "Change your mind and try some of this cheese. It really is delicious. I might be able to get you something without causing too much stir. A friend of a friend."

"I'd be very grateful."

"The only thing is—be careful!"

"Careful about what?" said Susan, startled by the urgency in her uncle's voice.

"About the way you use that knife. You should never cut a Stilton cheese vertically. Always horizontally. Let me show you."

"In many ways my education was sadly limited," said Susan. "Very little Latin. No instruction in cheese cutting."

Blackett knew, and Sam Lyon knew, that the Blackett empire was now easily the largest client of Messrs. Martindale, Mantegna and Lyon. He expected, therefore, a measure of deference when he visited their offices, but he never tried to ride roughshod over the senior partner. Sam was not only a shrewd accountant. He was personally very well acquainted with all Blackett's affairs. On this occasion he wanted some information from Sam. It was not directly connected with his own affairs, and he could not demand it as of right. He had to proceed cautiously.

After half an hour of professional discussion he said, "By the way, what's happened to that young man who used to help Hopkirk? Looked after some of my matters?"

"David Rhys Morgan, you mean?"

"Was that his name? He was certainly a Welshman."

"I'm afraid he was not satisfactory. Between you and me, he drank too much. He even brought drink into the office. We couldn't shut our eyes to that."

"Of course not. What became of him?"

"I was able to find him a job more suited to his—ah—talents. With a travel agency called Rayhome Tours. I understand that he conducts coach loads of trippers around the Continent."

"That was charitable of you, Sam. I suppose you had to tell his new employers about his habits."

"Certainly. They were not unduly worried. I gather that a measure of conviviality is an advantage in a courier. Actually, he was the second man I've sent to Rayhome. You don't remember Moule, do you?"

"The name rings a faint bell."

"In his case there was some excuse for his failings, poor chap. He was engaged to that very nice girl, Miss Blaney. Julius Mantegna's secretary. The one who was killed in that accident on Highgate Hill."

"I remember Phyllis Blaney very well, indeed. In Julius's day she looked after all my files, business and personal. She always knew where to put her hand on anything. Wonderful girl. Terrible tragedy." He paused for a moment and then said thoughtfully, "I hadn't realized she was engaged to one of your staff. Naturally, he'd have been upset."

"Personal life and business life don't always mix happily. Get a couple safely married, and they settle down. It's when they're in the betwixt-and-between stage that you get trouble. Up in the air one day, down in the dumps the next. That might

123

have been one of the reasons Morgan went to pieces. Gerald Hopkirk told me he'd had a blazing row with his girl friend. A very nice-looking girl. He brought her to our Easter office party. Intelligent, too. I gathered from the few words I was able to have with her that she was a qualified accountant but wasn't practicing."

"That sounds like a waste of talent," said Blackett. "Brains *and* beauty. I could probably find her a niche in one of my companies. Seriously, I'm always on the lookout for people like that. Do you happen to know her name or where I could contact her?"

"I don't. But Gerald will. I'll ask him and let you know."

"That would be very good of you," said Blackett.

— 16 —

The giant truck and trailer had been unloaded from the Channel ferry at Dover in the late afternoon and had come to London through Canterbury and the Medway towns. It was evidently following a route which had been marked out for it and was now stationary, halfway across the open top of Blackheath whilst Fred, the co-driver, tried to read a map by the dim light on the dashboard.

He said, "Right at that next roundabout, Charlie. Left again when you get to the bottom."

They ran down Maze Hill, swung left past the Royal Greenwich Hospital and right again, towards the river.

"If you ask me," said Fred, "this is bloody daft. Why didn't we go straight across the Heath? New Cross—Old Kent Road—New Kent Road. Straight into town. Left here, Charlie."

"Must be some reason for it, I suppose," said Charlie philosophically. "Do what you're told and don't ask questions. That's my motto." He was handling the monster with the light firmness of a man who has driven heavy-goods vehicles all his working life. "Less traffic this way, perhaps."

"Not much traffic anywhere."

The evening had closed in, and an early autumn mist was drifting up from the river. The yellow Continental-type headlights were a help, but they had to drive quite slowly.

"Right here," said Fred, "and left again at the end. Should bring us out into Tooley Street."

They were crawling along a completely empty stretch of road, bounded on both sides by shuttered warehouses. The overhead neon lamps shone through the mist with a bluish tinge.

"Turning coming up," said Fred. "Just round the next bend." And then, in a sharper voice, "Bloody hell! Watch it!"

Charlie's reactions had been fast. He had crammed on the powerful vacuum brakes.

A van was parked, just round the bend, broadside on, blocking the road. The giant truck juddered to a halt with its nose inches from its flank. The next moment the road was full of men. The doors of the cab were wrenched open. Fred, who resisted, got a punch in the stomach which sent him crowing and whistling into the gutter. Charlie, still being philosophical, was sitting on the pavement with a man standing over him with a pick helve.

Around them matters were proceeding in silence, without undue haste but with no waste of time. The padlocks on the doors of truck and trailer were cut with metal shears, and men became busy in both. Bales of paper were thrown out into the road. Other men cut the cords round the bales, stripped open the cardboard coverings and started to throw the contents into a great pile in the middle of the road.

Charlie watched, fascinated, as the pile grew. Other men were busy with jerricans of petrol, sousing the paper.

"Bloody Guy Fawkes won't be bloody in it when that lot goes up," said the man behind Charlie. "Better be moving back a bit, I suggest."

"Good idea," said Charlie. He shuffled farther along the pavement. Fred, who had got his breath back, crawled after him.

A second van had drawn up behind the truck, blocking the way back. It had a blue police sign on it. A car, coming up from behind, had been stopped, and at the corner a motorcyclist in police uniform was advising the driver to back.

"Lorry on fire round that bend. May go up any moment."

The car went hurriedly into reverse.

The truck and trailer were both empty by now. Someone tossed a bundle of lighted rags onto the pile and backed away quickly as the whole mass exploded in white flame.

Two minutes later the street was empty of everyone except Charlie and Fred, who sat with their backs to the wall, twenty yards down the road, looking at the bonfire.

"Better find a telephone, I suppose," said Charlie.

"Bloody nerve," said Fred.

Detective Chief Superintendent Morrissey, the big, white-faced Jew who had three times won the Police Heavyweight Boxing Championship and now headed the six Metropolitan Special Crime Squads, said the same thing to Detective Sergeant Brannigan.

Brannigan said, "Someone spotted the fire and put in an emergency call. By the time the first car got there everyone had gone except the truck drivers and this one young tearabout who'd been left on watch at the far end of the road, wearing, can you beat it, a police macintosh and motorcycle helmet. Turning motorists away. He tried to turn the squad car away." Brannigan gave a laugh. "That didn't go down big. They pulled him in. Boy called Colt."

"Any form?"

"He hasn't had time to collect much form. He's only sixteen."

"Get anything out of him?"

"Not to start with. Then someone got the bright idea of letting it slip out that his mates had left him behind on purpose. Got a grudge against him. Something about his girl friend. He fell for that and started to talk. Not that he knew a lot. Seems it was a package job. His mob, the Lewisham mob, the Water Rats and the Friary Lane crowd, Birnie Samuels, Ginger Williams, Monkey McVee, Big Pat, Scotch Jack, all that lot. They got a flat fee, paid in advance. The organization was done by the Friars, but they weren't paying for it. They were being paid, same as the others."

"Any idea where the money came from?"

"Colt didn't know. He said the buzz was it was a Trombo job. But dirty fivers are dirty fivers wherever they start from."

Morrissey thought about this. He said, "Water Rats? That's a new one."

"They come and go like Fourth Division football clubs," said Brannigan sourly. "The Rats are mostly sailors from the Baltic. Poland. Latvia. Places like that. The skippers know they'll hop ashore given half a chance. So they anchor in midstream and keep the lights on at night. But some of them always manage to slip through somehow. When they get on shore they've got no papers and they can't get jobs so they just naturally turn to villainy."

Morrissey scratched his thickened nose with a big thumb. He said, "Fourth Division clubs, eh? Give themselves a fancy name. Cause a bit of trouble. Then go too far and get stamped on. Small stuff. Small ideas. Small resources. That's the way it's been, ever since we put down the Krays and the Richardsons. Now it's a bit different. We've got to thank Mr. Trombo for that."

"I've heard a lot about him since I came here," said Brannigan cautiously. "He's quite a local character."

"He's a character, all right," said Morrissey. "No question. He's a Maltese. Was a mess steward, or something like that, in an A.A. Regiment in Singapore when the Japs took over. He wasn't a soldier, so they didn't put him inside. Made himself useful, running errands in and out of the camps. Made himself a bit of money, too. After the war he came back to England. Land of hope and glory and a spiv's paradise just then, by all accounts. Now he's what you might call an institution. You want a dirty job done, but you can't handle it yourself because doing dirty jobs isn't your scene. All you got to do is get in touch with Mr. Trombo. Pay him the rate for the job, and he'll organize it for you. Like you ring up Messrs. Whoosit and Whatsit when you want to put on a wedding reception. And there was one thing about any job he did. It'd be done proper. The people he uses do what they're told. No less and no more. Early on there was one time when someone wanted a restaurant in the Borough roughed up. Damage the place but not the people, Trombo said. He let it out to a small crowd from Stepney. They got overenthusiastic and messed about some of the girls. Trombo said, all right. You don't do what you're told, you don't get paid. Not a penny piece. They started to shout the odds. Trombo said nothing and he did nothing, for about a week. Then he brought a real heavy mob down from Glasgow, who stamped those Stepney yobs into the pavement. He hasn't had much trouble since."

Sergeant Brannigan was listening carefully. He knew that Morrissey didn't talk for the sake of talking. He said, "About that job yesterday. I did think the drivers must have been bought. If they'd kept to the main road there wouldn't have been much chance of an ambush."

"What did they say?"

"What they said was, they'd been given the route by the supervisor. He said he chose it special, because it was a quick way into the City. Cut out the traffic at New Cross and the Old Kent Road. Difficult to pin anything onto him or them."

Morrissey had lumbered to his feet and moved over to the window of the charge room in Flanders Lane Police Station. It was wide open, and the London summer smell of tar and diesel was blowing in, faintly mixed with the smells of the river. He said, "Mr. Trombo's got a good intelligence service. Half the barmen and taxi drivers and newspaper sellers in this part of London are on his payroll. He'll know, by now, that I've come to talk to you about last night's job. He'll know that we've picked up Colt and that he may very likely have started to talk. He won't be worried, but he'll be wondering what we're going to do next. What I like to do is the obvious thing—sometimes."

Morrissey's mouth opened in a grin which exposed two gold-capped teeth. It had been his tactic in the ring. To do the obvious thing when his opponent was expecting subtlety. "You say you've never met him. You ought to make a point of getting to know the local celebrities. Why don't you call on him?"

"I might do that," said Brannigan.

Later, he said to Detective Constable Wrangle, "The way the old man talked about him, it was almost respectful. Like as though he knew we should never pin anything onto him, so we ought to treat him gently."

Wrangle, who had worked with Morrissey before, said, "I wouldn't bank on it, Sergeant. I heard him talking like that about Paul and Abel Crow. That was a few weeks before he smashed 'em for good."

Brannigan said, "Well, I did think, for a moment, he'd gone soft."

Later that day he drove down to Burminster Street, which runs between Chain Walk and Stafford Quay, a corner of eighteenth-century London almost untouched by the hand of time. Trombo's shop was the biggest in the street. It specialized in kitchen equipment, and its two windows were full of grinders, mixers, choppers and knives. Knives of all sizes and shapes. There was one he noticed about fifteen inches long. Very heavy and sharp and tapering to a fine point. The card under it said, "All-Purpose Knife." Whilst Brannigan was wondering what those purposes might include, the door opened and a plump, middle-aged man looked out. Brannigan had no doubt that it was the owner of the shop. He said, "Admiring my new lines, Sergeant? We got them in last week from Sweden. You won't find a better piece of steel in Sheffield. Go through the toughest meat like a hot knife through butter."

"They look useful," agreed Brannigan.

"But you didn't come here shopping, I'm sure of that. Come inside."

The voice was difficult to place. It was almost classless, but Brannigan could hear the faint undertones of a foreigner who had learned to speak English almost, but not quite, young enough to forget his own language. In the officers' mess of the A.A. Regiment, or touting round the prison camps of Singapore?

He said, "I wanted a word with you."

"Of course. Come in. We can talk in my office."

They walked down the shop between the counters crammed with goods, each tended by a brown-faced, smiling boy. From the eastern end of the Mediterranean—Cypriots, perhaps, or Beiruti Arabs, Brannigan guessed. The office was an oasis of neatness among all this clutter. A table, a telephone, two chairs, a rolltop desk. Trombo waved the Sergeant into one of the chairs, sat down in the other, opened the desk and pulled out a box of cigars.

"Help yourself, Sergeant. Best Havanas. Smoked by Fidel Castro himself."

Without waiting for an answer he snipped the ends with a gold cigar cutter, handed one to the Sergeant, extracted a long box of matches and struck one.

"Never insult a good cigar with a cigarette lighter. I'm sure you know that. Good? That's right." He lit his own cigar and leaned back in his chair. "Now, Sergeant. Tell me what I can do for you."

Brannigan, who was conscious that he had been maneuvred into a false position, took his time over answering. Instead, he studied the face through the curling wreaths of cigar smoke.

Unquestionably there was authority, in the firm chin and the shaded eyes behind the gold-rimmed spectacles. Not the authority of birth or breeding, but of enterprise and success. An authority that came from challenging the world on its own terms and winning. He wondered what was wrong because, although the individual parts were agreeable enough, the face did not quite add up. Perhaps it was a hint of looseness in the mouth.

Brannigan realized that it was up to him to explain his visit. He said, "Did you hear of the trouble in Palmerstone Street last night? A lorry hijacked and its contents burnt."

"I not only heard about it, Sergeant—I read about it. It was in all the papers this morning. It seemed to me to be a singularly pointless piece of vandalism."

"What the papers didn't say was that we caught one of the men responsible."

"I'm sorry you didn't catch them all."

"And he seemed to have an idea that the whole affair had been organized by you."

"He said that?"

"Yes."

"I'm not surprised."

"Why?"

"Because, Sergeant, once you give a dog a bad name you can hang him twenty times over. I have never been able to understand how the theory arose that I was—what would you call it—a master criminal. But it is a fact that nowadays every episode of violence or law breaking which takes place in London is automatically attributed to me. If it was not so embarrassing, I should find it funny."

"It must be embarrassing," agreed Brannigan. "Can you tell me where you were last night?"

"You don't read your local newspapers?"

"I haven't much time for that."

"Then you missed an interesting news item. I was the guest of honor at the opening of the new Boys' Club in Lewisham. I accompanied the Mayor and other notables at the opening ceremony and spent the evening in the club. I played five games of table tennis and three games of darts and lost them all."

"I see."

"When you say, 'I see,' in that tone of voice, what you really mean is that you don't see. You don't see that the fact that I was not actually present in Palmerstone Street necessarily means that I didn't organize what happened there. You picture me as the spider in the middle of his web contriving illicit activities."

Since this was exactly what Sergeant Brannigan was picturing, he thought it better to say nothing.

Trombo leaned forward across the table. He had stopped smiling. His voice was serious. He said, "I am a law-abiding citizen. I pay my rates and taxes. I contribute as generously as I can to all local causes."

Brannigan knew this to be true. He still said nothing. He wondered what was coming.

Choosing his words with evident care, Trombo said, "I would give a great deal if my unfortunate reputation could be buried and forgotten. I have always been on the side of law and order. It would be worth a lot to me if I could feel that the forces of law and order were on my side. You are new to this district, Sergeant, and new brooms sweep clean. But they also signal a new start. I should like to think that you, personally, were able to disregard unfounded rumors and give me the benefit of that old legal adage that a man is presumed to be innocent until he is proved guilty."

As Sergeant Brannigan drove back to the police station, still smoking the cigar, which really was an excellent one, he realized that he had been offered a bribe. He realized, too, that it had been so skillfully done that a tape recording of their conversation, had one been taken, would have demonstrated nothing improper.

From Flanders Lane, Morrissey ambled gently through the sunny, smelly dockland streets towards Rotherhithe Station, where he caught a train to Whitechapel. As he got into the carriage one of the men already there pushed past him to get out, treading on his toes as he did so and moving away down the platform. Morrissey shouted after him, "Watch where you're putting your big, flat plates, Birdie." The man did not condescend to look round, but got into a carriage farther down and slammed the door. Morrissey grinned. He had put "Birdie" Redsell away three times for burglary.

At Whitechapel he changed onto the District Line train for

St. James's Park and walked across the road to the towering steel and glass building which was the new home of New Scotland Yard. He returned the salute of the constable on duty in the reception area and took the lift to the fourth floor.

The notice on the door said, "Arthur Abel." The man behind the desk had white hair, rosy cheeks and twinkling blue eyes. He would have passed, in any cathedral town, for a senior clergyman, possibly even for an archdeacon. He was head of the joint Metropolitan and City of London Fraud Squads.

Morrissey said, "I've come to waste some more of your time, A.A. Have you got anything for me?"

"It's never a waste of time talking to you," said Abel. "Sit down. You're getting fat."

"Fat and slow," said Morrissey gloomily.

"Nonsense. I expect you could still do a hundred yards in even time if you had to."

"If I had to run a hundred yards I should blow a valve."

Abel had produced an armful of folders from one of his filing cabinets and dumped them on the desk. They were full of company accounts and reports. He said, "I've had our legal branch working on this lot. It's an interesting organization that your friend Mr. Blackett has built up. It's based on four or five streams of companies which can intertrade without being legally interconnected."

"Keep it simple," said Morrissey. "Nothing more than two syllables if you can help it."

"Let me give you an example of one of the 'streams.' Then you'll see how it works. At the bottom you've got three small companies. Percy Cornford, who deal in paints and dyes; Harmond, who manufacture and sell printing ink; and Implex, who import paper from Scandinavia."

"All straight?"

"All perfectly straight. Old-fashioned family companies formed by the fathers or grandfathers of the present owners. Friendly connections with their suppliers, a good name in the trade. In each case they had got into difficulties after the war, trying to fight off the big combines. The trouble being that they were undercapitalized. Blackett supplied the capital."

"And took over the company."

"In fact, yes. Legally, no. He got fifty-one percent of the shares, but two percent of those went to his chauffeur. Who obviously does what Blackett tells him. But the fact that it's an obvious wangle doesn't alter the legal position."

Morrissey grunted. He had a low opinion of lawyers and their wangles.

"The next rank above them are two larger companies. One of them is a printing outfit, Sayborn Art Printers, the second is a property company, Cavaliero. It buys and sells and leases advertising sites. A very specialized job since the Planning Acts came in. Then, at the top of that particular pyramid you'll find Holmes and Holmes, which is one of the three largest advertising agencies in Great Britain. Do you begin to see the picture?"

"You mean they can take in each other's washing."

"Intertrading is the name of the game. The point of it is that the Revenue can only take a sizeable bite of a company's profits when they go above a certain figure. So if you control all the inlets and outlets you can arrange that this doesn't happen. Suppose Sayborn Art Printers looks like making too much money—they trade with other people, too, remember—all Blackett has to do is put up the price at which they buy from Cornford, Harmond and Implex. And vice versa."

"So what does he get out of it for himself?"

"Fifty or sixty prosperous companies, each paying him a fee *and* expenses as a consultant. The expenses being largely tax-free. It's not been an easy sum to work out, because some of the figures are guesswork, but he probably pulls in an income, after tax, of around eighty thousand pounds a year."

"*After* tax?"

"In his pocket."

"And there's nothing anyone can do about it?"

"They can nibble away at his expense allowances. But part

of his trade is international. This gives him an excuse for a lot of entertainment. Weekend house parties for foreign V.I.P.'s. If he's got friendly accountants, which he has, he can pretty well live on his expense account."

"Then what does he spend his real money on? Girl friends? Boyfriends?"

"I can tell you one thing he doesn't spend much of it on, and that's shares. If he did, we'd pick up the investment income in his tax returns. Probably he invests in things which don't bring in income. Like antiques and pictures and gold."

"I read a story once," said Morrissey, "about a man who bought a lot of gold. He filled his cellar with it. Gold pots and pans, trays and boxes and such. And because he didn't want anyone to know about it, he covered them all with black paint. Then he went and died in a car crash, and no one knew anything about them. They thought they were a lot of old rubbish and gave them all away to a jumble sale in aid of charity."

"A very moral story," agreed Abel gravely.

As Morrissey walked back down Petty France he was thoughtful. What he had said was true. He was getting slow. Slower at walking, slower at turning, slower at hitting. But not, he hoped, slower at thinking.

This was important. He was going to need all his wits about him, because a very complex set of arrangements, code name "Operation Snakes and Ladders," was moving steadily towards its climax.

— 17 —

"You've all worked like Trojans," said Martin Brandreth. "It was a close race. But Golden Apple was first past the post. And that seemed to me a good enough excuse for a party."

Laughter and cheers.

The typists' room at Sayborn Art Printers had been cleared of desks and chairs, and the tables which had been brought in from the Board Room held a noble assortment of bottles and glasses and a rather smaller supply of eatables.

"It's true that we were helped by an accident to the other side, but that doesn't detract in the least from your efforts. If we hadn't made the effort we did, and been on their heels all the way, we shouldn't have overhauled them in the straight."

"I suppose," said Eileen, "that you could describe their lorry being hijacked as an accident. From what I read in the papers it seemed pretty deliberate to me."

Simon said, in a fierce whisper, "You mustn't say things like that."

"Why on earth not?"

"It's asking for trouble."

They were standing on the fringe of the crowd, and Susan was the only person close enough to tune in to this exchange. She turned round and said, "I read about it as well. It did seem funny, happening just when it did. I thought perhaps Merry and Merry had upset someone, and they were getting their own back."

"I didn't think things like that happened here," said Eileen. "America, perhaps."

Simon had pointedly disassociated himself from this conversation and moved as far away as the crowd would let him. Susan thought, I wonder what on earth they did to him. He's still running scared. At this moment Martin Brandreth, who had been standing on a chair to address the troops, caught sight of her and beckoned imperiously. She edged her way towards him and was presented with a drink. Brandreth raised his own glass, said, "To my secretary. The busiest girl in the office," and downed half his own drink. Susan tasted hers cautiously. It seemed to be mostly gin. The crowd swirled and reformed, and Susan found herself next to Mr. Lambie. She said, "I'm not all that fond of gin. Do you think I could pour some of this into your glass. Hold it down, out of sight. No one will notice. That's fine."

"Anything to oblige a pretty girl," said Mr. Lambie courteously.

The room grew noisier and, although all the windows were now wide open, hotter. Faces were redder. Voices which had started at a moderate pitch had to be raised higher and higher in order to make themselves heard. Susan moved round the room as quickly as the crowd would let her. As secretary to the Managing Director she had to be agreeable to everyone and found that a lot of people wanted to be nice to her. Inevitably this perambulation brought her back finally to the top of the room, where Brandreth was holding court.

He had been waiting for her. On the table behind him was a full glass. He reached back and handed it to her. "A special drink," he said with a grin. "I've been keeping it for you. No heeltaps."

Susan took a cautious sip.

"What on earth is it?" she said.

"Firewater," said Brandreth. "Drink it and all your cares will fly away."

"Drink it and I shall be flat on the floor," said Susan.

At this moment one of the directors of Holmes and Holmes surged up and got between them. Susan backed away, holding the glass. She had a suspicion that it held neat vodka.

The crowd was thinning out now, and to repeat the maneuvre with Mr. Lambie would have been difficult. As she reached the back of the room she realized that a row was brewing. She heard Simon say, "Three's quite enough. If you drink anything more, I won't be responsible for getting you home."

"And who asked you to be responsible?"

"Your mother. Among other people."

"That was very kind of her. But quite unnecessary."

"If she'd known that you were going to stand here swilling gin all evening—"

"If you call three weak gin-and-tonics swilling, I don't. And what's more, you've got no right to count every drink I take."

To emphasize what she was saying, Eileen had put down her own glass on the table and swung round on Simon. It was a private battle, conducted with low-pitched venom, absorbing to the contestants and ignored by everyone near them.

The opportunity was too good to be missed. The glasses, hired for the occasion, were all the same shape and size. Susan placed her own on the table and picked up Eileen's. Then she set a course which would bring her back towards Brandreth. She was tired of his oafish tactics. She thought that the time had come to ring down the curtain on the act. Conclusively, but artistically.

With the departure of the Holmes and Holmes contingent there was only a hard core of drinkers left. Brandreth said to her, "When you've finished that drink, I've got a proposal to make."

"A proposal or a proposition?" Susan managed to get a little artistic thickness into her voice.

"A suggestion, really. As soon as we can slip away, I'll run you up to London and give you a proper meal. These bits and pieces are no fodder for a growing girl."

"Had you any particular place in mind?"

"When I celebrate I like to do it properly. I suggest La Terrasse."

"O.K. by me. But it's very popular just now. You probably won't get a table."

"I've already booked one."

The devil you have, thought Susan. What she wanted was a diversion. She was presented with one immediately. A table at the far end of the room went over with a crash.

Susan said, "That's Eileen. I'd better give a hand."

Several people were helping already. Simon, white-faced and furious, was saying, "She'll be quite all right if you get her outside. It was the heat."

Susan said, "We'll put her in the annex. If she's going to be sick, there's a lavatory there. You needn't all come. Put an arm under her shoulders, Simon. See if she can walk."

"I told her," said Simon. "It was that last drink that did it."

"It's always the last drink that does it. Put her in that chair by the window. I'll be back in a minute."

There were two telephones with outside lines. One was in her room, the other in Brandreth's. She thought it would be safer to use his. She hoped that the person she wanted was in and would answer her call quickly.

She was back inside five minutes. The room was nearly empty.

Brandreth said, "What's that silly girl been up to? I always thought she was a steady type."

"Showing off," said Susan. "They all do it. She'll be all right now."

"Then let's beat it."

Brandreth was a showy driver. His attention for the next forty minutes was devoted to passing cars, slipping between cars and beating traffic lights. Susan fastened her seat belt tight and uttered a short prayer to St. Christopher, patron saint of travelers.

Brandreth's luck was in. They arrived in one piece, and he even managed to find a parking space. He took Susan's arm as they went into the restaurant. The headwaiter said, "I have your table, Mr. Brandreth. We are a little crowded, but I have managed the additional place."

Brandreth stared, first at him and then at the table from which a middle-aged, grey-haired, grey-moustached man had risen politely to his feet. He knew him, of course. Andrew Holmes, senior partner of Holmes and Holmes, one of the largest advertising agencies in London and the principal customer of Sayborn Art Printers.

Holmes was holding a chair for Susan, who sank into it. Brandreth was very red and seemed disinclined to sit. Holmes said smoothly, "It seemed to me that we had a double event to celebrate, Martin. First our signal triumph over Merry and Merry. Hearty congratulations. A joint effort, but you did most of the work. Secondly, Miss Perronet-Condé's move to our firm."

Brandreth sat down slowly. He seemed to be having some difficulty in finding words.

"Since I have, as it were, intruded on this dinner party," continued Holmes, "I have compounded my offense by daring to order the first course. I hope you are both as fond of smoked salmon as I am. I have bespoken a bottle of Chablis Moutonne to go with it."

"Lovely," said Susan. "I've hardly had time for a drink all evening."

— 18 —

Rayhome had, once again, taken rooms for their party at the good-class hotel which overlooked the Filippo Strozzi Park. David was glad of this. He was bleakly conscious that all he had gained by agreeing to come on the trip was a breathing space. A very temporary breathing space. He was under no illusions about that. He was a prisoner out on bail, and at the end of the trip, or maybe sooner, his bail was going to be called in. Meanwhile he thought that he might as well enjoy all the comfort that was available.

The surveillance was extensive and unremitting. There was a new floor waiter on the fourth floor, a sulky youth who seemed to spend most of his time using the house telephone; a middle-aged lady in tight black who sat in the entrance hall doing an endless piece of petit point; and a gang of boys with mopeds, one of whom was always on duty outside the front door of the hotel and a second near the service door which opened onto an alley alongside the hotel.

In the galleries and restaurants, standing behind him admiring the pictures, or sitting at the next table intent on their meals, were different and heavier types of watcher, men who had the appearance of Milanese industrialists, but spoke with the accent of the south—serious men from Naples or Sicily.

The most alarming aspect of this surveillance was that it was carried out so openly. David wondered what would happen if he tried to break out. Suppose he jumped, without warning, onto a bus and went somewhere, anywhere, out of the city. Stupid idea. There were cars on call which could keep any bus under observation. Or dived down a side street where no car could follow. But there were few places where a boy, with or without a moped, could not keep on his heels.

"Take it easy, David, lad," he said to himself. "Don't let the bastards panic you. Let them sweat, not you."

Things were made a bit easier by the fact that he had found a drinking companion. Lewis Hobart, a cheerful brown-faced man of much the same size and drinking capacity as David, formerly a captain in the African Rifles, now on indefinite leave pending discharge.

"It's my eyes," he explained, indicating the tinted glasses which he wore. "Let me down badly; got what they call double sight. Thought I was aiming at a black buck and nearly shot the Adjutant. Bad show."

Captain Hobart's interest in museums and galleries was small and easily satisfied. As a companion David found him much preferable to Collings, and over a succession of evenings they drank and yarned together, mostly in Harry's Bar on the Lungarno, but sometimes in more disreputable places. David learned a number of curious facts about Africa.

"It really is a fascinating country," said Captain Hobart. *"Ex Africa semper aliquid nova.* That's what I learned at school, and it's true. You could find anything there, from diamonds to dinosaurs. A pity we've given it all back to the Africans. It's wasted on them."

Another thing David noticed, and it gave him a cold and uncomfortable idea of what he was up against, was that his watchers seemed to expect cooperation from the authorities. On one occasion, when a car which had followed him from the hotel to a restaurant had experienced some difficulty in parking, a patroling *carabiniere* had peremptorily ordered another car to move.

As the six days of their stay went by, under hot sun and skies as blue as they are in cinquecento paintings, David could feel the meshes tightening round him. He thought, not for the first time, that he should have cut and run for it when he was in London. There would have been immediate trouble certainly; but it would have been better than this cat-and-mouse game, and he would have been in his own country, with the police on his side and not, at the best, neutral or, at the worst, against him.

He realized that Italy was, for the time being, a country in which the rule of law had ceased to mean very much. Criminals and terrorists had got hold of the wheels. A politician who opposed them could be maimed in front of his family. A judge who condemned a criminal might be signing his own death warrant. Over this dark abyss the tide of tourism flowed, unknowing and uncaring.

On the last evening Collings had, unexpectedly, asked David to come out with him for a drink. It was unexpected because it was, on this occasion, unnecessary. On this trip the black bag was innocent of any illicit cargo and would remain so. Of that David was certain. He wondered what Collings, who had been unusually silent, could have to say to him.

When it came, it was startling.

Collings, his elbows on the table and his muddy face close to David's, said, "You know you won't be allowed to come back with us tomorrow."

"Who'll stop me?"

"The police. That boy who looks after us on the fourth floor is going to say you propositioned him. When he turned you down, you pulled him into the bedroom and tried to rape him."

"His word against mine. No court will believe him."

"It won't come to court. The men who take you away won't be *carabinieri*. They'll be in plain clothes. And they won't take you to a police station. They'll take you out to a farm.

Somewhere quiet, outside the city, where they can work on you."

David finished his drink and put the glass down slowly on the table. Then he said, "Perhaps you'll tell me what you're talking about."

"You know bloody well what I'm talking about. Last time we were here you took something out of the pocket in that bag and put something different back."

"For Christ's sake," said David, "stop talking like a bloody Dolgelly lawyer and say what you mean. You think that I removed six packets of high-quality heroin and substituted six similar packets of old-fashioned photographic developer. Then, when the Chevertons and their backers found out, you got stick. Because you were supposed to keep an eye on me and you fell down on the job. Right so far?"

Collings said sourly, "Put it any way round you like. It's you who's for it now, not me. They know you didn't bring the stuff back to England, so it must be here. If you don't hand it over, they'll make you talk. And once they start, there's no guarantee they'll stop, even if you do talk."

"I see," said David. He was trying to speak normally, but his mouth was dry.

Collings said, with a curious note, almost of pleading, in his voice, "I don't know what your game is, but if you've got as much sense as I think you have, you'll back down and do it quick. You're out of your depth. These people have got everything going for them. Police, politicians, the press, the lot. I'm telling you. If they came in now"—he looked at the door as he said it—"and picked you up, bundled you into a car, did whatever they wanted to you and dropped what was left of you into the river, do you think anyone would worry about it? With politicians blown up in their cars and policemen with their kneecaps shot off, you'd hardly rate a quarter column."

While Collings had been talking, David had been thinking. He said, "Suppose you're right. Suppose I did string along with them."

145

"Hand over the stuff?"

"Yes. But it's not all that easy. I haven't got it with me. I left it with a friend. And I'm not having him involved. He's got to live here."

"Fair enough."

"It's the timing I'm thinking about. It's in his office safe. The office doesn't open before half past eight. Our coach leaves at nine and doesn't hang about."

This was true. The congestion in front of the hotel was such that it was only by concession that the Rayhome coach was allowed to stop there for five minutes while the tourists and their luggage got aboard.

"However, I think I can manage it, if you'll settle up at the hotel and put my stuff on the coach."

Collings said, "If you get there only at the last minute, the people you give the packet to won't have time to examine it properly. They're a suspicious lot of buggers. They won't like it."

"Agreed," said David. "But don't forget, we're stopping that night at Como. They'll have all evening to check it as thoroughly as they like. Believe me, I'm not going to try any funny stuff. Como's still in Italy."

Collings thought about it, turning it all ways round in his mind, trying to shake the tricks out of it. He had seen enough of David in the past few weeks to distrust him profoundly.

He said, "I don't like it. They won't like it, either."

"It's the way I'm going to do it."

"How are you going to get to your friend without being followed?"

"I'll manage," said David.

Next morning he was dressed and ready and out of his room by eight o'clock. He sidestepped the sulky floor waiter, who seemed to want to say something to him, got into the lift and went down to the ground floor. As soon as he arrived, without getting out he pressed the button again and went up to the second floor. The corridor was empty, as also was the service room. David hooked down one of the long, white overalls which was the staff working dress, carried it to the service staircase and put it on as he was going down to ground-floor level. At the foot of the staircase a short corridor led to a side door opening on the alley.

Tuesdays and Fridays, as he knew, having studied the workings of the hotel, were rubbish collection days. There were six cans just inside the door. David hoisted one of them onto his left shoulder so that it hid his face, pushed open the door and went out swinging to the right and away from the watcher as he did so.

As soon as he was round the corner he put down the can, removed his white coat, stuffed it into the can, shut the lid and walked off down the street. Two girls who were passing observed his actions with surprise. David walked quickly away and out into the main street beyond.

His first call was at a shop he had already marked down, which sold all manner of stationery and office gadgets. Here he bought a stout padded envelope of the type used by publishers for the dispatch of books, a roll of reinforced tape, a stapler and six packets of envelopes. With these he retired to a café across the way and ordered breakfast. He had a feeling that it was going to be a long day and he saw no reason to start it starving.

When he had finished eating he got out his purchases. The six packets of smaller envelopes went into the large padded envelope, the open end of which he fastened with three separate strips of tape. He then stapled each piece of tape into position with four staples. When he had finished, he paid for his breakfast and departed, leaving the stapler and tape on a ledge under the table and putting the package inside the front of his jacket.

A quick walk through side streets took him to the mouth of the alleyway opposite the hotel and on the other side of the road. The time was a few minutes past nine o'clock. David peered round the corner.

The coach was there, the last of the luggage was being put aboard and Collings was standing beside the driver's seat looking worried. There were two men on the pavement in front of the hotel. Collings went across and had a word with them. The traffic policeman blew his whistle and waved to the coach. Collings came back and stood by the open door, looking up and down the street.

"Now for it, boyo," said David.

He sprinted down the alley, jumped into the coach and took his seat. Collings climbed in after him.

"It's all right," said David. "Off you go."

The policeman whistled again urgently.

David took the envelope out from under his coat, opened the black bag which was by the driver's seat and put it in as the coach moved off.

They stopped for lunch outside Bologna. David had time for a word with Collings. He said, "Sorry I was late. My friend didn't turn up until twenty to nine. I had to run for it."

Collings said, "Tell you the truth, I thought you'd bolted."

"I may be a fool, but I'm not such a bloody fool as that," said David. "Everything's all right now. The stuff's in that envelope. Nothing to worry about."

This was not true. There was still a good deal to worry about. But the situation had improved. He had had two reasons for suggesting a handover at Como. The first was that the opposition, although no doubt they would be there in sufficient strength, would be less well organized than in Florence. The second was that he was a great reader of escape stories. He knew that the only four prisoners of war who had got out of Italy before the Italian armistice had all gone the same way. By train to Como, then five miles up the road to Chiasso, then through the wire about a mile above Chiasso Station and so into Switzerland. He reckoned that, if he could get clear of the hotel, he could be in Switzerland in a couple of hours.

The thought kept him cheerful through the hot hours of the early afternoon. Most of the passengers were torpid and half of them were asleep. David had moved to the back of the coach to have a gossip with Captain Hobart.

They were ten kilometers past Piacenza when he realized that his plans had gone wrong.

The coach braked to a halt with a suddenness which made the passengers sit up. There was a barricade across the road, with an official-looking car beside it. David, looking down the length of the coach, recognized one of the two men who were strolling towards them. He had a remarkable bush of hair and a deeply cleft chin.

─── 19 ───

"Some trouble?" said Captain Hobart.

"Looks like it," said David. "I'd better go and see what it's all about." He opened the emergency door at the back of the coach and stepped out, shutting the door carefully behind him. Then he walked quickly back down the road, hidden by the bulk of the coach, jumped the ditch and found himself in a vineyard. This had been planted in the economical Italian fashion with vegetables sharing the beds with the vines, and it formed a useful screen. David got between two of the rows and started to run.

The slope of the field was downhill, and he was soon out of sight of the bus. The vineyard ended in a country road. Propped up, in the road, beside an opening in the hedge was a very old bicycle. David jumped onto it and pedaled off. As soon as he started he realized why the bicycle had been abandoned. Both the tires were flat.

Though uncomfortable, it was still rideable, and he had bumped along the road on the rims of the wheels for about a quarter of a mile when he realized that it was leading him back towards the main road. He had noticed the name of the town as they came through. Something like Fontenellato. It had a big church and a market square and looked quite a prosperous little place. It was the hour of the siesta, and the streets were empty.

David abandoned the bicycle and walked towards the square. Ahead of him he heard the sound of a heavy vehicle starting. He broke into a run. Sure enough, it was a bus and it was already moving.

The driver heard David's shouts and slowed to a halt. David threw himself on board, and the bus started up again.

"A narrow escape," said the conductor.

"Very narrow," agreed David.

"To what destination is the gentleman traveling?"

"Where does the bus go to?"

"Eventually to Piacenza."

"Then Piacenza is my destination."

An elderly gentleman in an alpaca jacket said, "It is dangerous to run in the heat of the day."

"I am in entire agreement with you," said David. "Such exercise is better taken in the cool of the morning, or perhaps in the evening when the sun is down."

"It is better not taken at all. A little forethought is all that is necessary."

"A last-minute decision."

The old gentleman pondered this remark. He said, "Since it would appear that you did not know where you were going until you had boarded this bus, how could you have come to any decision?"

"I have an impulsive nature," said David.

"You are English?"

"Certainly not. I am Welsh."

"A nephew of mine once spent a year in Cardiff," said the old gentleman. "He related to me some very curious stories about the Welsh."

The bus had left the main road and was making a circuitous route, stopping in each of the many villages which dotted the Lombardy plain to pick up or put down passengers. The old gentleman fell asleep. The countryside baked in the late afternoon sun. David was busy with his thoughts.

How long would it have taken his enemies to discover that he was not in the coach? When they did discover it, what would they do? If they assumed that he had taken to the fields they would be in some difficulty. Policemen with motor cars and modern communications could be very effective on main roads but at a loss in open country.

If they cast back to Fontenellato might they not pick up the story of the stranger who had run through the streets and clambered onto the bus as it was leaving? If they did, there would surely be a reception committee awaiting him at Piacenza.

On the whole, David thought this unlikely. Undoubtedly they would get onto his track in the end, but he thought that he had a head start which it was up to him to make the most of. He could have wished that the bus was not quite so deliberate in its approach to Piacenza, whose towers and office blocks he could already see ahead of him, but it got there at last and put him down outside the main-line station. He walked into the welcome cool of the waiting room and consulted the indicator board.

There was a train due in ten minutes, but this was described as *locale*, which meant that it would stop at almost every station. If he was prepared to wait for fifty minutes, there was an express train going directly to Milan. His instinct was to get away as fast as possible. His reason was against it. If a search was organized up and down the line, every intermediate station would be a danger point. Safer, in the long run, to wait.

It was a nerve-racking fifty minutes, which stretched to an hour, then to an hour and a quarter. David spent part of it in buying himself a panama hat, a pair of sunglasses and a cheap plastic briefcase, and the rest of it in the station buffet replacing lost moisture.

The shadows were already lengthening when a burst of activity announced the imminent arrival of the Bologna-Milano express. An official paced out onto the platform carrying a circular disc on the end of a stick, red on one side and green on the other. A boy wheeled out a trolley covered with drinks, sweets and newspapers. With important sighings and hissings the diesel-electric train slid into the station, and David climbed thankfully on board. He took his seat in the carriage just behind the engine.

The next hurdle was going to be the ticket barrier at Milan Central Station. There would be a lot of neutral observers around, and David reckoned that if any attempt was made to snatch him he could kick up enough fuss to attract attention and make things difficult for his assailants.

In fact, nothing happened at all, and David walked out into the station concourse with a feeling that he was now ahead of the game. Probably the opposition was still beating the coverts round Fontenellato. He hoped that they were getting good and hot. Speed was now going to be more effective than guile. He studied the timetable. The international express for Paris left at eight o'clock. He made for the ticket office. There were no *couchettes* left, but as the result of a last-minute cancellation there was a single *wagon-lit* apartment available. The thought of the privacy and the bed was irresistible. David had plenty of money with him. He booked the sleeper.

The next and most necessary step was to restore a measure of credibility to his appearance. He was aware that he looked more like a tourist who had been for a walk in the countryside than a respectable occupant of first-class accommodation in an international express.

Fortunately the shops were still open, so this was something that could be remedied.

At a men's outfitters in the Via Bolognese he bought a light traveling coat, a grey felt hat, some shirts and a pair of rather attractive Cambridge blue silk pajamas. At a chemist's he replenished his washing-and-shaving kit. Then he selected, to carry his purchases, a flashy-looking imitation pigskin suitcase. To give it a bit of weight he stopped at a kiosk and bought half a dozen magazines and a pile of newspapers.

A final thought occurred to him. A restaurant car, as he had discovered, was due to join the train when it reached Switzerland, and he would be able to have a comfortable dinner—comfortable in every sense, since his immediate troubles would be over. Nevertheless, he stopped at the nearest food store, bought a pork pie, a slab of chocolate and a small bottle of brandy, and stowed them away in his briefcase. Emergency rations, he said to himself—just in case he had to try an illicit frontier crossing on foot. He didn't believe it. It was the gesture of a man who is thankful for a run of luck, but touches wood.

By this time it was a quarter past seven. He made his way back to the station, located his *wagon-lit* and settled down to wait. The minutes passed slowly. He heard other passengers coming in and occupying their compartments. The only thing which struck him as odd was the nonappearance of the *wagon-lit* conductor. This official was usually on hand to check passengers' reservations, show them to their places and exact a tip.

It was nearly half an hour later that David became aware that something was happening.

He stepped into the corridor, lowered the window and peered cautiously out.

There was a group of half a dozen men on the platform. Two of them seemed to be station officials. The other two had the unmistakable look of policemen. There were three coaches of *couchettes* and *wagon-lits*, of which David's was the farthest away from the barrier. As he looked, the four men climbed aboard the first of the coaches.

"Search party," said David. "And they'll be here inside five minutes."

There was only one course open to him. He left his new suitcase on the bed and dropped his new hat and coat ostentatiously on top of it. The longer they thought he was somewhere on the train the better. Then, picking up his briefcase, he made his way along the corridor towards the far end of the train.

It was a long train. By the time he reached the head of it, he had put eight more coaches between himself and the pursuit. The engine had not yet been backed into position. The far end of the platform was dimly lit. David stepped out of the carriage and dropped down onto the line in front of the front coach.

His train was on the outer of six lines. He crossed the other five lines carefully and regained the far platform. He had two choices. To get back onto the station concourse and mingle with the crowd or to get onto the train which was standing farther down the platform.

It was a *locale,* second-class carriages only, and it was crowded enough to suggest that it was ready to start. David looked at the destination board. Lodi—Piacenza—Parma—Reggio Emilia—Bologna—Firenze.

"The hunted fox," he said, "when hard-pressed, will sometimes find safety by doubling directly back on his tracks."

He boarded the train, choosing a carriage which was already occupied by an Italian family. A mother, a father, a small girl, a smaller boy and a very small baby. Also a grandmother, a formidable grenadier with a moustache and a bonnet. David inserted himself between the father and the small girl, and the train moved off.

It seemed, to start with, that his intrusion was going to be resented, but, as happens on such occasions, the advent of mealtime broke the ice. Under the supervision of the grandmother a basket of provisions was brought down from the rack, portions of chicken leg and pasta were distributed, two bottles of wine were uncorked and an agreeable picnic got under way. David produced his own food and was invited to share in the wine. In return he distributed pieces of his chocolate, a gesture much appreciated by the boy, who coated his mouth and chin with a brown layer.

In the middle of the meal a ticket inspector arrived and prepared to take a serious view of the fact that David had boarded the train without a ticket. The grandmother took up the cudgels on his behalf. Whether this was because she approved of David or simply because she enjoyed an argument was not clear. She went straight over to the attack. There had been a long queue at the booking office, but only one of the ticket windows had been open. Why was that? If there was a long queue waiting, why was the second window not open? Was it because they were short of staff? It could hardly be that, when one considered the price one paid for a ticket—

At this point the inspector gave up. He accepted the money David was offering him and withdrew, slipping on a grape which the boy had dropped—an accident which caused general satisfaction.

By the time the train reached Bologna, David had discovered the names of the three children and of three other children who had been left at home, and had entertained them with an account of his misadventures on a walking tour in the Italian Alps. Between Bologna and Florence the children and the grandmother fell asleep, the mother cross-examined David about the cost of living in England and the father about the religious beliefs of the Welsh.

On arrival at Florence complicated arrangements had to be made to disembark the family. David, having one hand free, offered to carry the baby, an offer which was gratefully accepted. He walked out of the station and accompanied his new friends to the family flat in the Via Torta. They parted on the doorstep with expressions of mutual esteem, and David made for the nearest telephone booth. It was ten minutes short of midnight, but he did not think that the Aldinis were people who went to bed early.

Clarissa answered the telephone herself. She seemed pleased and unsurprised. Certainly there was a bed available. She couldn't guarantee how soon he would get into it, as there was a bit of a party going on.

It turned out to be, apart from Clarissa, an all-male party, consisting of two architect colleagues of Carlo Aldini; a man with a bushy red beard, whom David supposed to be an artist, but who turned out to be the Assistant Procurator Fiscal of Glasgow; and a serious young man in steel-rimmed glasses whom David diagnosed, correctly this time, as an American professor.

It was the sort of party where everyone talks at once. David had now got his second wind. He talked to one of the architects about the scandal of modern office building, to the Procurator Fiscal about football and to the professor about a new theory that Shakespeare was the illegitimate son of Henry the Eighth. It was three o'clock when he tumbled into bed, wearing pajamas borrowed from his host, and eleven o'clock when he opened his eyes to find Clarissa standing beside the bed with a cup of coffee in her hand.

"You could have something more elaborate if you liked," she said, "but actually it's nearly lunch time. And you can borrow Carlo's shaving things—that is, if you don't happen to have brought any with you."

Her unconcern as to the reason for David's unceremonious arrival was so splendid that it made him laugh. Clarissa laughed too. David thought she looked terrific and in any other circumstances would have invited her to jump straight into bed with him. He rejected the idea regretfully and said, "Sit down for a moment. I'm not going to tell you the story of the last few days, because you wouldn't believe it. I've been engaged in my favorite pursuit of running away. It's the thing I'm best at."

"You did tell me that you never went into a restaurant without looking for a way out through the kitchen."

"I'm looking for a way out now. Out of this God-forsaken country. I'll need a bit of help."

"All right," said Clarissa placidly.

"Nothing criminal."

"I'm glad about that. Italian prisons are places to keep out of, so my friends tell me."

"If you look in the breast pocket of my coat you'll find a passport. That's the one."

Clarissa examined it critically. She said, "It seems to belong to a man called Lewis Hobart."

"A good type. I'm certain he won't mind lending it to me for a day or two."

"Won't he be needing it himself?"

"They don't bother to look at them at the Italian frontier. Sometimes not even at Calais. It'll be wanted at Dover, but that's tomorrow night, and I'll be back in England by then, I hope."

"You don't look much like him."

"Like enough. In passport photographs it's only the externals that count. I'll need a pair of tinted glasses with frames like his. You can buy them at any optician's. Explain they're for amateur theatricals. Then see if you can pick up a brown-and-white checked coat, like the one he was wearing when the photograph was taken. And some suntan lotion."

"Also for amateur theatricals?"

"Right. He's a bit balder than me, but if I comb my hair right back it should get past. Then you go to that travel agency in the Via Tornabuoni, I forget the name, but it's next to the American Bank. See if you can book me a sleeper or a *couchette* on the night train from Livorno this evening. The one that goes to Marseilles."

"In the name of Lewis Hobart."

"Captain Lewis Hobart. Late of the King's African Rifles."

"Anything else?" said Clarissa, who was making a list.

"One or two things. I'll need another suitcase. And some washing and shaving things. I don't think I'll bother about shirts this time."

"What happened last time?"

"I had to leave them behind. Two shirts *and* a pair of Cambridge blue pajamas."

"You'd have looked very tasty in them," agreed Clarissa.

"Oh, boy," said David to himself. "This is a girl in ten thousand."

"You're a girl in ten thousand," he said.

The arrival of Carlo saved him from what would unquestionably have been an indiscretion.

When Clarissa got back from her shopping expedition, having got all the things David had asked for, including a *wagon-lit* reservation on the Livorno train, she said, "I couldn't help noticing that the *carabinieri* were clustered rather thickly round Central Station. They seemed to be particularly interested in English passengers. Why don't I run you in my car to Empoli? Most of the Florence–Pisa trains stop there. No one will think of watching out for you in a small place like that. Then, if you get out at the stop before Pisa, you can take a bus into the town."

"A girl in a hundred thousand," said David.

The first part of the plan went well. He took an appropriate farewell of his guardian angel at the quiet end of Empoli Station platform and by three o'clock in the afternoon had reached Pisa, where he picked up a stopping train for Genoa. There was no sign of the opposition. He had dinner at the station restaurant and by nine o'clock he was sitting on the bed in his *wagon-lit* watching the Mediterranean coast slip past.

On one point he had made up his mind. He would not go to sleep until the train was out of Italy and over the French frontier. He had surrendered his passport and ticket and had filled in the customary declarations. In the ordinary way he would not be disturbed again.

He lay down on top of the made-up bed and devoted thought to the future. If he got back to England undetected, and he thought that the chances were now in his favor, he would have taken an important step forward on the tortuous track that he was following. No. That was wrong. Not forward. Downward. And it wasn't a track, it was a ladder which he was descending. When you were on a ladder, it was dangerous to look down, particularly when the bottom of the ladder was resting in a pit of warm darkness.

The train stopped with a jolt.

David opened his eyes and sat up. It was broad daylight.

His watch told him that it was six o'clock, and the board outside the window of his carriage told him that they were at Marseilles. Time for breakfast.

An unhurried morning took him across the South of France and up the west coast of Nantes. The sight of some cows in a field made him laugh. He was thinking of Mrs. Fairbrass and the first Rayhome tour that he had conducted. It seemed light-years away.

At Nantes he got a taxi out to the airport and booked a seat on the afternoon flight to London. The plane left at three o'clock. French clocks being an hour ahead of English, it reached Heathrow at ten past three. By a quarter to four he was on the Underground train heading back for central London.

There was one more urgent job to do. If Paula had done her stuff, there would be a parcel waiting for collection at the Poste Restante at Burnt Oak. Also, possibly, a letter.

He had chosen Burnt Oak because it was on the Northern Line and had one smallish post office, in a quiet street near the Underground station.

He reconnoitered it carefully.

A man on the corner selling evening papers. He remembered him there before. A woman pushing a pram with one child in it and another walking beside her. A female traffic warden inspecting a line of cars at the far end of the street. Nothing out of the ordinary.

David walked into the post office, his eyes open for trouble. At the far end of the long counter a youth with a startling crop of pimples was selling a postal order to an old man. At the end near the door there was a middle-aged lady who smiled pleasantly at him and handed him, without demur, the package and letter he asked for.

David walked out into the sunlight. The child in the pram had thrown a toy dog at the other child. The traffic warden had spotted a defaulter and was sucking her pencil. Life was proceeding normally.

David let out the breath which, unconsciously, he had been holding and made for the Underground.

Once he was safely on the train he opened the letter. The message was typed on plain paper. It said, "In answer to your query: There are a number of doctors who are suspected by the police of dealing illicitly in hard drugs, including heroin. List of names and addresses herewith."

He studied the list. There was really only one of them that could have matched the description given him by Watterson. "Dr. Ram Jam or something" with a surgery "down near the Surrey docks."

By eleven o'clock that night David was drifting through the empty streets of dockland. Barnabas Road, Lavender Steps, Winnipeg Street, Rat Alley, Moscow Street and so into Pipe Street. He picked his way up Leonard Mullion's front path, avoiding Uncle Tom Cobley on one side and the Big Bad Wolf on the other. He used the key that Leonard Mullion had given him and opened the front door as quietly as he could.

There were no big bad wolves in the dark little front hall or in the room on the first floor at the back, which overlooked a garden the size of a billiard table, crammed with roses, wallflowers and pinks.

David opened the window, and the massed scents invaded the room. He took a deep breath. Against all the odds, he had made a home run.

Less than a mile away the old tramp was settling down in his nest of newspaper. He was settling down to talk, not to sleep, because sleep was hard to come by, and when it did come was full of dreams which slid into nightmares of such horror that he woke shaking and dribbling and running with sweat.

Irish Mick, who dossed down in the straw beside him, was usually willing to do his share of talking, but tonight felt sleepy and disgruntled at a turnup he had had with an officious policeman.

He said, "You're a great one for talking, Percy. If it's a big secret, the way you say it is, why don't you do something about it? Turn it into cash. That's the thing to do with secrets. Sure an' someone will buy it from you if you take it to the right market."

The tramp said, in his educated voice, "There are some chances which one can take and some chances which one cannot."

"Sleep on it, chummy. Sleep on it," said Irish Mick.

20

"I'm beginning to think," said Trombo, "that we may have underestimated Mr. Morgan."

Neither of the Chevertons had anything to say to this.

"If I am right," continued Trombo, in a level voice, which had a definite undertone of menace in it, "it may be very serious. Serious for all of us. Our Italian contacts are not people to play games with."

Ronald said, "It was them who made a mess of it. Not us."

"I don't agree," said Trombo sharply. "The mess was made when you hired Morgan without making any proper enquiry into his background. What did you know about him? Well?"

"We knew he came from a firm of accountants in the City. The same firm one of our earlier couriers came from. A man called Moule."

"Never mind about Moule. What did these City accountants tell you about Morgan?"

"Sam Lyon, he's the senior partner, wrote him a goodish testimonial. Then he got on the phone to me and gave me the real story. He said that Morgan was a man who hit the bottle and would pinch the petty cash if he got half a chance."

"Which made him, no doubt, the ideal man to act as courier to your parties."

"In a way, yes. We fixed him with his own bag. If there was any trouble, *he* was going to be on the spot. The worse his character, the more likely the dirt was to stick."

"Myself," said Bob, "I always thought he might have some form."

"I'm not interested," said Trombo, "in whether he has been to prison or not. My principals want him found and dealt with. They have been made to look stupid. They will not tolerate that. They have ways of making their displeasure felt. You understand me?"

The Chevertons looked at each other. Bob said, "We must have an address for him somewhere. He won't have gone back, of course. But we might be able to pick up the trail from there. Let's ask the girl."

Paula was summoned. She said that the only address she had was the Radstock Hotel in Lucas Street. She had telephoned them already. He had given up his room when he left on the last Italian trip.

Bob said, "He didn't leave a forwarding address, I suppose."

"The only forwarding address he ever gave me was one for Mr. Moule."

Paula was not an observant girl, but it did seem to her that this remark was greeted with unexpected interest. For a moment no one spoke. Then Trombo leaned forward and said, "Why should a forwarding address have been necessary for Moule? He left here over three years ago."

"David—I mean Mr. Morgan—said something about meeting him."

Paula was flustered. The atmosphere had suddenly become unpleasant.

"Go on," said Trombo.

"He said, if a parcel arrived for Mr. Moule, would I forward it to this address. Poste Restante, it was. At Burnt Oak."

"And did a parcel arrive?"

"That's right. The day after he left for Italy. I thought it was a funny thing, because the parcel was from Florence, and as he was going to be there himself in a day or two I wondered why he couldn't have picked it up—"

No one seemed to be listening to her. Trombo said to Ronald, "Have you got a telephone? With an outside line. In a room where I can be private."

The girl behind the counter looked up when the two men came in and managed a smile although neither of them looked worth it. The larger of the two had red hair and the flat, white face of a boxer. The smaller had an oddly squashed nose which made him look like a bad-tempered monkey. It was the small man who did the talking.

He said, "Anything here for me? Name of Moule. Spelt with a *u*."

The girl flicked through the contents of the M-N-O slot and said, "Sorry. Nothing here."

"You sure? It'd be a large envelope or a small parcel."

The girl looked again, rather more quickly this time, and said, "Nothing for Moule."

She had a fat envelope with foreign stamps on it in her hand as she said this.

"That could be it," said the small man.

The girl stowed it away without bothering to say anything.

"Mind if I look?"

"I'm sorry. No one's allowed this side of the counter."

"Too bad," said the small man and climbed over.

The youth at the far end said, "Hey, mister—you can't do that—" and moved towards the girl.

This brought him within range of the red-headed man, who stretched out a long arm, caught him by the lapel of his coat with one hand and his hair with the other and banged his face on the counter top.

"Keep an eye on the door," said the small man.

He was rifling through the contents of the Poste Restante cupboard, picking out the larger envelopes and flat packages and putting them on one side.

The girl had got out a handkerchief and was trying to mop up the blood which was pouring out of the youngster's face.

The small man finished what he was doing, hopped back across the counter and said, "You'd better not follow us. I've got friends outside."

The girl looked at him scornfully. She was dialing the local police station by the time the men were going out of the door.

Three minutes later an area car, which had been on patrol, reached the post office. The operator said, "A big chap with red hair and a small, ugly chum? We'll see what we can do." He spoke on the car wireless. A hastily organized dragnet found the packages. They had been ripped open, searched and dropped in the gutter. There was no sign of the two men.

A report on the matter went out on the general telex link to the Incident Room at Scotland Yard and came, in due course, under the eye of Chief Superintendent Morrissey.

It was the name Moule which interested him.

He spoke on the telephone to Sergeant Brannigan, at Leman Street. He said, "You've got a man down there who knows all the local villains. Been on the Station some time."

"Wrangle."

"That's the one. Send him up to Burnt Oak Post Office to get a description of the two men who assaulted a post clerk and ripped a lot of stuff out of the Poste Restante and strewed it round the streets."

"If he gets anything, do I send it to you at the Yard?"

"You can tell me about it personally," said Morrissey. "I'm coming down. Things are starting to move."

When Morrissey reached Leman Street he found Brannigan alone in the detective room. Wrangle had not yet reported back. Brannigan was looking at a cedarwood cabinet which stood open on the table. He said, "It came this morning. Addressed to me, at my flat. We don't often get parcels. My wife was sure it was a bomb."

"It's not a bomb," said Morrissey thoughtfully. "It's more

what you might call a booby trap. Lucky you're not a booby."
In the box, carefully arranged, was a set of ten kitchen knives,
beautiful pieces of craftsmanship, each with its black wooden
handle, copper tang and shining steel blade.

"When my wife saw those," said Brannigan, "she couldn't
hardly keep her hands off them."

"From Trombo, I suppose."

"That's right."

Morrissey had taken out the biggest of the knives. It had a
razor edge and a massive backing of steel which gave it weight
as well as sharpness.

"Take off a man's hand with that easy," he said. He slotted
the knife back into the box. "Must be worth the thick end of
two hundred pounds, a set like that. Restaurant stuff. They'll
have to go back."

"That's right," said Brannigan, with a grin. "I thought I might
take them back myself. Tell him what I thought of him."

"I wouldn't do that. Just send them back." A clatter of feet
on the stairs announced the arrival of Detective Wrangle. He
looked pleased with himself. He said, "Not much doubt who
the men at Burnt Oak were. Ginger Williams and McVee."

"Monkey McVee?"

"That's right, sir."

"That makes it the Friary Lane crowd. Operating out of
their territory, weren't they?"

"That's what I thought, sir. They don't often go north of
the river." Wrangle was looking curiously at the knives. "Are
we starting a butcher's shop?"

"Many a true word spoken in jest, son. That's just what we
may be starting." He thought about it, staring out of the window. His lips were moving as though he was working out a
sum. Wrangle, who had worked with him before, felt a prickle
of excitement. He had thought there might be something in
the wind. Now he was sure of it.

Morrissey swung round. He said to Brannigan, "Is there anywhere round here we could keep men under cover?"

"For how long?"

"A day and a night, maybe two nights."

"There's the drill hall in West Street."

"Who's it belong to?"

"The army, I suppose. It hasn't been used for some time. You'd need to get the water and gas and electricity turned on."

"See if you can do it quietly. Just tell them you need it for training purposes. Bills go to Central. Right?"

"Do what I can," said Brannigan. "How many men had you got in mind?"

"Up to a hundred," said Morrissey.

Susan's job with Holmes and Holmes was proving a lot more interesting than anything she had done before. It involved no shorthand or typing. Her main duty seemed to be keeping people away from Andrew Holmes, but doing it without irritating them. It involved a lot of eating and drinking.

On her third morning there she sidetracked the Managing Director of a wholesale clothing firm by taking him to lunch at the Savoy. When he had got over his annoyance at being sidetracked, which took about ten minutes, he started to enjoy the experience of lunching with a girl who was easy to look at and easy to talk to. Susan had spent ten minutes reading up the last few annual reports and accounts of her guest's company and was able to display an informed and flattering interest in its prosperity. When they got back to the offices of Holmes and Holmes in Theobalds Road, he seemed sorry to exchange her for Andrew Holmes, who was now ready to see him.

Two days later she entertained a Saudi Arabian Minister, who spoke excellent English and was, as she quickly discovered, just as intelligent as she was. On the following week she found herself in charge of four Japanese businessmen.

It was a routine which did not leave much time for gossip, but sometimes, in the early evening when he was waiting for his letters to sign, Andrew Holmes found time to talk. She discovered from him that he was a keen fisherman and, from other people, that he was a formidable poker player—two appropriate pursuits, it seemed to her, for the head of an advertising agency.

Inevitably, sooner or later, the talk turned to Blackett. "In his own way," said Holmes, "he's one of the most remarkable men in England. He's taken on the system, on its own terms, and he's beaten it. The Inland Revenue would give its collective back teeth to catch him out. They've had two shots at him, one with the General Commissioners and another with the Special Commissioners, and they lost them both. He's too big for them."

"Too powerful, you mean."

"No. Too big. He understands every ramification of his own business machine. The people who try to investigate it only manage to see and understand about a fifth of it. They're like children trying to chase a grown-up through a maze which he built himself. He understands all the twists and turns and blind alleys and comes out of the exit, laughing, while they find themselves exhausted and back at the entrance."

"They're very patient," said Susan. "The tax people, I mean. They don't give up easily."

"Certainly. They keep after him because they hate him and envy him. A senior tax inspector—perhaps he's a man at the top of that particular tree, living in his suburban semi-detached, driving a five-year-old car and worrying about the way the electricity bills keep going up—finds himself dealing with a man like Blackett, who has a house in ten acres of ground near Virginia Water, a full staff of servants, including a gardener and a chauffeur—"

"I've seen him," said Susan. "A big, blond brute."

"A heated swimming pool, a private squash court and a cellar full of vintage burgundy and claret. What's his reaction?"

"Perhaps his reaction ought to be that Blackett works harder than he does?"

"Don't you believe it! His reaction is that he'd like to catch the bastard out and extract a walloping fine from him or send him down for a couple of years."

"The Inland Revenue can be ruthless, too," said Susan. "Don't forget they got Al Capone after the F.B.I had given up!"

On another occasion it was Susan who introduced the topic. They had been having a difficult time with a client who didn't seem to know quite what he wanted except that it was a lot of advertising for a little money.

"You have to make allowances, I suppose," said Susan.

"Why?"

"He had a beastly time during the war. He told me all about it. Four years in a Japanese prison camp. It must have affected him. Mentally as well as physically."

"Blackett took damned good care that it didn't affect him. Do you know what he did with his gratuity? People who'd been in Jap hands got treated quite well. I think he collected eight hundred pounds in back pay and such like. Quite a substantial sum in those days. He spent the lot on a three-months' course in a Norwegian health clinic. The sort of place that started with sauna baths and relaxation classes and finished with P.T. and ski-trekking. That was to take care of the physical side. When he got back to England he put in for a government grant and qualified as an accountant in record time. It was immediately after the war, and service people were allowed to cut corners. As soon as he was qualified he took himself off to America. In contravention, incidentally, of the terms he'd got his grant on. He wasn't looking for money just then. He was looking for know-how. He got a job with a firm of international insurance brokers—if you know what they do."

"More or less," said Susan cautiously. "They find re-insurance for U.K. risks in the States and vice versa, don't they? What did he do when he came back?"

"He got a job with Morphews Van Nelle, the Merchant Bankers. Am I boring you?"

"Success stories are never boring."

"Up to that point, what I've been telling you is public property. The *Chronicle* did a profile of him last year. 'Captains of Industry.' A clever piece. It made him sound like a mixture between Horatio Bottomley and Father Christmas. I don't think Blackett liked it much, but the facts about his early life were there, all right. It's after he left Morphews and founded his own company, Argon, that the record gets a bit elusive. There was one other director, a retired army man, Colonel Paterson. A nice-enough chap who liked to take two hours over his lunch and left all the real work to Blackett. Argon was just a medium-sized run-of-the-mill finance company until it had the good luck to pick up the shares in a property company called Blackbird."

"It wasn't luck," said Susan. "It was Harry Woolf getting cancer."

"Now how on earth would you know that?"

"I was told about it by Mrs. Woolf. She's a friend of my grandmother."

She explained about her grandmother.

"Then you know more about that bit than I do," said Holmes. "The buzz round the City was that he'd borrowed the money to buy Woolf's shares, on pretty steep terms, from a character called Arnie Wiseman. I always thought he had a bit of luck there."

"Lucky being able to borrow the money, you mean?"

"That was lucky. But it wasn't what I meant. The point is that Wiseman would certainly have insisted on early repayment of his loan. And the only way Blackett could get the money was by selling off a lot of the actual Blackbird properties and hanging onto the options. Which is certainly what he did in the summer and autumn of 1972. Then, in December 1972, the property bubble burst. I expect you remember it. A lot of investment companies and private banks went under. Argon was laughing. It was practically a cash company by that time. Blackett got a lot of credit for having seen the slump coming. And that sort of credit is mighty useful to a man in his position.

· And as I said, I think in that case it was nine parts luck."

"That's a useful commodity, too," said Susan. What happened to Arnie?"

"No one knows. He must have been sitting pretty. He'd got his money back and he'd have got all the collateral benefits he'd bargained for, too. He was a director of Argon, with a good service contract, I'd guess, and a fat expense allowance. Practically he could milk the company of anything he wanted. And then he disappeared."

"Post hoc, but not *propter hoc,"* said Susan smugly.

"So! A Latinist *and* an economist."

"Not really. It was a tag I picked up the other day. I was longing to work it off on someone."

"Blackett was right. You're an unusual girl."

"Did he say so?"

"He's certainly interested in you. No doubt about that. Why do you think you've come up three ladders in record time? You're being groomed for stardom."

"What sort of stardom?" said Susan doubtfully.

"Sooner or later—and my guess would be sooner—you'll find yourself working directly for Blackett."

"I'm not sure that I should like that."

"Most people would jump at it. And when I say that he's interested in you, don't misunderstand me. I don't mean that he's attracted by your appearance, although that's quite attractive enough for any normal person. Blackett's not a normal person. Sexually I should guess he's a virgin. What I meant was, quite literally, that he finds you interesting. And when Blackett finds someone interesting, he likes to take them to pieces to discover what makes them tick."

— 21 —

Blumfield Terrace, S.E., had some pretensions to gentility. The houses were old and mostly subdivided, but front steps were holystoned, windows were curtained and there were flowers in the tiny gardens. Number 17, which carried the plate of Dr. Ramchunderabbas, M.B., M.I.P.D., was at the far end, where the road, which had been cut off by the railway, ended in a brick wall. At this point, if you were on foot, a passageway took you down, under the railway bridge and out into Blumfield Road, parallel to Blumfield Terrace and to the south of it.

At the open end of the Terrace there was a small, steamy café. Most of the work in it was done by a homesick Welsh girl of sixteen, who had no objection to David spending long hours over a single cup of tea, at a table in the window. What she made of him, apart from the fact that he was a fellow exile from the valleys, it is difficult to imagine. His clothes suggested the final step down before destitution. A flannel shirt, without a collar, a grubby windcheater, blue list trousers and gym shoes. Clearly he had no job, or he would not have been sitting about all day.

It took David three patient days to establish the doctor's routine. There were two normal surgeries, one between ten and twelve in the morning and the other between five and six in the evening. But he gained the impression that there was a third and rather different surgery, which started after the last regular patient had left.

It was difficult to be certain, but he guessed that these visitors must be coming up the passage and getting into the house without showing themselves in the Terrace. The surgery, he now knew, was the room on the first floor. He caught occasional glimpses, through the window, of Dr. Ramchunderabbas, a burly figure in a white coat, and of other men as well. Men he had not seen approaching the house.

He realized that he was going to need a closer observation post, and this presented difficulties. Many of the houses in the Terrace were occupied by elderly ladies, who spent most of their time at their front windows, spying on their neighbors.

Accordingly, when he left the café that evening, he made a detour, down the High Street, along Blumfield Road and up the passage from its bottom end. Just short of the top he stopped. His guess had been right. There was a doorway in the wall on the left of the passage which must lead to the back of the doctor's house. The wall on the other side was high, but not too high for an active man. He jumped for the top and pulled himself up until his chin was level with the coping. What he could see beyond the wall was a derelict triangle of land, knee-deep in nettles and separated by a high wire fence from the railway line.

He thought it would serve.

On the following night he was back at the same spot at ten o'clock, carrying a small knapsack over one shoulder. A quick pull-up, and he was over the wall and down among the nettles. As he arrived a train rattled past on the line. He noted that the wire fence was close-meshed enough to mask him from casual inspection from the train. The nettles were the only drawback.

From his knapsack he took a hammer and three short lengths of angle iron, flat at one end and cut to points at the other. Using the hammer cautiously, he drove these pegs into the brickwork of the wall. The first one went in three feet up, as a step; the other two a couple of feet higher, as a platform. When he had hoisted himself up onto them he found that he could see the length of the passageway as far down as the railway bridge and, immediately opposite him, the door into the doctor's garden.

On four occasions in the next hour footsteps approached up the passage, and David got into observation. The first time it was a policeman, who walked solidly past, his helmet inches from David's nose. The next three were all patients of Dr. Ramchunderabbas. They drifted up the passage, phantom figures, making little noise and hugging the shadows, paused at the garden door, darted a quick glance to right and left, then pushed the door open and went through, closing it softly behind them. It was too dark to see faces, but David could hear that one of them was crying softly.

The last of the visitors arrived at half past ten. When he left, the light in the first-floor window went out, and a minute later the light in the ground-floor front room came on. David clambered down stiffly from his perch. He had discovered what he wanted to know. He left the pegs in position, hoisted himself back over the wall and made for his bed.

Sleep proved evasive. The nettles had uncovered gaps in his defenses, and his calves and ankles were burning.

He turned over and made a determined effort to compose himself, but he could reach no more than the borderland of sleep. It was a land of shadows, where darker shadows moved. Helpless, hopeless ghosts who turned their faces away when he tried to identify them and wandered off, sobbing. It was daylight before he dozed off.

At eleven o'clock on the following evening he was ringing the doctor's bell. The surgery window was dark, confirming that the last of the evening callers had gone, and there was a light on in the front room downstairs, from which he could hear the sound of music.

For a long minute after he had rung nothing happened. He

noticed that there was an optic in the door and guessed that he was under observation. Then the door swung open and Dr. Ramchunderabbas said, "The surgery's shut. What do you want?" He was a burly figure and was standing in a way that blocked further advance.

David said, "If you'll allow me inside for a few minutes, I'll tell you. I've got a message from your suppliers. It's for you, mister, not for the whole street."

There was another long pause. What was evidently puzzling the doctor was the discrepancy between his visitor's disreputable appearance and the authoritative way in which he spoke.

Then he said, "You can come in, but no funny business."

David followed him into the front room. A cold meal was laid on the table, and a television set was humming softly. The doctor switched it off and said, "Well?"

By this time David was feeling a lot more comfortable. If the doctor had been on the level he would have slung him out and telephoned the police.

He said, "I understand that you've been experiencing some difficulty over some supplies."

"Supplies of what?"

"Heroin."

"So?"

"I am afraid that the difficulties are going to increase. There has been a hitch."

"I've no idea what you're talking about."

"If you don't know what I'm talking about, I'm wasting my time and yours."

David swung on his heel and made for the door.

"Don't let's play games," said the doctor. "If you've got something to say, come back, sit down and say it."

David came back, perched himself on the edge of the table and said, "The people you get your heroin from were swindled over the last consignment. They'll have considerable difficulty in replacing it. In fact, supplies may dry up altogether, for a time."

"And what has that got to do with you?"

"As it happens, I am in a position to offer you an alternative supply."

He put a hand into the top pocket of his windcheater and drew out a plastic packet. There was no doubt, now, about the doctor's interest.

Bad trouble with his patients, David diagnosed. Keep at him. You've got him rolling.

"You can test it if you wish. I imagine you have the apparatus."

"No need for apparatus," said the doctor. He opened the package, spilled a few grains from it onto a spoon from the table, held it up to the light and examined it closely. Then he touched a grain with his tongue.

He said, "How much are you asking?"

"There, now," said David, "I like a man who knows his own mind and comes straight to the point."

"How much?"

"If you weigh the packet you will find that it contains exactly twenty grams of top-grade heroin. The open-market price, I understand, is twelve thousand pounds a kilo. By my calculation that makes this lot worth two thousand, four hundred."

"You're talking curb-side prices. I don't deal in that market. First, I shall have to have the powder converted into regulation hypodermic tablets. That is an expensive process."

David knew that this was true. A doctor would have a small legitimate supply. But it would be in tablet form. If he dispensed the drug in powder form and it was traced back to him, he would be in bad trouble.

"I'll give you eight hundred pounds. Not a penny more."

"That wasn't the sort of price I had in mind."

"If you don't like it you can take the stuff somewhere else."

"What I proposed," said David placidly, "was to give you the packet."

The doctor stared at him.

"In exchange for some information. And a little help."

"So?"

"I will go further than that. If the information you give me proves correct and your help is effective, I will present you with a similar packet, also for free."

The doctor, who had been standing, sat down in the chair at the head of the table and closed his eyes.

Just as if he was going to say grace, thought David. "For what we are about to receive—"

After a long pause, the doctor said, "You are prepared to pay so handsomely for this information that it makes me wonder what it is and why you want it."

"Then let me explain." He extracted a snapshot from his wallet and laid it on the table. "I've every reason to believe that this is a photograph of one of your patients. It was taken some years ago, and the man will have changed a lot by now. But I think, if you look at it carefully—"

The doctor examined the photograph for a long minute. Then he said, "Perhaps."

"You do know him?"

"If it is a man who looks like a tramp and speaks like a gentleman."

"Yes, indeed," said David softly. "That will be the man."

"What do you want with him?"

"I've come a long way to find him." David put the photograph back in his wallet. "And I want you to help me."

"How?"

"Very simply. I have observed that you have regular days and times for the patients who visit you in the evenings."

"Certainly."

"Then you know when this man will come here next."

"He comes once a month. He has some allowance, I believe, from a family trust. He collects it in cash and comes here that same day. I sell him a month's supply in tablets."

"Which is how much?"

"All he can afford. Sixty tablets of one sixth of a grain each. He will be here next"—the doctor consulted a black covered book on the table—"on October fifteenth. That is in just a fortnight's time."

"You're quite certain?"

"Unless he dies in the meantime," said the doctor, "which is quite possible. Or if, by chance, he happened to get his hands on some other money, he might try for an earlier appointment, but I think that is unlikely. In the last two years that has happened only once."

"What is the routine for your patients? I'm sure you are very careful."

"Very," said the doctor, with rather a grim smile. "Each patient has a name. Not his real name, of course. A name by which he is known to me and to me only. He speaks it into the answer-phone at the back door, and I can release the door lock from here."

"Then, as soon as my man speaks his name, turn off your surgery light, keep it off for five seconds and turn it on again."

"Is that all?"

"Not quite. When he comes in you will explain to him that there has been a hitch in your supplies. You are having to ration all your patients. You can spare him only forty tablets."

"There'll be trouble. You don't know these people."

"It's the sort of trouble I expect you can deal with," said David. "Anyway, that's the proposition. And let me tell you one thing more. If you take my stuff and don't keep your side of the bargain, there will be another sort of trouble. My suppliers are hard men."

The doctor thought about it. Then he said, "I have told you that I cannot absolutely guarantee that he will be here on that date. It is a ninety-five percent probability only."

"In the changes and chances of this mortal life," said David, "how can one hope for more than ninety-five percent?"

In the fortnight that followed, a close observer would have noted the tiny successive steps in David's descent from poverty to destitution. The hair growing longer and greasier, the ruinous overcoat which he donned as the weather sharpened, the trousers collapsing at the bottom over boots which had started worn and now sported holes, stuffed with paper, in both toes.

In that fortnight, David explored the kingdom of the tramps. He came to know their enemies and their friends. The police who bullied them, the societies who afflicted them with tracts and prayer and the householders who were good for a cup of tea and an occasional small gift of money. He discovered that certain seats in parks and public places were their preserve and that the routes between them were preordained. When you went from Byland Street to Porthead Road you took the circular route, west of Rotherhithe Park, never the more direct route to the east of the park. Why? No one knew. The procession of the tramps was as immutable as the procession of the planets.

He also discovered, in time, some of their favored sleeping places. These were closely guarded secrets and were referred to only by indecipherable code names. The Villa, the Blink, Up-and-Under, Calcutta, Rats' Castle. As dusk fell the waif-like figures would melt into the shadows, moving first slowly and with caution and then very quickly, to reach their secret lying-up places.

On the first night of real cold and rain, David made for a tramps' lodging house in Stepney which had been recommended to him as a superior doss. After a night between dirty blankets on an iron cot without a mattress, in a room holding twenty-four men, half of whom snored and half of whom coughed and all of whom stank, David decided that he would prefer to brave almost any weather in the open.

By luck, on the very next night, he located the Blink. This was a corner of a bricked-up railway tunnel, the door to which someone had found a way to force. It was a snug place, lined with sacks. David had to fight to establish his right to a bed, but was finally accepted and even became friendly with one of the "owners." Dai, a fellow Welshman, had one eye and an ingratiating smile. He called himself the Minstrel Boy and made a living by busking the cinema queues in Leicester Square. He instructed David, "When you come into a place like the Blink and no one knows who the hell you are, you don't just barge in, see. What you do is, you say, 'Who's the big man, then?' Right? Then people know you're a scrapper and mostly you won't have to fight. Tramps are peaceful people, see. Live and let live."

"Why do you call it the Blink?"

"Ah, that's easy. British Rail is zinc pail. Zinc is blink. Right?"

"Right."

"It's easy when you know, isn't it?"

"Everything's easy when you know," said David. But in the days that followed this was the only code name he did unravel.

All of his fellow tramps smoked. He decided that one of the reasons that they shuffled along with their eyes on the ground was so as not to miss the smallest abandoned fag end. Three or four of these could be collected, unraveled and re-rolled. They would drink anything they could get when they could get it. A much-fancied tipple was a well-known brand of cough mixture, which was obtainable on National Health and was said to taste like sherry. "Strengthen it up with a drop or two of paint stripper," said Dai, "and it's a real knock-out."

The only drug which was used at all regularly was glue. This could be taken at night with the head inside a plastic bag. Hard drugs were a rarity. The cautious questions that David put out produced no more than the fact that some people knew someone who knew someone else who was a sniffer or a popper or occasionally a main-liner. The point was that people who used such things must have money; and money was the rarest commodity of all in the kingdom of the tramps.

After dark on October fifteenth David was back at his observation post. It had crossed his mind that the doctor might have arranged a reception committee for him, and he had approached with great care, crossing lower down and working his way up the side of the railway. The nettles welcomed him like an old friend.

It was another wet and miserable night. Summer was a distant dream. Five patients came and went, and the surgery light shone steadily out through gusting curtains of rain. David shivered and cursed and wiped the drops from his nose on the cuff of his filthy coat.

Suddenly he stiffened to attention. The surgery light had gone out. He counted—one, two, three, four, five. The light came on again. David jumped down from his perch, moved back to his crossing place lower down and took up the position he had chosen, in the doorway of a shop opposite the lower end of the passage.

He waited for a full ten minutes, and it crossed his mind that his quarry might have taken advantage of the darkness and the rain to leave by Blumfield Terrace. He was wondering whether to risk a dash up to the corner of the main road when the tramp appeared. He materialized, like a shadow, at the end of the passage, and like a shadow he drifted off up the road.

In the hour that followed David realized that the wind and the rain were his friends. On a fine, still night he must have been spotted before he had gone a hundred yards. He had to keep close behind his man. He had the impression that if he took his eyes off him for a moment he would dematerialize. And there were curious variations in the speed of his progress. Sometimes it was very slow, sometimes surprisingly fast. David decided that the pace depended on the street lighting. In the brightly lit main roads, the tramp scudded along as quickly as possible. In the dim side streets he shuffled and loitered.

David had long lost any idea of where they had got to and where they were going. His only guides were the east wind, which blew the rain steadily into his face and a feeling that they were going downhill and therefore must be heading for the river.

"East and south. It's dockland, for a bet," said David. "Is the old coot going to wander round all night?"

They were in a long, straight road, which was totally deserted and lit by overhead lights. This forced him to fall back, waiting until his quarry had disappeared into the gloom between two widely spaced pools of light and then sprinting to catch up with him.

Between two lamps, his man had disappeared.

David was sure that he had not passed the second lamp. He could never have climbed the high plank palisades which fenced the road. He must have found some way through.

It took David five minutes to locate the loose plank, during the whole of which time he cursed steadily and obscenely to himself. It would have been unthinkable to have come so far and suffered so much and to have failed at the finish.

As the plank swung inwards under his touch he breathed again. The cinder path inside was easy to follow. It led him, between the heaps of rusting and abandoned machinery and pits of black water, dimpling in the rain, to what had once been Messrs. Hendrixsons' offices and store.

He saw a massive, brick-built, three-sided block, rectangular and open on the fourth side. The back and the right-hand wing had, at one time, been offices. The glass had been smashed, but the iron-framed windows and doors still barred entrance. The left-hand wing was open-fronted and had once been a store. Here it is, thought David.

He felt his way in, treading carefully among the rubble, and found the wooden staircase which led upwards.

His nose told him that he had come to the right place. As he came up through the trap door there was a rustling and whispering among the paper and straw which covered the floor a foot deep, and someone grunted out what sounded like a warning or a challenge.

David said, "Who's the big man, then?"

There was a moment of silence.

Then the rustling started again, but it was not aggressive.

People were turning over and settling back to talk, or sleep if they could.

Taking as much care as he could not to tread on any of the recumbent forms, David made a slow way to the far corner. Here, he found a free place to curl up in. He thought that the less he disturbed the debris the better, but he managed to detach some sheets of newspaper which seemed to be fairly clean and he covered himself with these and settled down, with his back against the wall, to wait for the morning.

To most people it would not have seemed an attractive situation, but David was well content. The shy and furtive little animal he had been chasing for six months was now within a few yards of him. It had been a long, winding, downhill track, but he had touched bottom at last. The thought was so agreeable that he managed to fall asleep. No dreams, this time.

—— 22 ——

On Monday morning, when Paula arrived at the Rayhome offices, she was surprised to find the door locked. Repeated ringing of the bell eventually produced the lady from the basement, who doubled the jobs of concierge and cleaning woman.

She said, "It's no good ringing. They've gone."

"Gone?"

"That's right."

"Where?"

"How'd I know? You work here?"

"I thought so," said Paula.

"They paid up the rent and cleared out Friday evening. Gave me a month's pay for notice. What about you?"

Paula reflected. She was paid monthly, in advance, and it was only halfway through the month. Looked at from that point of view, she had two weeks' pay in hand. All the same, they might have said something.

"Didn't they give any reason for clearing out?"

"Not to me, they didn't," said the lady. "I've spoken to the agents. They'll soon have the board up. We'll get someone else, easy enough. You leave your address with me, love. Then, if the new lot want someone to help in the office, I'll pass it on."

"Well, ta," said Paula.

During the first few weeks that she worked for Holmes and Holmes, Susan began to appreciate why top secretaries earned top salaries. It was no nine-to-six job. She was expected to be available whenever Andrew Holmes had to entertain important clients to drinks or dinner. On one occasion she had been landed with the wives of three American tycoons and told to look after them whilst Andrew spent the evening talking business with their husbands. In desperation she had taken them to the Palladium, where Tommy Steele was at the top of the bill. They had occupied a stage box and enjoyed themselves thoroughly.

It was not only the long hours. It was the fact that she had to keep her wits about her all the time. She had to have a mental picture of how Andrew planned to spend his day. What could be squeezed into it and what could not. And, occasionally, what was so important that someone, less important, had to be squeezed out—and how to do it without giving offense.

On a rainy evening in the third week of October, she had been allowed home, for once, in good time. A solid lunch at the Savoy had taken the edge off her appetite. She boiled herself an egg, made some toast and coffee and settled down in front of the fire.

Under the light of the single table lamp, which emphasized the vertical lines on her face, she looked not only tired, but fine-drawn—as though she had been working towards a goal which was in sight, but still beyond her reach.

She was almost asleep when the telephone rang.

She said, "Hullo." And then, with a marked lack of enthusiasm, "Oh, it's you, is it."

"It's me," said David. "And I'm in trouble."

"You're always in trouble."

"You don't understand. For the last six weeks—I can't describe it—"

"I'm sure you can if you try," said Susan coolly. Her hand went out to the switch under the telephone table.

"I've been living like an animal."

David was speaking slowly, dragging out the words as though he, too, was tired to death.

"A lot of animals I know of seem to live very comfortably."

"In casual wards. Sleeping rough. In holes and corners. My clothes rotting on my back."

"Truly? Or are you making it all up?"

"No fooling, love. I'm a sight for sore eyes. Holes in everything. It's not right, in weather like this."

"What do you want me to do about it?"

"Want? I want you to give me some money for a start. You can spare it."

"How much?"

David seemed to be thinking.

He said, "Ten pounds. That would do me. For a start."

"I'm not exactly rolling in money right now. I've just had to pay the rent and rates. Both of them up."

"Five pounds, then. Four. Even three would help."

There was a clear note of desperation in his voice.

Susan said, "Well, I might—"

"You've never starved, have you? Weeks without proper food. Cold and wet all the time."

"I've never starved," agreed Susan.

"I'm finished if you don't."

Susan seemed to relax. She said, "All right, David. If you're finished, I'll have to see what I can do. Where do you want the money sent?"

"Send it to the Rayhome office," said David. He, too, seemed to be happier. "I'll pick it up there. Good-bye."

"Good-bye," said Susan softly.

She put back the receiver, extracted the tape recorder from under the table, set the speed to slow and took down the conversation, word for word, in shorthand. Then she transcribed it into longhand and read it over to herself. It seemed to cause her some satisfaction. Her face had lost its drawn look and was almost serene.

On the following afternoon, in a burst of fine mid-October weather, Chief Superintendent Morrissey called on Arthur Abel at New Scotland Yard. He found A. A. looking cheerful. His table was covered with dockets and loose papers, and there were files on another table behind him, and more on the floor beside him. Abel said, "I think we're getting somewhere. You know, I've always realized that the key to this whole business was the one hundred thousand pounds that Arnie Wiseman lent Blackett so that Blackett could buy the remaining seventy-percent interest in the Blackbird Property Company from Harry Woolf and his wife, so I've been concentrating on that."

He cleared a little space on the table, spread a fresh sheet of paper on it and drew a diagram.

"This is how it went. Argon, remember, already held Blackett's thirty percent of Blackbird." He drew two squares and joined them to a third with a green arrow. "Blackett now gets hold of the remaining seventy percent and transfers it to Argon." A second green arrow. "You see what that produces?"

"Three squares and two arrows."

"It means that Blackbird became a wholly owned subsidiary of Argon. And that means that it could declare a group dividend."

"So what?"

"So all the money in Blackbird, which was a wealthy company already and became a lot wealthier as its properties were sold off, could go into Argon *free of tax.*" Two more arrows, this time in red. "Right. So Argon now has a great deal of money. Now watch this. Here comes Arnie."

"In that yellow circle?"

"That's him. He doesn't take any of the actual shares in Argon, note. But he becomes a director. Along with Blackett and that army chum of Blackett's, Colonel Paterson. And he starts to milk the company. In the first year he was modest. Comparatively. He had a salary of five thousand pounds and an expense account of around eight thousand." Blue arrows. "That was for starters. The next year his salary went up to ten thousand, his expenses to nearly fifteen thousand *and* he borrowed another twenty thousand from the company, free of interest." More blue arrows. "Now tell me this. *Why did Blackett let Wiseman do it?*"

Morrissey was staring in a bemused manner at the diagram, which was sprouting more arrows than St. Sebastian. He said, "I dunno. Perhaps it was because he owed him all that money."

"But he didn't."

"I thought you said—"

"He paid back the one hundred thousand pounds in six months, with the proceeds of the first property sales. After that he didn't owe him a penny."

Morrissey grunted. He was beginning to get an idea of what Abel was driving at. Two sides of his puzzle were beginning to link up.

Abel said, "After the money had been repaid, there was no reason in the world for Blackett to put up with Arnie's tarradiddles. He controlled Argon. He could throw Arnie off the Board whenever he wanted to. And if he did allow him to stay, he could monitor his expenses and refuse to make him interest-free loans, or any other sort of loan at all. *So why did Blackett stand for it?*"

"Because Arnie had got him by the short and curlies. That what you mean?"

"That's exactly what I mean. Somehow, when he loaned him that one hundred thousand pounds, Arnie put Blackett on the spot. I've got one or two ideas about how he could have fixed it, and if I could only get a sight of the documents they signed at the time—"

Morrissey banged his large fist down on the table and said "Moule."

"Mole?"

"Moule with a *u.*"

The two sides were coming very close now.

"Let me tell you something for a change," said Morrissey. "The way this all started was I got a buzz from one of my pet grasses that a hopped-up old toe-rag was wandering round South-East London claiming that he'd got some *papers* stowed away somewhere which would blow the great Randall Blackett sky high. So why didn't he use them? Answer—because if he did, Blackett's friend Trombo would cut him into small pieces with one of his lovely knives and feed the pieces into a mincing machine."

"And the tramp is Moule."

"I'm beginning to think that must be right. Listen. Moule used to work in the offices of Blackett's accountants, someone, somebody and Lyon. It was the senior partner who looked after all Blackett's affairs. I've forgotten his name."

"Martindale, Mantegna and Lyon."

"Bang on. It was Julius Mantegna. He'd be one man who'd have been able to tell us exactly what was in those papers. So would Blackett's partner, Colonel Paterson. He'd have had to sign anything involving the company. The only other person who *might* have known the details was Mantegna's confidential secretary."

"Then couldn't we ask—"

"You won't be able to ask any of them anything. They all went under a five-ton lorry on Highgate Hill in a rain storm."

Abel thought about it. Then he drew an oblong in black, round three smaller circles, and put three little crosses on top of it.

"What you're saying is that, from that moment, the precise details of Blackett's bargain with Wiseman were known only to him and Wiseman."

"Correct."

"And Wiseman started behaving like a pig who's got his nose in the trough. And ended up in Trombo's mincing machine."

"It fits together, dunnit? Because I'll tell you something else.

Ever since Arnie disappeared, Blackett's been paying Trombo money. A regular fee every quarter. That's what makes Trombo such a bloody menace. No one else in his line has got that sort of backing. He can pay for any muscle he wants. Bring villains down from Scotland or in from abroad if he needs them. Cut off his money supplies, and we'd cut him down to size quick enough."

"Can you prove that Blackett's financing him?"

"No. The payments are made in notes. I guess Blackett draws the money originally as expenses, but it changes hands half a dozen times before his boy, Harald, takes it down personally to Trombo's shop. And Harald's incorruptible."

"How do you know?"

Morrissey said, with a grin, "Because I tried to corrupt him. I soon saw I wasn't going to make any distance that way. It had to be done from the other end. First find Moule, quietly and without alerting anyone to what we were up to, which was easier said than done. Get hold of these papers he talked about, if they existed. Then we might know just what Arnie had on Blackett. That would give us Blackett's motive for having Arnie put away. Then we'd be getting somewhere. I set up this operation. I made it a double one. I borrowed Morgan from our Welsh friends. I needed someone whose face wouldn't be known in this town. To see if he could work his way down to Moule. Then I got one of the girls in the Fraud Squad. Her job was to work her way up, to Blackett. I don't mean vamp him. He's not built that way. But he's always had a reputation for using smart people when he can find them. I was going to call it 'Operation Hunt the Slipper.' Then I got a better idea. One going up, one going down. I called it 'Snakes and Ladders.' Remember it?"

"Yes," said Abel. "Yes, I remember it." He was back in the nursery, himself and three sisters, poring over the new and exciting game they'd been given for Christmas. The ladders, shortcuts which led you upwards; and the bright, evil, twisting snakes which snatched you back.

"If I remember it rightly," said Abel, "the really tricky bit came at the end. You had to throw exactly the right number to get you onto the hundredth square. If you overdid it, you went back again and there was a very nasty snake waiting for you on square ninety-seven which could send you nearly down to the bottom again."

"That's right," said Morrissey. "We don't want any slipups."

Abel said, "I'm not sure that I understand all the details of your game, even now. But I'm beginning to realize one thing. You're pointing Morgan at Blackett to get Trombo. You don't care a damn about Blackett, really. It's Trombo you want."

Morrissey looked disconcerted, but only for a moment. He said, "I suppose you could put it like that."

"Isn't it a bit dangerous for Morgan?"

"Morgan's crafty. He's a professional, and he's dead careful. We fixed up, when he started, that he was going to operate on his own. No direct communications. He was right about that, too. However careful you are, messages from public telephone booths, that sort of thing, people notice. And I've an idea Trombo's got someone on his payroll in this building."

Abel looked upset, but not incredulous. He said, "Any idea who?"

"No. Probably someone unimportant. On the telephone exchange, or a messenger. They're the people who pick things up. That's why his messages don't come through police lines at all."

"But he can communicate?"

"Certainly. The last communiqué I had said he was in touch with Moule and things were coming to a head in about three weeks' time. Until then, we've got nothing to do but wait."

"And hope."

"That's right," said Morrissey. He sounded unusually serious. "And hope."

— 23 —

Having found him, David experienced no difficulty in getting alongside Moule. The only thing tramps were not short of was time. When the weather was fine they spent long hours sitting on their favorite benches or huddled together in quiet corners, talking about all the things they had done in the past and things they hoped to do in the future. David had prepared an elaborate account of his earlier wanderings in Wales, but his fellow tramps were not curious. Their minds were concentrated on themselves, their own hopes and fears and small ambitions.

Moule, he found, was different from the others in a number of ways. It was not only his superior habit of speech. It was known that he had a small but regular income which he collected each month and almost the whole of which he spent on heroin as soon as he laid hands on it.

David studied his routine with interest. Twice a day, once in the morning and once in the early evening, he extracted a single precious tablet from his store, dissolved it in distilled water and filled the hypodermic syringe which lived in a leather case in his coat pocket. Then he injected the magic directly in the veins of arm or leg. For an hour or two afterwards he was dead to all that went on around him. His body slumped, his head nodded and his pupils contracted. He seemed to be asleep, but in fact he was wandering freely in his own world of beauty and hope and youth restored. Then he would return, often quite abruptly, to the prison of the present. For a few hours he would be a tolerable, talkative companion. Then David would note the symptoms, the yawning and sneezing and scratching, as impatience developed beyond impatience into longing and beyond longing into a twitching lust for the next shot. But he had retained just sufficient strength of mind not to anticipate it. His life was ruled by the white tablets and the syringe. He would have fought to defend them with nails and teeth insanely, using any weapon he could lay hands on. Even his most light-fingered friends knew this and left him alone.

After a few arguments and one fight, David succeeded in establishing a sleeping place alongside him. The fight was with Irish Mick, who had previously regarded himself as Percy's particular friend and confidant and resented the shift in his allegiance. The fight had not been a long one. David had tripped Mick and sat on him long enough and heavily enough to convince the Irishman that he was a stronger and fitter man. Peace had been patched up.

David had then clinched his hold over Moule by indicating to him, indirectly and under the strictest promises of secrecy, that he might have an available source from which further supplies of heroin could be obtained.

"For a price," said David. "It's not given away."

"I have the money," said Moule. This was true. Money was only important to him as a key to the white tablets. Since he had not been able to buy more than forty, barely a three weeks' supply, the money he had not used was wrapped in a handkerchief and tucked away in one of his many coat pockets. He spent very little on food and nothing on anything else. The money was there. What he needed was the drug. Towards the end of the second week, under renewed pledges of secrecy, David produced six tablets. They were part of a much larger supply which he had extracted from Dr. Ramchunderabbas when he handed over the promised second installment of heroin. He sold the tablets to Moule for three pounds in cash, and from that moment his bondage was complete. David was master, he was slave.

Twenty times a day he said to David, in a voice which trembled with anxiety, "You will find it for me. You've got a supplier. I've got the money. I'll pay for it."

"When the time comes," said David.

"You're sure."

"Rest easy."

He knew, to a day, how long his slave's supply would last.

Night was the time for confidences. In the warm and stinking darkness, as the aftereffects of his evening shot wore off, Dennis Moule would talk. Long, rambling discourses, covering his early life, unhappy times at school—he still remembered the name of a boy who used to bully him—happy holidays with his widowed mother, who spoiled him. Early days as a trainee accountant. Some reminiscences of his life with Martindale, Mantegna and Lyon, where he had worked his way up to be chief assistant to Julius Mantegna. Occasional references to the young lady he had hoped to marry, but nothing on the topic that David was waiting for. At that point, a curtain came down.

David was careful not to force confidences. He knew that his time would come.

Only once was he given a glimpse behind the curtain. It started with discussion of something which had been reported in the papers. Two boys had found an old tramp, asleep and bemused with methylated spirits. There was some left in the bottle beside him. They had poured this over his legs and set fire to him. The tramp had died of shock and burns.

"Dangerous louts," said David. "I hope they catch them and put them away for a good long stretch."

"Louts, yes," said Percy in his schoolmaster's voice. "But not dangerous. If you have met really dangerous men you would not trouble your head about boys."

David grunted encouragingly. Moule seemed to be considering whether he would go on. In the end he said, "I told you that I used to work for this travel agency."

"You did mention it."

"After I had been there about a year, I found out that they were using me to carry drugs. In a secret pocket in my courier's bag. I thought I would take a little for myself. Why not? It was I who was taking the risks. There were a number of packets and I took a little, a very little, out of each. But of course, they found out. One evening two men bundled me into a car and drove me down to a place not far from here. It was dark, but I could see it was a shop. I was taken into a room at the back and strapped to a chair. The man who seemed to be in charge—I found out afterwards that he was a Maltese—quite an ordinary-looking man, rather tubby, with glasses, said, 'Put your hand flat on the table and don't move it until I tell you to.' I did what he said. I was so frightened by now that I was pissing in my trousers. Then he took up a big, heavy knife and he said, 'You helped yourself to a little of my friends' goods. I'm going to help myself to a little bit of your hand.' And he brought the knife down, smack, and cut off the very tip of my middle finger."

"So you got back into line and did what you were told."

"Good God, yes."

"And have stayed in line ever since."

"After I left the agency, I had no occasion to interfere in things of that sort."

"Not in the drug-running business. But there was something else, wasn't there?"

"What do you mean?"

"I've heard stories," said David. He had moved up, in the darkness, so that his head was close to Moule's, and he had dropped his voice to a trickle of sound. "People do say that you've got some secret. Some sort of papers, which might incriminate a big businessman."

"No."

There was a long silence.

David was close enough to Moule to feel that he was shaking.

"Nothing in it, eh?"

"I don't want to talk about it. I won't talk about it. I can't."

"All right," said David agreeably. "Let's talk about something else, then."

"Blackett wanted me to go down on Thursday and stay the night," said Sam Lyon. "He wanted to talk to me about the implications of the new Finance Bill. He must have forgotten that I was going to be in Switzerland on Thursday. I shan't be back much before midnight. When I told him, he suggested that you went, instead."

"Me?" said Gerald Hopkirk a bit blankly.

"Why not? You know all about his affairs. When I retire, you'll probably have to take him on."

"Then don't retire," said Gerald.

Sam Lyon accepted the compliment with a smile. He said, "You're scared of him."

"Certainly I am."

"He won't eat you. You've never been down to his house before, have you?"

"Years ago. I took some papers down for him to sign."

"He's a good host. He'll make you very comfortable. Take your dinner jacket."

"That's all very well," said Gerald. "But I don't know a lot about the new Finance Bill. What *are* its implications?"

"There was a very good crib in the *Economist* last week. I imagine it's the company 'see-through' provisions he's worried about. Have a look at Section 18 and 19—"

The discussion became technical.

"And one word of advice," said Lyon. "Don't drink too much of his port. I made that mistake last time I went down and very nearly fell asleep in the middle of a technical discussion on underdistribution."

Thinking about it afterwards, Gerald could not have explained why he had felt uncomfortable about a perfectly ordinary business trip. He had visited clients at their homes often enough and had once spent a weekend in the castle of an impoverished Scottish laird who wished to discuss the economics of grouse shooting. It is true that the standard of living at Blackett's Virginia Water house was several degrees plusher than anything he had encountered before. There was a manservant who devoted himself silently to his comfort and succeeded in making him thoroughly uncomfortable. The household obviously ran on oiled wheels; and the garden, in which he strolled before dinner, was large and was maintained to a pitch of neatness that he had previously associated with public parks.

Blackett, who had met him at the station, drove him back to the house. He said, "Let's keep business for after dinner."

When Gerald went up to his room to change, he found that his suitcase had been emptied of its scanty contents, his dress clothes laid out and a bath run for him in the bathroom which was en suite with his bedroom. A small decanter of whisky had appeared on the table beside the bed, with a thermos flask of iced water. Remembering Sam Lyon's warning, he helped himself to a very modest peg, had his bath and began to feel better.

When he got down to the drawing room he discovered, to his relief, that he was not the only guest. A South African, with a chin like the prow of a battleship, whom he was invited to address as Barney, and a smooth Kuwaiti Arab whose name he never discovered were already there, drinking very cold and very dry martinis. They were joined by Barney's wife and a pleasant middle-aged lady called Mrs. Arbuthnot, who seemed to fill the function of hostess.

It was as good a dinner as Gerald had ever eaten, beautifully cooked and served with the unobtrusive efficiency of a top-class French restaurant. The details of the food escaped him, but the wine remained in his memory. A white wine which was as cold and smooth as the ice maiden's kiss and a robust red burgundy which laughed all the way from the glass to his palate. After the meal coffee was served in the drawing room, round a fire of applewood. Gerald, who had lost most of his inhibitions by now, said, "Sam warned me about your port, Mr. Blackett."

"He gave it a bad name?"

"On the contrary. Too good a name. He said that I should allow myself two glasses, but no more."

"In South Africa," said Barney, "we have excellent Burgundy, but we've never produced any port worth drinking. Burgundy's a technique. The production of port is an *art* known only to the Portuguese." He proceeded to give them a ten-minute lecture on wine making, either unconscious that he was monopolizing the conversation or not caring. At the end of it he said, "We'll have to be getting back now. We can fix up the final details when you meet my Board on Monday." He collected his wife, and they made for the door. Blackett went with them. The Kuwaiti had not joined them for coffee, but had made his excuses and gone straight up to his room.

When Blackett returned, Mrs. Arbuthnot said, in the tone of voice of someone who has said the same thing before without any expectation of attention being paid to it, "You men mustn't sit up gossiping until all hours," and took herself off.

Blackett filled Gerald's nearly empty glass from the decanter and said, "Now, what about this bloody Finance Act?"

It took them half an hour and a further glass of port to straighten out the Finance Act. Gerald was relieved to find that his views on it largely coincided with his host's. He was wondering whether it would be politic to make a move towards bed when he found that his glass had been refilled.

Blackett cut short his protests. He said, "Sam's a good chap. I'm prepared to accept his views on accountancy, but, like most people, he talks nonsense about wine. Vintage port doesn't give you gout and it doesn't send you to sleep. It simply complements the meal." He added, suddenly and with no particular relevance to what had gone before, "Do you remember a man called Moule in your office? Or was he before your time?"

"Dennis Moule. I knew him well. We came into the firm almost at the same time."

"Then you can advise me. I had a letter from him the other day. Not very legible, but I made most of it out. He wanted a job. Any sort of job. Commissionaire, post-room, odd-job man. It struck me as an unusual request from a qualified accountant."

"I haven't seen him since he left, but I did hear that he'd—well—gone downhill."

"In what direction?"

"Drink, to start with."

"Then drugs, I suppose."

"I did hear something of the sort."

"I don't want to break any confidences, but if I'm going to employ him, I'd better know the worst."

"It wasn't entirely his fault. I don't think he was what you'd call a strong character, but he was perfectly all right until his fiancée was killed in that accident. I expect you remember it."

"I not only remember it," said Blackett, "you could say, in a way, that I was responsible for it. Ian Paterson and Julius Mantegna were driving up to North London, looking for me, when it happened. I didn't realize it had such a traumatic effect on Moule."

"I don't think I shall ever forget that day," said Gerald. "February fourteenth, St. Valentine's Day, but not much love around the office. It wasn't only the rain, which never let up for a moment. Julius was in a bad frame of mind, which was unusual for him. I gathered from Miss Blaney that he'd taken home some papers to read the night before and he was very worried about them."

"Do you happen to know what the papers were?"

"Not really. They were confidential. A client had done something stupid, without telling Julius. That's the trouble with clients. They consult you *after* they've put their foot in it."

"Just so," said Blackett, with rather a grim smile.

"Of course, we knew nothing about the accident until we got to the office next day. The rain had stopped overnight, and it was a lovely morning. I was feeling particularly cheerful, for some reason I can't now remember, and I'd got in earlier than usual. The cleaners were just finishing their morning chores. One of them said something about 'poor Mr. Moule.' I couldn't make out what she was talking about. At that moment the door at the end of the passage swung open—it was a little room where we keep our photographic machine—and Moule came out. I noticed that he was carrying a folder of papers and I said, 'Hullo, Dennis. You're up early,' or something like that. He pushed past me, without a word, and went into Julius's room and slammed the door. As he went past, I got the impression that he'd been crying. Then Sam Lyon arrived and told me what had happened, so of course I realized what was wrong."

"Do you know," said Blackett, "you've got a selective visual memory. Tell me, can you remember what sort of folder he was carrying?"

"As a matter of fact, I can," said Gerald. "It was an Oxford blue folder. I remember being slightly surprised, because it's a type of folder we use for confidential papers, and they are usually kept by partners in a locked filing cabinet."

"But Moule, being Mantegna's number-one boy, would have had a key of his cabinet."

"I expect he would have done. Why?"

"It's an extraordinary thing," said Blackett. He had picked up his own glass and was staring into its red depths. "What you've been describing happened eight—nearly nine—years ago. A lot of interesting and exciting things must have happened to you since then, but I doubt whether you can remember them with anything like the same particularity."

"That's true," said Gerald. He was beginning to feel very sleepy. "I suppose it was the shock of hearing about the accident that printed it in my mind. Three deaths—"

"People sometimes overrate the importance of death," said Blackett. "Did you know that I spent some years in a Japanese prison camp?"

Gerald nodded. It was easier than speaking.

"We thought a lot about death in that camp. One of the things we had managed to smuggle in and conceal were a few cyanide pills. They had been issued to men who worked behind the Japanese lines and might have been caught and tortured. If one of our people was taken out to be flogged, he would take one of the pills, hidden in his mouth. We were paraded to watch the punishment. It wasn't normally designed to kill, but it was very severe. Yet I never knew a man bite into that pill. They hung there by their hands, in the hot sun, with the flesh stripped off their backs, but they wouldn't do the one thing which would have given them instant relief. They were a lot braver than I was, or perhaps more stupid. I shouldn't have hesitated. My dear fellow, I do apologize. I'm talking too much. I've been boring you."

"Not bored," said Gerald. "Just sleepy. I'll go up now."

"Would you like Harald to give you a hand? He's somewhere about."

"No, I can manage. Goo' night."

"Good night. Sleep well," said Blackett.

After Gerald had gone, he sat for a few minutes in front of the dying fire. He said to himself, "The photographic room. Extraordinary! I ought to have thought of that." He got up and touched the bell. When Harald appeared he said, "Did my guest reach his bedroom?"

"He accomplished it," said Harald. "It was a brave effort."

"Sit down for a moment and listen. Tomorrow you will see Mr. Trombo, taking the usual precautions, and this is what you will say to him."

Blackett spoke slowly and when he had finished, Harald repeated, word for word, exactly what Blackett had said.

"Good. And remember, this is so important to me that it is not to be delegated. I insist that he handles it personally."

"It is so important," repeated Harald, "that Mr. Trombo must handle it personally."

"I hope you had a pleasant evening," said Lyon.

"Very nice," said Gerald. "And I agree with you about the port."

"I thought the Burgundy was worth drinking, too."

"Perhaps," said Gerald judgematically. "But one has to remember that Burgundy making is only a matter of technique. The production of vintage port is an art known only to the Portuguese."

"I can see that you enjoyed yourself," said Lyon with a smile.

24

Viewing it by daylight, David decided that he had hardly ever
seen a more dangerous and more unpleasant spot than the
one he had landed in.

It was not the smell. He had got used to that. It was the
danger inherent in the setup. The room was full of the most
combustible material, occupied by an unstable group of men,
and it had one narrow exit through a square hole in the floor
and down a flight of wooden steps.

"Rats' Castle," he said. "And if anyone came after us, we'd
be rats, no mistake, and if someone dropped a match in this
stuff, we'd be roast rats. You've got to find a way out, boyo.
And if you can't find it, you've got to get busy and make it.
No choice."

He was able to survey the unhappy prospect at leisure, because the loft was, as far as he knew, empty. With the first
light of dawn the dozen regular lodgers disappeared, slipping
out quietly and vanishing like ghosts who have heard the crowing of the cock. David had gone with them, but had managed
to slip away and hide, in the half-darkness, behind a pile of
machinery. When the last of its nighttime occupants had gone,
he had climbed back into the dormitory and viewed it, in all
its horror, by the light which seeped through the single tiny

barred and filthy window at the far end.

"It's a dump," he said. "A bloody awful, stinking, dangerous dump."

The only part of it which offered any hope at all was the far corner, where he had spent his first night in the place. It seemed that, when Messrs. Hendrixsons had been in occupation, some operation had been carried out in the loft which demanded heat, and there were signs that a stove had been installed. The stove itself had disappeared, but the iron backing sheet was still there, with a circular hole in it through which the stove chimney had been passed.

David descended the steps to the ground floor and found, as he had hoped, that there was a fireplace underneath and in line with the stove in the loft. This argued the existence of some sort of chimney built into the thickness of the brickwork with shafts connecting the two fireplaces; the fireplace on ground-floor level was heavy and firmly fixed, but the iron sheet in the loft was a temporary job, and it took David only a few minutes' work with his clasp knife to hinge it back.

The shaft behind sloped upwards at a steep angle. It was lined with corroded soot and an overlay of loose, grey dust. By pressing his back against one side and his feet against the other, in the manner of a climber in a rock chimney, he found that he was able to squeeze himself upwards without too much difficulty. The disadvantage of this method was that it brought down both soot and dust in choking clouds.

Ten feet up the shaft, David reached the point where his tributary met the main chimney. There was light above his head, dim but sufficient for him to assess the position.

It was not encouraging.

Above him he could see that the chimney narrowed until it reached the single pot through which he caught a glimpse of the sky. The difficulty was that, even if he could discover some method of shifting the pot and the solid pediment on which it rested, the last section of the chimney was clearly too narrow to admit even his agile body.

As he was thinking about this the light through the pot was blocked. A starling had poked its head through to look at him. He could see now that there was a nest of ragged sticks on a ledge just below the stack.

"If I was a bloody starling," he said, "I wouldn't be standing here with cramp in my legs and a mouth full of shit. I'd fly out of that bloody chimney, wouldn't I just?"

The starling put its head on one side, as if considering the pronouncement, and then flew off with a clatter of its wings.

"So what now?" said David. "No good just standing here like bloody Father Christmas."

If he managed to lower himself down the main chimney, he could, no doubt, reach the point where the shaft from the downstairs room came in and could descend that. But even if he could shift the fireplace which blocked that outlet, this merely got him back to the ground floor, which was not where he wanted to be.

"Only one thing for it," said David. "Have to go through." He considered the plan of the building. The loft, which was about eight foot high, had a ceiling of planks. Above this was a sloping roof. If this sort of construction continued all the way round, there must be an open space, two or three feet high, between the ceiling joists and the roof.

This would provide a perfect back door. *If* he could break into it.

"Only one way," said David, looking with distaste at the blackened brickwork of the chimney on a level with his eyes. "Get some of those bricks out. And you're not going to do it with your clasp knife. You'll need a cold chisel and a hammer and plenty of time."

Having reached this conclusion, he slid back down the shaft, swung the sheet iron into position, brushed himself down as best he could and made his way out. He knew of only one place where he could get what he needed, and it would not be safe to approach it before dusk. Also, he wanted a further word with Moule.

Moule found him. He came up to David, who was killing time sitting on a seat in a secluded corner of the small Rotherhithe Park and Recreation Ground, sat down beside him and grabbed his arm with surprising strength.

David said, "So it's you. What do you want?"

"You know what I want."

"Suppose I do."

"You promised."

The grip on his arm tightened.

"All right," said David. "Lay off the judo. So I promised."

"I told you I had enough for twenty days. I used the last one last night. I've got no more left." The whine had become almost a snarl. "You said you'd get some for me."

"Let go of my arm," said David, with sudden ferocity.

Moule stared at him for a moment, then let go of his arm.

"That's better. Now listen to me. How many of your friends know you're on hard stuff?"

"Some of them."

"And do they know you're short of supplies?"

"They might. I'm not sure."

"Don't arse around," said David sharply. *"Who have you told?"*

"I told Mick. I thought he might be able to get me some."

"Just as I thought. So if they see you're stocked up, they'll know you got it from me. And they'll know I've got a source. And that puts *me* on the spot."

"Mick won't talk," said Moule. The whine was back in his voice.

"Maybe, maybe not. But we've got to be careful. I can only stock up in the evening. And I can't get more than two or three tablets at a time. I'll need the money in advance."

Without a word, Moule put his hand into the inside pocket of his overcoat, pulled out a handkerchief, unknotted it and pushed across a wad of screwed up and filthy pound notes. "There's twenty pounds there," he said. "Take the lot."

"You don't listen, do you?" David unpeeled five of the notes

207

and handed the rest back. He spoke slowly, as though to a child. "I can get you two or three tablets this evening. Because that's the way my supplier works. And maybe another two or three tomorrow evening. And so on. I'll pass them to you, but it's got to be done so that it doesn't attract attention. I'm moving my bed into the far corner, by the old fireplace. You shift yours up alongside. That gives us a bit of privacy, see?"

"Yes," said Moule. "I'll do that. Only you won't let me down."

"I'm promising nothing," said David. "You'll have to wait and see what turns up, won't you? And don't tag round after me, or you'll get nothing but a boot on the arse. Understand?"

His slave said, very humbly, that he understood.

Trombo was able, whenever he wanted it, to have the exclusive use of a room on the first floor of the Lord Mornington public house—which was hardly surprising, since he owned the place. To it, that same morning, came the representatives of the three most powerful criminal armies in South-East London. The Friary Lane lot, led by Ginger Williams and his chief lieutenant, McVee; the Bravos from the Elephant and Castle, who operated under Birnie Samuels; and the newly formed Dock Rats, deserters from foreign ships, shunned by the locals and tolerated only on account of their single-minded ferocity. It was not an easy alliance and one which only Trombo could have put together.

When they understood what was wanted, Williams protested. He said, "Don't like it. It's stupid. What does it get us?"

Trombo recognized Williams as the strongest man there, indeed a possible successor to his own empire. He said, coldly, "What it gets you is what you always get when you work for me. Money, as promised, paid on the nail."

There was a murmur of agreement.

"I'm not objecting to the money," said Williams. "It's just that—well—who wants to go chasing round after a lot of stinking old toe-rags? Myself, I wouldn't want to get within a yard of one. Leave alone talk to him."

"I wouldn't expect you to do it yourself. You must have plenty of boys who aren't so particular."

"Besides which, if you do ask them a question you get nothing out of them but a load of old cock. And once the word gets round you want to know something, they'll clam up, just to be bloody-minded. I'm telling you. They're dirt."

"It might help," said Nicholas the Pole, leader of the Dock Rats, in his careful English, "if you could explain why you want this done."

"I can't explain," said Trombo, "but the terms are as stated. I want this man found. There's a hundred-pound bonus for the man who locates him. Then I want to know where he sleeps. Probably not at a regular spike, but in some hole and corner. There's a further hundred for the man who does that. That's in addition to the regular rate for the job."

"It'll be like raking through a heap of shit with your bare hands," said Williams. He still seemed to resent the whole thing as a personal affront. "What a way to spend a working week."

"I can't give you a week," said Trombo shortly. "The job's got to be done as quickly as possible. A day or two at the most. And there's one other thing. We're not the only people after him. There's a Welshman called Morgan. If you locate him, like as not he'll lead you to the other chap. In fact, that may be the best way of working it."

"It'd be easier," said McVee, "if we had a photograph, or some sort of description."

"You won't need a photograph of Morgan. You've met him. You remember the man who worked for Rayhome?"

McVee said, "Yes." It came out, from his squashed face, as a noise which sounded like "Uss."

"What, that bastard?" said Williams.

"That bastard," agreed Trombo pleasantly. "Find him, and you find the other chap. That's the first and most difficult part of the job."

"What's the second part?"

"I can't tell you until I know exactly where he lies up at

night. We may have to make alternative plans. But I promise you it'll be interesting and remunerative. Now, if there are no more objections—"

Leonard Mullion looked with disapproval at his lodger.

"You're a mess, Dave," he said.

"I'm afraid I am."

"You're going downhill."

"Wrong," said David. "I've reached the bottom of the hill."

"I got what you were asking for. A chisel, a hammer and a claw."

"Good on you, Len. How much?"

"The man I got them from charged me a fiver, which was a bloody sauce, seeing I happen to know he'd lifted them."

"Five it is," said David. He handed over the notes Moule had given him. Mullion looked at them in horror.

"You've been keeping 'em in your socks."

"They're a bit the worse for wear," agreed David. "But I'm told that as long as you can recognize it's the Queen and not Mae West they're lawful currency."

"I'll tell you something," said Len. "You better put that stuff out of sight. A bluebottle sees you with that claw, he'll run you straight in on suss. I got a little sack you can borrow."

"They do look a bit incriminating," agreed David. He was handling the hammer. It was a beauty, heavy in the head and whippy in the shaft. "Just the job."

"If you're thinking of breaking into the Bank of England, you might bring me out a bit of gelt."

"I'll do that," said David. "You're a real friend."

"Then here's a bit of friendly advice," said Mullion. His long face was suddenly serious. "Watch your step. There's something going on. I got the tip this evening. The word is, keep off the streets after dark."

"Bad as that, is it?"

"There's a game on. The boys are after someone. They're shaking down every toe-rag they find. One poor old sod gave them some back answers and got his ears cut off. That was the Dock Rats. Nasty heap. Furrin muck. Keep clear of them, Dave, that's my advice."

"As a matter of fact, I'm planning to stay out of sight all tomorrow. Maybe the next day as well. I'll need some food and a bottle of cold tea."

"Tunneling job, is it?" said Mullion with a gleam in his eye.

"That sort of thing."

"I'll see what I can get together. And here's something else. Just an idea I had. If you *should* be on the run."

He had produced a local street map, which looked as if it had been torn out of a shopping guide. "See that bit of green? That's Rotherhithe Park. The small one, where I work. Now if you should be on the run—"

He demonstrated his idea.

David said, "You're wasted in your present job, Len. You ought to be at the War Office. You've got real tactical sense."

David had once spent an unforgettable and unforgotten six months as a trainee miner. But for the technique this had given him for working in a confined space, he would have given it up as impossible.

The first brick had been desperately hard to move. He was working in the dim light which filtered down the chimney, was balanced on the edge formed by the meeting of his shaft and the main chimney and was using a hammer which he had no room to swing and a chisel which constantly threatened to slip out of his sweating hand and disappear down the shaft.

When this had happened twice, and twenty minutes had been wasted on each occasion retrieving it, David tied the end of a piece of string round the handle of the chisel and the other end round his wrist.

At intervals, through that endless day, he climbed back into the loft and lay flat on the floor easing the cramp out of his tortured leg muscles.

"You're a bloody fool, David, boy," he said. "But so what?

You've been a bloody fool all your life. Too late to change now."

The masons who had built the chimney had known their job. It was only with infinite pains that David drove his chisel through the rock-hard mortar on each side of the brick he had selected. Then he enlarged the hole on one side of the brick until it was big enough for the claw to go through. Then he used his weight on the end of the claw and felt the brick shift.

He celebrated this success with a quick snack and a drink of cold tea. Thereafter the work was a little easier. By the time he knocked off, six bricks were out and had been dropped down the main shaft. David replaced the sheet iron carefully and tidied up.

Moule was one of the first of the lodgers to arrive. He came straight over to his corner and grabbed him by the arm.

"You've got it for me. You promised you would."

"Relax," said David. "And leave go of me. You must know by now that when I say I'll do something, I do it."

"That's right. I know I can rely on you."

"Two tablets. Two quid."

The exchange was made, and the ritual of the injection took place.

Hours later Dennis Moule came slowly back to earth. By this time all the regular lodgers had arrived. None of them came near the corner where David and Moule were lying. It was recognized by now that they had something going between them, and they were left to themselves.

This was the time for confidences. Having been deprived of the drug for twenty-four hours and then taken a double shot, Moule was closer to his old civilized self than David had ever seen him. At one moment he startled him by breaking off a long, whispered monologue, saying, "Who are you and what do you want?"

"Wassat?" said David. He was desperately sleepy after the efforts of the day.

"I said, who are you?" To his surprise, Moule was chuckling. "What the hell are you doing here? You don't really belong. You can't fool me. You've got some game on, haven't you?"

"Shurrup and go to sleep," said David.

Moule chuckled again. He was back, God knows where, in one of the long corridors of his youth. The rain, which was beating down on the roof, seemed to remind him of something. He said, "It was raining hard on that afternoon. I shall never forget it. Never. They were worried about something. I could see that. Phyllis told me. She said, 'Blackett's in bad trouble, and Julius'—she used to call Mr. Mantegna Julius, though not to his face of course—'is worried stiff. Blackett ought to have showed him the papers *before* he signed them, not afterwards.' But that's clients all over, isn't it? Get themselves into trouble and then come along when it's too late and ask you to get them out of it. That's right, isn't it?"

"I don't know what the hell you're talking about," said David. But he was wide awake now.

"Phyllis showed me the folder the papers were in. A blue folder. She was putting it away in the private cabinet. Do you know what she said? She said, 'This folder's dynamite.' And I said, then you'd better lock it up before it goes off, hadn't you?"

This piece of repartee seemed to amuse Moule, and he started to laugh. The laugh turned into a cough, and quite suddenly David realized that he wasn't laughing any more. He was sobbing.

"What is it?" he said. "What's up?"

"They all died," said Moule. "That same afternoon. In the rain."

And that was all he would say.

—— 25 ——

"You think it'll come to a head tonight?" said the Assistant Commissioner.

He was looking out of the window at the weeping grey sky.

"Tonight or tomorrow night," said Morrissey.

"And you're leaving the ring clear and watching to see which way it goes."

"That's right."

"It's a bit cold-blooded."

"We're dealing with a cold-blooded type," said Morrissey. "I'm aiming to stay out of it as long as I can. But, if I have to go in, I've organized a force big enough to swamp any opposition."

"What have you told the men?"

"Nothing." Morrissey grinned. "But one of my sergeants let it slip, casual-like, that we expect trouble at the National Front rally in Lewisham."

"We may get that, too."

The Assistant Commissioner had known Morrissey since they had worked together, twenty years before, at the rough end of Southwark. He said, "I'd be happier if I could see how it was going to come out. You realize that if they catch up with Morgan, he'll be in real bad trouble."

Morrissey said, "The thing Morgan's best at is getting out of trouble. He's an expert at that."

"I saw him playing rugger once," said the Assistant Commissioner. "For the Glamorgan Police against the London Welsh. He was playing scrum half. One moment he'd be at the bottom of a heaving mass of forwards. You'd think they were murdering him. The next moment he'd be ten yards away up the field. A remarkable performer. I believe he'd have got a cap for Wales, except that they've got more scrum halves than they know what to do with."

The second day's work was easier. The removal of the first few bricks had made all the difference. There was one interruption, when David heard a fearsome scream from below. He came down quickly. At the far end of the loft an old tramp was sitting up in the straw, his face purple. As David looked at him, he fell back. David could smell the methylated spirits, before he saw the empty bottle with which the old man had been dosing himself. He was breathing in huge, tortured gasps. There was a rattle, and the gasping stopped. The man was dead. There was nothing David could do about it. He covered him with newspapers and straw and went back to work.

By midday the hole was large enough for him to wriggle through. He had a small torch, which he used sparingly, as the battery was on the blink.

He had broken into the space between the top of the ceiling and the underneath of the tiles. Its floor was formed by ceiling joists, and this made progress slow and painful. He worked his way along the main building on the east side of the block and turned the corner, which brought him above the shorter, southern, wing. When he had reached what he judged to be the middle of this, he broke through the ceiling by stamping a hole in the lath and plaster and peered down into the room.

"Easy does it, now," he said. "Got to think about getting back again."

The problem, once posed, was not too difficult. He saw that

the mistake he had made was breaking through the ceiling in the middle of the room. What he had to do was break through again alongside the room wall. Then it would be possible to scramble back. It proved even easier than he had thought, since his second entrance point was immediately above the mantelpiece.

"Forethought, boy," he said. "That's the ticket. Forethought." He found he was talking to himself a good deal. He had eaten very little and slept hardly at all for the past two days, and he was beginning to feel lightheaded.

The room he had broken into had once been an office. Rather a superior office, with two good southern windows. The iron frames were rusted, but David got one of them open and peered out.

With the approach of evening the rain had eased off and was now a drifting curtain.

"Just what the doctor ordered," said David. It was a fair drop to the open ground at the back of the building, but negotiable at a pinch. The windows at ground-floor level would, he guessed, be barred.

A staircase led down into the front hall. This had two doors on either side of it and a small, walled-off cubicle at the far end. David reconstructed the setup in his mind. This was the reception area. Visitors would come through the front door and would be put into the smaller front room on the left to wait. The cubicle would take a receptionist and maybe the telephone exchange. He walked up the hall and looked in. There was a hatchway which gave onto the second larger room on the left. General office, thought David. The heart of the organization. The inner citadel, held by the remnant of the garrison as the enemy closed in round them. The scene of the last stand.

One battered desk and two chairs had been left behind when they went. There was a double row of lockers on either side of the fireplace in the far wall. David walked in and opened them. They were all empty except one, which contained a milk bottle filled with a fine growth of matured mold. The light was growing dim now, but he could make out graffiti on the bare plaster walls. Most of them were pictures of girls drawn by an artist with more imagination than sense of perspective.

Underneath, in smeared letters, someone had written, "The sun never sets on the British Empire" and underneath that, in another hand, "Why, 'cos there ain't no Empire left for it to set on."

David shivered. The room was dank and horrible and desolate. The weather would soon be bringing in the homeless men who had inherited the building. There would be less of them tonight. The cold and wet would have driven some of them to the discomforts of the spike and the tramps' lodging houses. He climbed back the way he had come, refixed the plate of sheet iron and settled down among the debris to wait. He was still shaking. Cold and lack of food, he told himself. But he knew that there was more to it than that.

Moule was among the first to arrive. In his eagerness to reach David, he tripped and finished the journey on hands and knees. He was in a pitiable state, dripping with moisture, his face yellow and his teeth chattering.

"We're a pair," said David. "That's what we are. A pair of real beauties." He handed over the two tablets. Moule's hand was shaking so badly that he could hardly hold the syringe. In the end, David had to give him the injection. He needed Moule back to some semblance of normality. The difficulty was staying awake himself. To give himself something to do he shifted two large empty cartons, which somewhat increased the privacy of their corner.

A succession of racking coughs was the sign that Moule was wrenching himself out of Arcady and back into the grey, unprofitable present. Presently he yawned, hoisted his back half up against the wall and said, "You're still there? I'm glad of that. I dreamed I'd gone a long way away and lost you for good."

He put one thin hand on David's arm as if to make sure

that he was really there. David switched on his torch. Its feeble light produced an illusory effect of snugness and security.

He thought, "We're two explorers, in a cabin, at the top of a high mountain. We're shipwrecked sailors on a raft in the middle of the wide, grey sea. We're the last men on earth, the only two survivors of an atomic holocaust."

Moule seemed to be reading David's thoughts. He said, "There's something wrong with you. What's happening?"

David said, with calculated brutality, "What's happening is that I've had enough. I'm getting out."

Moule stared at him. Then he said, "What about me?"

"I'm not your father and mother. I'm not your bloody nurse. What about you? What the hell do I care about you?"

"You promised—"

"Anything I promised, I've done. And done more than I promised."

"Yes, yes." The slave was anxious to propitiate a master who had turned suddenly stern. "You've been very good."

"And I could be better. Look at this, will you?" David had an envelope in his hand. He said, "Hold the torch. I want to count." He spread a khaki handkerchief onto the straw between them and trickled out onto it first ten, then another ten, then a final ten of the white tablets.

"Thirty," he said. "Thirty of them. Now say that I don't keep my promises."

Moule's voice was shaking. He said, "Oh, you do. You do. I haven't quite enough money for all of them—"

"I'm not interested in money," said David. He was tipping the tablets carefully back into the envelope as he spoke. The last one escaped and rolled into the straw. David shone the torch down, located it and picked it up. He did all this slowly and deliberately.

There was a moment of silence in their tiny bivouac. Then Moule said, framing the words with difficulty, "Please—please tell me what you want."

"You know what I want."

"I don't. Really I don't."

"I want those papers. The ones you hid."

Moule didn't pretend not to understand him. He was leaning back, his face working. If he doesn't break now, thought David, he never will. Deliberately he crushed the tablet he was holding and scattered the white powder into the straw.

"One of those goes away every minute until you make your mind up."

The tortured indecision on Moule's face was horrible. As David took a second tablet out of the envelope he said, "Stop. Don't do that. Wait for a moment. You don't understand. If I tell you and you take the papers, people will know."

"Know what?"

David turned the tablet over between his fingers.

"Know that I've told you."

"Your name won't be mentioned."

"They'll guess."

"It's up to you."

Moule gave a dry sob. It was like a boy who has been beaten so often that he can cry no more. He said, "All right. I'll tell you. It was the audit."

"What audit?"

(Keep him talking.)

"I used to do audits for Mantegna. It meant going out and spending the day—several days—in the office of the firm we were auditing." Moule had lowered his voice to a confidential whisper. David turned off the torch. Darkness might help the confessional. "When you'd done the same audit for several years, you got to know the chief accountant quite well. It was a sort of joint effort, to get the accounts presented in good order. You weren't on opposite sides, really. You were on the same side. You understand?"

"I understand," said David.

"This cashier and I became very friendly. He—well, he liked to take a drop from time to time, and I was a bit that way myself. It was on account of Phyllis."

"I know about Phyllis. Go on with the cashier."

"He always had a bottle of Scotch handy. Of course, we used to wait until the junior cashiers had gone to lunch; then he'd pull it out and we'd have a small one, or maybe a couple. One day the Managing Director came in and nearly caught us." At this point Moule giggled. "I got the bottle into the wastepaper basket, just in time."

(Don't be impatient, boy. We've got all night in front of us.)

"Well, anyway, the point was, he had a particular place where he kept this bottle. He didn't want some nosey typist finding it, you see, and reporting him to the boss."

"Creepy Crawley."

"What was that?"

"Just a thought. Go on. Tell me. Where did he hide it?"

"There were these lockers, on either side of the fireplace. They were built up on a sort of stand. The wooden piece at the bottom looked solid, but if you got your fingers round one corner—that was on the fireplace side—you could move it out. I thought of this afterwards, you see."

"After what?"

"Why, after the firm went bust. We were put in by the liquidator. I suppose I was one of the last people to use the place—after everyone else had gone away."

The truth, the incredible truth, was beginning to dawn on David at last.

He said, in a voice which he tried to keep matter-of-fact, "What was the name of this firm?"

"I told you, didn't I? Hendrixsons."

"This place?"

"That's right. That's why I used to come back here. I felt I was sort of keeping an eye on the papers."

"You put those papers under the lockers, in the cashier's room?"

"I knew they were going to shut it down. All the places round here were being closed down. It seemed a very safe sort of place."

'It was an excellent place," said David. "Oh dear, yes. It was the best place you could possibly have thought of, in the whole wide world. You've no idea how excellent." He had clambered to his feet.

"What are you going to do?"

"I'm going to get them."

"You can't get in. It's locked and barred."

"That's just the point, my lovely boyo. I *can* get in and I'm going to get in. I'm Father bloody Christmas with a difference. He comes down chimneys, I go up them."

He had moved the sheet of metal and was starting on his way up the shaft when it happened.

A strong beam of light shone up through the hole in the floor, and a voice—loud, confident, authoritative—bellowed, "Come out of it, all you stinking toe-rags. Come out quick, or we'll burn you up."

Smoke was already trickling up between the floorboards.

— 26 —

There was a squealing and a scurrying like a rats' nest disturbed by terriers, as a dozen frightened tramps rolled from the straw and made for the one exit.

It turned out to be more smoke than fire. Trombo and his assistants had set fire to bales of straw and doused them with water as soon as they were alight. The tramps tumbled, one after another, down the steps and were seized by the men there and pushed up against the inner wall, where they stood blinking under the powerful headlamps of three trucks which were parked in the yard.

Trombo stood in the middle of the open space. He was wearing a long-skirted, belted seaman's coat, and the rain had smoothed the hair over his curiously rounded head. Irish Mick was standing beside him, examining each of the tramps as they were dragged forward for inspection.

"That's Percy," he said. "That's him."

"Ah," said Trombo. "So this is my old friend Mr. Moule. And where is his friend Mr. Morgan?"

Mick darted up and down the line of tramps and came back, shaking his head. "He's not here," he said. "He must be hiding upstairs. He's there, all right. I saw him come in."

"Roust him out," said Trombo. "Take a couple of lamps. This is the only exit."

Birnie Samuels appeared from behind one of the vans. He was a stout and cheerful Jew. He was carrying a short-handled pitchfork. He said, "This might be useful. We'll soon dig him out for you."

He and McVee disappeared up the steps, and they listened to the thumping and bumping as they searched. A few minutes later Samuels reappeared. He said, "No sign of Morgan. It's a stinking muck heap, and there's a dead man in one corner."

"Dead?"

"Big, fat fellow. Been dead some time by the look of him. If anyone else wants to search, they're welcome."

No one seemed anxious to volunteer.

"You're sure he's not hiding? He's a slippery customer."

"He didn't slip past Monkey and me," said Birnie. "We turned over every lump of shit and corruption in the place. He must have got out before we came."

One of the tramps, a wizened man with a high-pitched voice, squeaked out, "Ask Percy. They used to doss together like a pair of poofs."

"I don't know that I'm all that interested in Morgan," said Trombo. "It's Mr. Moule we've come looking for. Put him up where we can all see him."

Moule had collapsed into a squatting position on the floor. Ginger Williams grabbed him by the coat collar and dumped him on top of a packing case. A nail which was sticking out of the wood went into his leg, and he gave a little squeal and was silent again. His eyes were glazed with terror.

"I seem to remember," said Trombo comfortably, "that you and me have had words before."

Moule shivered.

"That being so, you know that I'm a man of my word. If I tell you that I'm going to tie you up in one of those straw bales and set fire to it, you know I'll do it."

Moule shivered again. Then he said, in his oddly pedantic

voice, "There is no need for threats. I will tell you anything you wish to know."

"I was sure you would. It's a little matter of some papers—copies of papers, I think they were—that you stole from a friend of mine and hid somewhere. Well?"

"I will show you if you wish. They are not far from here."

"That's friendly," said Trombo.

"It will mean breaking down a door."

"No problem."

Moule pointed across the courtyard to the front door of the office block, which was covered by a padlocked metal grill.

"Turn that van, so we can get some light on the job," shouted Ginger Williams. "Mace, you and Scotty attend to the door."

Two blows with a sledgehammer dealt with the padlock. The door was a tougher proposition. It took a full minute to demolish it.

Williams said, "We don't want everyone coming inside." There were a dozen men in the courtyard, most of them sheltering from the rain in the vans and another lot crowded into the open space under the loft. "Birnie, McVee, Mace and Scotty. Bring those torches with you. The rest—stay out here."

If Trombo noticed that Williams seemed to be taking over the operation, he gave no sign of annoyance, but followed the men in.

"Where now?" said Williams.

They were in the entrance hall, with the two doors on either side and the small partitioned cubicle at the end.

"The door on the left. The second one," said Moule.

Williams said, "Birnie, stay outside and keep in touch with the rest of the crowd. Put one of them outside the front door and tell the others to get the vans turned and facing outwards. If we have to scarper, we don't want to waste any time."

Birnie Samuels nodded his understanding.

"All right," said Williams. "Let's get on with it."

The rest of them had already moved into the big office room. Three powerful torches lit up the lockers which flanked the fireplace.

Moule went down on his knees in front of the left-hand set, fumbled for a moment and drew away the strip of wood which formed its base. He put in his hand, felt around and drew it out again.

"Well?" said Trombo.

"Could you give me one of the torches? Thank you."

He held the torch at ground level and knelt to peer in.

"Well?" said Trombo again.

Moule said, "They were here. Someone must have found them. They're gone."

"So we see," said Trombo.

"I swear I put them there." The panic note in his voice was pitiful. "No one could have got them. The place was locked up. See for yourself." Moule was still on his knees. The words tumbled out of his mouth, disjointed and almost inaudible.

Williams took the torch out of his shaking hand and shone it down onto the floor in front of the fireplace.

"Someone's been here, no question," he said. "Look at those marks in the dust."

Trombo peered over his shoulder.

"So it would seem."

"And not long ago." Williams jerked Moule to his feet. "If you were the only one who knew, you must've told someone." He gave Moule a shake. "That's right, isn't it?"

"It would seem to be the only possibility," said Trombo. His voice had thickened. There was a treacly note in it which was more menacing than threats. "Put him on the desk."

Handling Moule as though he were a child, Williams placed him on the desk, gripping his match-stick arms above the elbows. All the torches were focused on the scarecrow figure.

"Now," said Trombo gently. "The truth, please."

Moule opened and shut his mouth, but no sound came out.

Trombo clenched his right hand and hit Moule a savage clout on the left side of his face, a blow hard enough to jerk his head round on his shoulders.

"Think again. You don't want me to get rough."

"I didn't." There was a pause. Moule's voice was low, but quite distinct. "I didn't."

This time the blow came from Trombo's left fist, jerking Moule's head straight again. Then, without pause, from the right and the left and the right. The force of the final blow knocked Moule off the desk, which crashed over with him onto the floor.

"Hold it," said Williams. He lifted the desk and peered down at the figure sprawled there. "I think you've done him."

The crash of the desk going down had brought Birnie Samuels into the room. For a moment no one had eyes for anything but the bundle of rags on the floor. No one saw the shadow which slid down the hallway outside the open door of the room and vanished up the stairs.

During all this time David had been in the old telephone cubicle at the end of the passage, having dived in there at the last moment for safety as the front door went down. The hatchway had given him a view of what was happening in the office, and he had stood there, impotent to help but unable to move as long as Samuels was outside the door.

He had now only one idea in his head. To get away as fast and as far as he could. He had little doubt that Moule was dead. In his weakened state any one of those blows could have finished him.

He had left the window of the upstairs room open when he came down. He peered out. The rain had thickened again, and a freshening east wind was driving it up river. The night was as black as the far side of hell. He was glad he had reconnoitered the spot by daylight. He could hardly have risked a blind drop.

He lowered himself out of the window, hung on by both hands for a moment, used his knees to push himself slightly away from the wall and let go, flexing his knees and rolling as he landed.

"A perfect parachute drop, without a parachute," he said. He was winded, but undamaged. He scrambled to his feet and trotted off down the cinder track which led to the fence.

He located the swinging plank without difficulty and pressed it outwards. Halfway up it seemed to stick.

As he crouched down and put his shoulder to it, a bright light came on in the road outside, and a motor horn blew three short, three long and three short blasts.

Cursing under his breath, David went into retreat, trying to think as he stumbled back down the path. He had not gone far when he stopped. Trombo, as always when an emergency arose, had taken charge. He was speaking through a loud-hailer.

"We know he's somewhere in here," said the booming voice. "And he can't get out. The gates are guarded, and there are cars outside. There's nowhere he can climb the fence without being spotted. What we're going to do is beat this whole area and drive the Welsh rabbit onto the guns."

A rumble of laughter.

"We'll have three men on the cross tracks at the west end. You, you and you. The rest of you spread out, starting at the east end. Keep in touch and move as slowly as you like. The trucks can keep in front of us, one on each track, with headlights full on. Any questions? Right. Then, let's get moving."

David thought about it, and the more he thought about it the less he liked it. He had explored the area by daylight and he knew that the high fences of small meshed wire were impossible to climb without tackle. And even if he could get over, a car in the road outside with headlights on would pick him up at once. Alternatives? He could try to hide, in or under one of the piles of rusty machinery, but forty men, with torches, would be sure to find him sooner or later.

The voice boomed out again. "I'll give you something to play for, lads. There's two hundred for the man who first spots the rabbit. And five hundred for the man who lays the first hand on him."

It had become a game for them. A game played on a board half a mile square, full of rusty machinery and deep pools of stagnant water and crossed by rutted tracks. A scientific game. Not quite chess, perhaps. Fox and geese, with himself as the poor, bedraggled fox.

While he was thinking this out, he had been moving, keeping parallel to the main cross path, but edging slowly towards the western fence. He could see the lights behind him now. The firefly flicker of the torches and the tigers' eyes of the headlights.

He stopped. He had come to the first of the cross tracks, and a man was standing there. David recognized the stunted figure he had seen before in the Rayhome office. It was McVee.

It would be easy enough to creep past him, in the rain and darkness, but what good would that do? He would be pinned against an unclimbable fence, in the headlights of the advancing trucks. Probably the only result would be to put seven hundred pounds into McVee's pocket.

It was when he was thinking about this that the plan came to him. It was a plan born of desperation. It depended on split-second timing and was based on greed and surprise. It contained a dozen imponderables. All that could be said for it was that it was better than no plan at all.

Just beyond the point where McVee stood was one of the largest of the abandoned pools, fifty yards across and brimful of water. McVee had his back to David and was standing on the far side of the track staring down into it.

If David was going to do what he had in mind, he had to wait until the advancing truck was on the point of swinging round the bend twenty yards away.

Not a second too soon. Not a split second too late.

One eye on the truck, one eye on McVee.

Wait for it.

Count five.

McVee had shifted his position, half turning to look at the truck, whose headlights could be seen.

Just beginning its swing round the corner. Now.

David took three quick steps forward and kicked McVee in the middle of the back. He shot forward, teetered for a moment on the slippery edge and then fell with a splash into the water.

The van was round the bend now and coming towards him, accelerating and breaking sharply as it came up.

David was standing in the middle of the track, waving his hands in the air. "I saw him," he shrieked. "I saw him. I was first. Then he went into the water, and I couldn't get him. He'll try to swim for it, and I can't swim."

The driver was already out on the path.

"I can," he said briefly.

McVee was floundering in the water, splashing feebly, three yards from the edge. The driver jumped straight into the pool. But no more quickly than David jumped into the cab of the van.

It was an old Bedford Woodman, of the sort he had driven as a boy on his father's farm. He slammed it into gear and was moving before the man in the water had had time to turn his head.

"No stopping now," he said. The van had both accelerator and hand throttle. "Made for the job." By the time he rounded the last bend and sighted the gate, he was moving fast.

"Slow it a little, boy. No need to risk a broken leg."

Through the bars of the gate, which was a massive, padlocked affair, he could see the radiator of a car and a man standing in front of it.

He twisted the hand throttle, feeling it take over from the accelerator, opened the door and put one foot on the step. Then he aimed the truck at the middle of the gate, opened the throttle wide and dropped to the ground. The truck leaped forward and hit the gate squarely. There was a scream of metal on metal as truck, gate and car went over together in a thrashing heap, and David was across the road and over the fence beyond.

He had landed in long, wet grass, and he crouched there for a minute getting his breath and his senses back. He could hear sounds from the other side of the fence. Someone alternately retching and cursing. He guessed it was the second man, behind the car, hit by some fragment of the general convulsion. The man who had been standing in front was almost certainly finished. A second car was coming up fast. It was time to move.

He started to crawl. It was not good ground for crawling, the long, sodden grass being full of thistles and dwarf thorn. But David persevered. The thing that mattered now was keeping out of sight. If he was spotted and had to run, he'd be done.

He was a long way from being out of the woods. The streets round the dock area would be patrolled by Trombo's mercenary army, and he was now such a conspicuous figure—muddy, bedraggled and tattered—that he would be identified at sight. He wondered if they could pick up his trail. A lot depended on whether the second man had seen him go over the fence. Anyway, it was a possibility that would be explored as soon as Trombo had the pursuit reorganized. He did not underrate that bald Napoleon.

A second fence.

David examined it. He was becoming an expert on fences. This one was diamond mesh, but the meshes were larger and offered a toehold. He scaled it cautiously. The wires at the top had been twisted upwards and formed an uncomfortable obstacle. He left further fragments of his trousers in it. A plain trail for the hounds, but it might not be picked up in the dark.

The bank on the other side was steep and slippery. He turned over on his back and slid, feet foremost, clutching at tussocks to slow his progress. It was quite a long drop. As his feet grounded on what felt like rough stones, he realized two things simultaneously. He was on a railway line, and a train was coming.

He flattened himself on the flint beside the track. An electric train rattled past a couple of feet above his head.

Electric train? Live rails. Dangerous at any time. Murderous when wet.

Try to think.

Were the live rails on the outside of the ordinary rails, or were they together on the inside, and, if so, how far apart.

David decided that it would be stupid to electrocute himself and that he must wait for the next train. Its lights would show him what he wanted to know.

He waited for ten minutes. It was a bad ten minutes. Twice he thought he heard voices in the field above his head, and twice he decided that it was his imagination. His head was full of strange sounds, buzzing and clacking and, behind them, in a swelling diapason, the glorious hymn which he had heard rolling round Cardiff Arms Park.

"Feed them till they want no more."

Yes, indeed.

Here came the train. By its lights the position was made clear. There were two live rails, between the tracks and less than three feet apart.

"You'll have to step like a bloody ballet dancer," said David. "An *entrechat* or *pas de deux*."

He advanced towards the live rail, lifted one foot over, felt himself sway, said, "Don't be bloody silly, now. A child could do it." Lifted the other foot over. Repeated the process. Cleared the second live rail. Took two quick steps forward, tripped over the outside rail and fell flat on his face against the far bank.

Compared with what had gone before, this seemed a minor matter.

"Nearly out now," he said. And no sooner said it than he realized that there was a difference between sliding down a steep, muddy, twelve-foot embankment and climbing up one.

There were moments in the time that followed when he nearly decided to give up and spend the night beside the railway. For every six inches he went up he seemed to slip back five. His nose was never more than an inch from the slimy surface. Handholds came away as he grabbed at them. He discovered one unexpected advantage from having no caps to his boots. His bare, protruding toes could seek out and dig into the smallest crevices, and it was this, in the end, which enabled him to lever himself onto the top of that nightmare bank and climb the fence beyond it.

He found himself on a rough track which paralleled the railway running past the ends of a number of small back gardens. He guessed that there must be side roads or alleys leading from it into the High Street, which cut across at this point. The important decision now was whether to turn right or left. He tried to visualize the map that Len Mullion had showed him. He thought that he would go left and take the next opening that offered. If he was wrong he would have to go back and try again in the other direction. His wristwatch, after he had scraped the mud from its glass, showed the time to be ten minutes after midnight.

The High Street, fronted by rows of locked shops, was silent and empty, the rain slanting down under the yellow neon lights and bouncing back off the black surface of the road. As David peered out, like some troglodyte intruder, from the mouth of his alleyway, a car turned the corner and cruised towards him.

He drew back and waited, counting slowly.

When he had reached fifty, a second car appeared and followed the first.

What David was looking for was one particular turning off the High Street on the other side.

A third car came past. The patrolling was regular and unrelenting. As soon as the car was out of sight, David scurried across the road and started to trot down the pavement. The side road ahead of him looked as though it might be the one he wanted. Another car. He dived into the entrance of a jeweller's shop and pressed himself back into the darkness.

For a heart-stopping moment he thought that the car was slowing. Then it was past him and driving away.

As soon as he reached the corner he knew that this was the road he had been looking for. It was a cul-de-sac, leading down past the Borough Primary School, which loomed up on the right, locked and empty. Two more fences now, but easier ones. The first let him into the school playground. He padded across and turned the corner of the building. The low roof of a bicycle shed gave him a leg up over the second fence, and he was in the smallest of the three Rotherhithe public parks.

Len Mullion's instructions had been clear. Follow the path along the north side of the park, nearly to the end. Turn right and you'll find it, tucked away behind a clump of bushes.

It was a tiny, cylindrical building, like a pepper box in brick and tile. It was the place where the park keeper kept his tools and spare equipment. David had been carrying the key, strapped by sticking plaster to his leg. There had been times that night when the feel of it had been almost the only thing which had given him the courage to go on.

He pulled off the plaster, took out the key and unlocked the small door. It was stoutly made, with wrought-iron hinges, like the door of a vestry.

There was one thing he had to do before he went inside, and it took an effort of memory and will to do it. He retraced his steps until he found a wire-mesh refuse basket beside the path. He unhitched it, carried it out and dumped it, in full view, on the grass. Then he went back to the tool shed.

He went in, locked the door behind him, sat down on the floor and took six very slow, deep breaths. When he took out his torch he found that it had expired. He discarded it and clicked on his cigarette lighter.

Len had done everything that he had asked him.

The single small window had been carefully blocked with brown paper pasted on the inside. There was a hurricane lamp on the bench beside the sink. David lit it, putting it down on the floor to avoid any chance of the tiniest chink of light showing.

Under the bench he found a bulging kit bag and an old army bedroll.

In the kit bag was an outfit of coat, trousers, shirt, shoes and socks. Len's taste was a little more dashing than David's, but they were new and clean. There was a washing and shaving kit and a pair of pajamas. Flanelette and striped, not silk and Cambridge blue. How long ago had that been? There was a thermos which turned out to contain soup, almost too hot to drink, and a small flask of brandy. There was a large, rough towel.

"Len," said David, "you are all the angels in Heaven rolled into one. Gabriel. Azrael. Ithuriel. Michael."

He stripped off every stitch of his sodden and filthy clothing and toweled and pummeled his naked body. Then he put on the pajamas which were too large for him, sat down on the floor and drank the soup, cooling it with alternate mouthfuls of brandy.

The desire for sleep was overpowering. He unstrapped the bedroll, for which there was just room among the flowerpots on the tiled floor, crept into it, blew out the lamp and dropped down into a black pit, full of ghosts and shadows, men and half-men who wept and giggled, and one ghost in particular who said, "I didn't, I didn't, I didn't," to the rhythm of an electric train.

Unconsciousness came at last.

— 27 —

With the first drowned glimpses of morning, Len Mullion might have been observed, had there been eyes watching him, walking along Byland Street at the back of Rotherhithe Park. He plodded along with the steady deliberation of a man making his way to an unloved, early work shift.

Halfway down the street there was a wicket gate, not available to the public, used by the park keepers. Len had the key ready in his hand, opened the gate, slipped inside and relocked it. A moment later he was out of sight behind a bank of laurels. A cautious advance from here brought him to a point where he could see the central stretch of grass. There was still not much light in the sky, but enough for him to see the refuse basket lying on its back on the grass.

Len breathed a sigh of relief. So David had made it. He'd never doubted that he would. Corner a crafty Welshman? You might as well try to pick up a blob of mercury in your fingers. He made his way back, through the shrubbery, to the pavilion tucked away in the northwest corner of the park. A second key opened the door. There was a telephone inside. Len dialed the number of Flanders Lane Police Station.

Morrissey took the call. He had been sitting for the best part of six hours beside the telephone and was so stiff that he nearly fell out of his chair when he got up to answer it. He listened carefully, said, "Stay where you are, Len. I'll ring you back in five minutes." Kicked Sergeant Brannigan, who was snoring on the floor beside him, and said, "Wake up. We're off." He was already dialing another number.

It rang for some seconds before it was answered. Morrissey said, "You all asleep at that end?"

"Sorry, Superintendent," said a brisk voice. "Actually, I was shaving."

"Well, when you've cleaned your teeth and brushed your hair, suppose you get moving. Operation Dawn Raid is on. I want all the men on those lists pulled in. All except Trombo. For questioning in connection with a breaking and entering in the docks area. No charges yet. Understood?"

"Understood."

"And send a car to Rotherhithe Park. The back entrance in Byland Street. I'll have it open for you. There's a man to pick up. Bring him straight back here. I need his story before the questioning starts. Understood?"

"Understood."

Andrew Holmes was worried.

He had noticed lately that his secretary was getting tired and had been thinking that a holiday, backed by a large bonus, might be the right medicine. Now, for two days, she had looked more than tired. She had done her work well enough, but the signs of strain had been too marked even for an unobservant man to miss; and Andrew Holmes was far from unobservant.

However, he had got something for her that morning which might cheer her up. He said, "Blackett just telephoned. He wants to look at the Planetarium papers. He knew you'd done a lot of work on them and suggested that you brought the file down yourself."

"A suggestion?" said Susan sharply. "Or an instruction?"

Holmes looked surprised. "A bit of both, I suppose. Do you mind? I thought you'd like a trip this beautiful morning. He's sending his car for you."

The rain had stopped, and a bland autumn sun was apologizing for the past.

"Now? Right away?"

"Immediately after lunch, he suggested. Is there something wrong?"

"Not really."

"Play your cards right and you'll end up working for him. Then you really will be at the top of the ladder. Not that I want to lose you. Don't think that. You've been absolutely splendid."

"Is there somewhere I could telephone, without the call going through the switchboard?"

"There's one outside line. It's in the cashier's office. Ted's away this morning. If you want to use that you won't be disturbed."

Susan said, "Thank you, Andrew," and went out. It was the first time she had used his Christian name. Holmes looked after her thoughtfully.

When she came back five minutes later the change was extraordinary. She looked her own self again. He said, "I gather the news was good."

"Very good."

"Then I'll give Blackett a ring and tell him to expect you."

"Blackett?" said Susan. She sounded almost as though she had forgotten about him. "Oh, yes. That'll be quite all right now."

Morrissey finished reading the five sheets of official blue paper, shuffled them together, stapled them in the top left-hand corner, took off his glasses and said to Sergeant Brannigan, "Now, I think we might pay a visit to Mr. Trombo."

"Just you and me?"

"What do you suggest? A squadron of Sherman tanks?" Morrissey was in a high good humor.

"I just wondered."

"You could have a car standing by if you're feeling nervous."

"I'm not nervous," said Brannigan indignantly.

"There'll be no trouble. These boys are only dangerous after dark. We'll take Bob Wrangle with us and leave him outside in the car."

When they reached the shop in Burminster Street and had pushed open the door, they sensed the thunder in the air. The polished brown boys behind the polished brown counters looked up and looked down again and said nothing.

"Mr. Trombo at home?" said Brannigan.

One of them jerked his head towards the room at the far end of the shop. The two policemen stumped up the open space between the counters, and Morrissey opened the door without knocking.

Trombo was sitting behind the table. Morrissey strode across, stopped just short of collision point and said, "Get up." When Trombo didn't move, he bent his head forward and roared at him. "On your feet, you yellow monkey."

Trombo got up slowly. The two men were so close that their noses were only inches apart.

"Just giving you a bit of practice," said Morrissey. "The next time someone tells you to stand up it'll be the judge at the Bailey, and you'd better jump up quicker than that, or he'll add another year to the fifteen he's giving you, just to teach you manners."

"I don't know what you're talking about."

"Oh, yes, you do. You know bloody well what I'm talking about. Shut that door, would you, Sergeant. I'm talking about you standing trial for the murder of Dennis Robert Moule. Killing the poor old sod by hitting him on the head. Left, right." Morrissey swung his great fists, missing Trombo by a fraction each time. "Then another right and a left and a right. Not a great boxer, Dennis. Not good at blocking head punches. Particularly when his arms were being held."

Trombo said nothing.

Morrissey backed away slowly and parked himself on the edge of the table. He said in a more relaxed voice, "Don't think I'm bluffing. I've got it in black and white, signed on

238

the dotted line, from that oaf Williams. He was in what you might call a ringside seat at this demonstration of fisticuffs."

"Evidence from a man like that. Given to save his own skin." There was a hint of relief in Trombo's voice. "You won't get any court to convict on that."

"Right," said Morrissey. "But he won't be the only witness. McVee. Mace. Scotty. They were all there. When they heard Williams had sung, they all sang too. In unison."

"Men with criminal records, who'll say anything the police teach them to say. You're going to need more than that to put me down."

"The same massive thought had occurred to me," said Morrissey genially. "So I'll let you in on another little secret. Do you remember that cubbyhole at the end of the passage? Samuels was standing outside it, until he heard Moule hit the floor and had to poke his nose in, to see what was going on. That was when the man who had been in that cubbyhole got out. Having seen everything that happened, through the shutter. He was a police officer, name of Morgan. You spent the rest of the evening trying to catch him, but you didn't, did you?" Morrissey was smiling broadly now. He seemed to be visualizing the scene. "So we can have it all explained to the court. Every move made by everyone in that room. Every word spoken. And all corroborated by a police officer handily placed in the next room. You're dead meat, Trombo. Dead and stinking. Fifteen years! You'll be lucky if you don't get life. Not to be let out in less than thirty years. That's the dose they're handing out now."

Trombo said nothing. He seemed unable to speak or move.

"However, like I said once before, you're a lucky man. You must have been born under a lucky star. Because maybe—I only say maybe—you won't be charged at all."

The pink end of Trombo's tongue came out and was passed over his lips.

"To tell you the truth and between these four walls, I'm not all that interested in Moule, poor old sod. He was on the

239

way out. This winter or next he'd have gone. Not that I'm
going to repeat that in court, so don't start banking on it."
Morrissey's grin was ferocious. "There's a man I'm a lot more
interested in than you or Moule. I've been after him for a
long, long time. You help me to land Blackett, and everything
else is forgiven and forgotten."

"You mean—?"

"I mean just this. You give me the truth about what happened
to Arnie Wiseman, and I'll give you an indemnity for any part
you had in it."

"Arnie?" said Trombo thoughtfully.

"The truth, the whole truth and nothing but the truth. How
much Blackett paid you to do it, where you put him, all the
details. Because now we've got those papers we know *why*
Blackett wanted him out of the way. You give us the story,
you get the usual indemnity and we forget all about your part
in it."

There was a long silence.

At last Trombo said, "How do I know you'll keep your
word?"

"I always keep my word," said Morrissey. "That's how I get
results. Right, Sergeant?"

"Right," said Sergeant Brannigan.

There was another long pause. Then Trombo said, "Very
well," and sat down.

"In your own handwriting," said Morrissey.

"Before we discuss the Planetarium," said Blackett smoothly,
"there was one other matter I wanted to deal with."

They were alone in the drawing room at Virginia Water.
It was a lovely room and impersonal as a stage set.

Susan said, "I was so certain that you didn't want to discuss
the Planetarium that I didn't even bother to bring the papers
with me."

If Blackett was surprised, there was little sign of it in his
face, only an additional hardness in his voice. He said, "Then

we can get straight to the point. I've known for some time that you had been planted in my organization. I thought at first that you were an agent of the Inland Revenue. Your background and training suggested it as a possibility. In my frequent brushes with that Department, they seemed to suffer from not knowing half as much about my business as I did. It would have been sensible to instal one of their own people to investigate it from the inside."

"And when did you decide that I wasn't a tax inspector?" Susan's voice was coolly amused.

"When I unearthed your connection with—how do I describe Morgan?—your boyfriend."

"I think he is a little old for boyfriend," said Susan gravely. "Gentleman friend might be more appropriate."

Blackett looked up. There was something in Susan's manner that puzzled him. He said, more sharply, "After that it was an obvious precaution to have your telephone tapped and to have one of your intimate and touching telephone conversations recorded."

"I hope you found it entertaining."

"Enlightening more than entertaining. It wasn't a very difficult code, was it?"

"It depends which one we were using. We had two or three different codes. Sometimes it was the second word in every sentence. Sometimes it depended on numbers."

"Let me remind you. In the case I had in mind, Morgan started by saying, 'For the last *six* weeks—' After that it was the sixth word each time he spoke. Right?"

"I expect that was it," said Susan politely.

"And what an interesting message it was. Short and to the point. *Animal in sight. Give me three weeks.* The animal being, one assumes, a down-at-heel ex-accountant called Moule."

"That would seem to be a logical interpretation," said Susan cautiously. Blackett's smooth tone was slipping. Prod him. He was soon going to blow his top. "If you thought so little of our efforts," she said, "why did you let them worry you?"

241

"I wasn't worried. Puzzled, rather. I couldn't imagine why the police—give them their due, they are professionals—should have handed over this job to a pair of amateurs with the adolescent mentality which one associates with Boy Scouts and Girl Guides."

"David a Boy Scout?" said Susan. "In shorts and a shirt covered with badges for woodcraft and cookery. I find it hard to visualize. But tell me, if what he was doing didn't worry you, why did you try to stop him?"

"I don't like the word *try*," said Blackett. His breath was coming more quickly. "If I have to abate a nuisance, I take appropriate steps. I abate it."

"So he hasn't heard yet," thought Susan.

"If people annoy me, I punish them appropriately."

"Like when Phil Edmunds pulled your leg about your Guards' tie, and you did your best to ruin him."

There was a moment of silence. Susan could hear a motor mower puttering at the far end of the lawn. Then Blackett said, "Who told you about that? Would it have been young Harmond? I always thought he was soft on you. I think it must have been him. Not very wise. I shall have to punish him."

Susan said, "Don't be so infantile." Blackett stared at her. "You're behaving like a nasty little boy who pulls his sister's hair and breaks her toys because she's got the better of him in an argument."

Blackett's face had gone deep scarlet. "I don't suppose anyone's talked to him like that in the last thirty years," thought Susan. "One more crack and he *will* pull your hair." She said, "What are you going to do? Call in Harald and tell him to beat me up? He's a nice boy, and I doubt if he'd do it."

When Blackett spoke, his voice was so thick with spite and venom that the words could hardly force their way through. He said, "Certainly not. That would be stupid. And I'm not stupid. But you'll find that I've a lot of good friends. Not nice people, perhaps, but effective. In five or six months, or maybe longer than that, when your friends in the police have relaxed their efforts to guard you, you might come home one evening and find everything in your flat destroyed. Broken, defiled, stamped into pieces, burnt with acid. Or perhaps you might be walking home at night. Things happen to girls who walk home at night. And when I read about it in the papers next morning perhaps I should be sorry for you."

"Perhaps you would and perhaps you wouldn't," said Morgan. He had come in quietly through the unlatched French windows. He looked brown and thin, but seemed cheerful. "However, it doesn't arise. Because you won't be in any position to carry out your threats. And the people who might have carried them out for you won't feel inclined to do so. Not once you're inside."

Blackett had not taken his eyes off David from the moment he had come into the room.

"It's all right," said David. "This *is* me. David Rhys Morgan, the great escaper. The original india rubber man. Now, if you've finished trying to frighten Susan—which I assure you is almost impossible—let me put you briefly in the picture. At eleven o'clock this morning your friend Trombo started writing out a statement. I'm told that it took him a full hour, but he had a lot of ground to cover. He was dealing with the disappearance of one Arnold, or Arnie, Wiseman."

He stopped as if inviting comment.

"Nothing to say? I'm surprised, because, according to Trombo, you instigated the whole thing and have been paying him a regular fee ever since to keep his mouth shut. For other services, too, of course. But what may be news to you is this. Before they finished Arnie off, the boys got him to make a statement in writing, explaining just how he'd maneuvred you into an awkward corner. One imagines he made the statement in the hope of saving his own life, but it didn't do him a mite of good, because, before the ink was dry, he was strangled and buried in Epping Forest. The police have already located the remains and are happy they'll be able to identify them by the dental work. Arnie's statement, coupled with the papers which I handed over early this morning—damp, but still legible—give them the whole story and so, not to put too fine a point on it, you're for the high jump."

Blackett said, "They wouldn't—they couldn't—" and then seemed to lose the grasp of what he was going to say.

David said, "Don't fool yourself. It's open and shut. The charge will be conspiracy to murder. Your motive is established. The star prosecution witness will be the man who carried out your orders. The only doubt is how long you'll get. The betting at the moment is seven or fifteen, with a slight shade of odds on seven, but I shouldn't bank on it."

David looked at his watch.

"Some visitors will be arriving shortly. The Chief Constable, Chief Superintendent Morrissey and one or two stalwart constables. They should be here in about ten minutes. You'll have things to arrange before they cart you off, so we'll be on our way."

He walked across to the window. Susan followed him. Blackett said nothing. As they crossed the lawn, the motor mower swept past them. It was driven by a boy who looked as happy as if he was taking a racing car round Brands Hatch.

As the noise died across the wide space of the lawn, Susan said, "Will he—?"

"Kill himself?" said David. "Of course he will. That's what he's been given ten minutes to do. Save a lot of trouble."

"But *will* he?"

"When it's a matter of exchanging all this"—David indicated the house and garden asleep under the autumn sun—"for a ten-foot-by-six cell with a homosexual in the bunk underneath. Being shouted at by warders and bullied by the other prisoners. They like to have a gent to take it out of, I'm told. Slopping out every morning and jam twice a week if you're good. Of course he will. I could see him making up his mind to do it before we were out of the room."

"Would you mind—?" said Susan.

David looked at her in alarm and got an arm round her.

"Can you hold up for about twenty yards? The car's behind that hedge over there."

"I'll be all right in a moment. Stupid of me. It's just that I'm not quite as cold-blooded as you seem to think."

"And when I'd been building you up as the original iron lady."

He kept his arm round her until they reached the hedge. Harald was standing beside the car. David said, "Don't do anything you might be sorry about afterwards."

Harald said, "Why not?" and took a light step towards them. He looked like a boxer advancing into the ring.

"Two reasons," said David. "First, because a car load of top coppers will be here in a few minutes. Second, because you're needed up at the house. Badly needed."

They heard the sound, distant but unmistakable, like, but not quite like, the slamming of a door.

Harald turned and started to run back towards the house.

"Section 54," said Abel. "I'd more than a suspicion that it might be. It was about that time the Selangor Rubber Estate case was on, so naturally it would have been in Arnie's mind. A company giving financial assistance for the purchase of its own shares. You follow me?"

"No way," said Morrissey.

Abel was smoothing down the four stained and battered papers on the table in front of him with loving fingers.

"A company minute, appointing Arnie Wiseman a director of Argon. A service contract for Arnie, on pretty generous terms. A contract under which Arnie loans Blackett one hundred thousand pounds to be used in buying out Harry Woolf. And here"—Abel held up the document in triumph like a surgeon who has just fished out a difficult appendix—"is the key to the whole thing. A charge on all the assets of Blackbird to secure the loan. You appreciate that under Section 54—"

"No," said Morrissey. "Don't explain it. He'd done something he didn't ought to have done. Right? So what was the penalty?"

245

"That's just it. It's the only section of the Act which carries criminal sanctions. If you commit a deliberate breach of Section 54 you can be sent to prison. Even if it only meant a heavy fine and a ticking off by the judge, it would have finished Blackett in the City."

"And that gave Arnie a handle to squeeze him."

"Certainly."

"So Blackett got hold of his old acquaintance from Jap prison-camp days and said, 'Throw a scare into Arnie.' Instead of which Trombo first winkled a written statement out of him and then finished him off. Thus putting Blackett in *his* pocket."

"All he'd done," said Abel, "was change paymasters."

"And now that Blackett's dead, we've got Mr. Trombo where we want him."

Abel looked at him in some surprise. He said, "If you try to use that confession, won't he say you got it out of him by promising him an indemnity?"

"Certainly."

"Well, then—"

"No need to use his confession. He's not going to be charged with killing Arnie Wiseman. The charge is the murder of Dennis Moule. We don't need any confessions for that. We've got enough witnesses to prove it six times over."

"But I thought you promised him—"

"People sometimes don't listen careful enough to what's being said to them. Particularly when they're scared. The only promise I gave Trombo was that I'd give him an indemnity for any part he took in removing Wiseman. I didn't say nothing about Moule."

Abel took some time to think this out. Then he said, as though he had suddenly seen the light, "Then it *was* Trombo you were after all the time, not Blackett."

"Wrong," said Morrissey. "I was after both of 'em."

"Good God. David!" said Gerald Hopkirk. "What are you doing here?"

246

"Just dropped in to look up my old friends," said David.

It was five o'clock, and the offices of Martindale, Mantegna and Lyon were beginning the business of closing down for the night.

"Nice to see you, anyway."

"I hear Sam's in trouble."

"He's not exactly in trouble. He's up at Scotland Yard with his solicitor, protesting against their efforts to get their hands on Blackett's private papers. He says that Blackett was never actually charged with anything, and suicide isn't a crime, anyway."

"If I was Sam, I wouldn't bother," said David. "Blackett's dead. His empire's disintegrating. He wasn't a very worthy citizen."

"I don't know," said Gerald. "Private enterprise and all that. England needs a few Blacketts, in my view. I didn't know him well, of course, but he asked me down to his house last week, and I thought him nice enough. Did you ever meet him?"

"Once," said David. "Very briefly. Come and have a drink. I've found a lovely little place, just off Cornhill."

"Well—"

"Then we can go back and have dinner at my place. Susan was saying only this morning that she'd like to see you again."

"You're back with each other, then?"

"Certainly. Like I told you. These things never last long. After a bit we both realize what we're missing. An armistice is declared. Until next time."

"Well, then—"

"A celebration is called for. We'll get Fred to come along, too. And look who's here! Would you care to join us for a drink?"

Miss Crawley gave him a look of loathing and scuttled off.

"On the whole, just as well," said David. "I have a feeling she wouldn't have added to the gaiety of the occasion."